VANISHING
POINT

VANISHING
POINT

MARCIA MULLER

NEW YORK   BOSTON

This book is a work of fiction. Names, characters, places, and incidents are the product of the author's imagination or are used fictitiously. Any resemblance to actual events, locales, or persons, living or dead, is coincidental.

Mysterious Press
Warner Books

Time Warner Book Group
1271 Avenue of the Americas, New York, NY 10020
Visit our Web site at www.twbookmark.com.

The Mysterious Press name and logo are registered trademarks of Warner Books.

Printed in the United States of America
First Edition: July 2006

10   9   8   7   6   5   4   3   2   1

Library of Congress Cataloging-in-Publication Data
Muller, Marcia.
    Vanishing Point / Marcia Muller.— 1st ed.
       p. cm.
    Summary: "Sharon McCone is hired to investigate the 22-year-old cold-case of a housewife and artist who vanished inexplicably in the central part of California"— Provided by publisher.
    ISBN-13: 978-0-89296-805-3
    ISBN-10: 0-89296-805-2
    1. McCone, Sharon (Fictitious character)—Fiction. 2. Women private investigators—California—Fiction. 3. Missing persons—Investigation—California—Fiction. I. Title.
    PS3563.U397V36 2006
       813'.54—dc22
                                                                    2005034180

For Alison Wilbur—
finally, one under your real name—

and

Larry Griffin—
your own big-girl thriller!

Special thanks to:

Melissa Meith, my expert on legal matters—and mothers!

Bette Lamb, extraordinary nurse, artist, and writer.

And, as always, Bill Pronzini:

Dammit, why are you always right?

VANISHING
POINT

VANISHING POINT

1. a point of disappearance, cessation, or extinction
2. (in the study of perspective in art) that point toward which receding parallel lines appear to converge

—*Random House Unabridged Dictionary,* 2nd edition

Sunday

·

AUGUST 14

"My God, what's going on down there?" I asked Hy.

He peered through the Cessna's side window as I banked over Touchstone, our property on the cliffs above the sea in Mendocino County. "Hate to say it, but it looks like a party."

"Oh, hell, I never should've called the office from Reno."

It did indeed look like a party: tables dotted the terrace, their brightly colored cloths fluttering in the sea breeze; smoke billowed from the barbecue; a crowd of people stood on the mole-humped excuse for a lawn, staring up and waving at the plane.

"There's Mick," Hy said. "And Charlotte. And Ted."

"Probably the instigators." I banked again and began my approach to our dirt landing strip along the bluff's top. "How on earth did they organize this in just a few days?"

"Well, your people're nothing if not efficient."

"Yours, too." I pointed down at Gage Renshaw, one of Hy's partners in the security firm of Renshaw and Kessell International. "He made it up from La Jolla in time."

"Nice of him. And I see Hank, Anne-Marie, and Habiba.

And Rae. But all these people kind of put a damper on the rest of the honeymoon."

"Oh, Ripinsky, we've been honeymooning for years."

"That's a fact."

I concentrated on making a smooth landing, then taxied toward the plane's tiedown, where my nephew Mick Savage, his live-in love, Charlotte Keim, and several other friends had converged. When I stepped down, I was smothered in one hug after another, while Mick helped Hy attach the chains to the Cessna. The hugging and exclaiming continued as we started toward the house, and then I heard someone singing.

"Tough lady thought she couldn't be caught by the rhythm of the blues

Till she fell right hard for a flyin' man who had nothin left to lose . . ."

The voice belonged to my former brother-in-law, country music star Ricky Savage. The song, apparently, was one he'd written especially for Hy and me.

"So did you get married in a wedding chapel?" Hank Zahn, my former boss and closest male friend, asked.

"Plastic flowers and a rented veil?" This from his wife and law partner, Anne-Marie Altman.

"Were there Elvis impersonators?" The dark eyes of their daughter, Habiba Hamid, sparkled wickedly.

"You guys are thinking of Las Vegas," I told them. "We spent the night in Reno, then drove to Carson City, the state capital, applied for a license, and were married that afternoon by a judge. It was nice. Private. Tasteful, even."

Hank and Anne-Marie nodded approval, but Habiba looked disappointed. She was a teenager who probably would have delighted in the image of Hy and me rocking-and-rolling down the aisle.

"What, no ring?" Ted Smalley, my office manager, demanded.

"Neither of us likes to wear rings. Besides, we feel married enough as is."

"Nobody can feel too married," his partner, Neal Osborne, fingered the gold band that matched Ted's. They'd exchanged them at a ceremony at San Francisco City Hall, during the brief period when the mayor had declared the clerk's office open for the issuance of marriage licenses to gay couples.

"I guess not," I said. "And you two are a good example for all of us."

"Tell that to the governator."

"He'll be told, come next election. You're married in the eyes of your friends, and someday you'll be married in the eyes of the state."

"Sure is nice to be working for an honest woman." Charlotte Keim, my financial operative, punctuated the comment with a bawdy laugh.

My nephew Mick said, "I think that's a hint. She wants to fly off to Reno like you did."

"Flatter yourself, already!" Charlotte elbowed him in the ribs.

"One of these days I just might weaken and ask you."

"One of these days I just might weaken and ask *you*."

"Well?"

"Well?"

I smiled and left the happy couple to their half-serious standoff.

*   *   *

"So, McCone, you gonna tame him down?" Gage Renshaw, one of Hy's partners, smiled slyly at me, dark hair blowing in the wind off the sea.

"No more than he's going to tame *me* down."

"Yeah, I guess that would take some doing."

Gage never discussed personal things with me. I glanced at the champagne in his glass, wondering how many he'd had.

"In my experience," he added, "a man gets married, he gets cautious, loses his edge. In our business, that makes for mistakes. And mistakes can be fatal."

No, Gage wasn't drunk; he was trying to send a message.

"I hear you," I said, "but you're talking to the wrong person."

"Don't think so. We've got a situation coming up that's gonna require all our resources. See that your man's ready for it."

Nice wedding gift, Gage.

Hours later, clouds had gathered on the horizon, orange and pink and purple in the afterglow of the sunset. The others had retreated from the clifftop platform to the house, presumably to raid the dessert table, but Rae Kelleher and I remained behind to take in what, to me, were the most spectacular moments of the sunsets here on the Mendocino Coast. Rae—my onetime assistant, close friend, and near-relative, having married Ricky after his divorce from my younger sister Charlene.

I said, "Nice song Ricky wrote. On short notice, too."

She laughed. "He wrote it a year ago. He's been waiting for the two of you to get married before he performed it."

"Oh, and he really expected that would happen?"

"We all did—except for you."

I sighed. Sometimes our friends and relatives know us better than we know ourselves.

"It'll be on his next CD," she added.

"Our little piece of immortality."

"Well, we all want that, don't we?"

Did we? It seemed to me that right now I had everything I'd ever wanted. Even if I hadn't realized how much I'd wanted it until Hy turned the plane toward Reno a few days ago.

We sat silent for a moment. The surf boomed on the rocks in the cove below, eating at the steep cliffs. What was it the geologist who had inspected our land before we sited the house had said? Something about it possibly sliding into the sea if we intended to live there for more than a thousand years.

Right now I felt as if I could live forever.

Rae said, "What was it that tipped the scales in favor of marriage?"

"It just seemed right. Hy's been wanting this for a long time, you know. But he had a good first marriage, even if Julie was very sick for years before she died. My history with men, on the other hand—"

"Right. No need to rehash that." Rae looked down at her diamond-studded wedding ring. "Or to rehash *my* checkered past. What a bunch of losers—including me, for getting involved with them. What did your mother say when you told her the news?"

"Which one?" I had two: the adoptive mother who'd raised me and the birth mother with whom I'd finally connected a couple of years ago.

"Both."

"Well, Ma carried on as if I'd announced I'd won the Nobel Peace Prize; then she had me put Hy on the phone. To him she said, 'Congratulations on joining our family.' And then she laughed and added, 'Well, considering the family, maybe congratulations aren't in order.'"

"Oh my God. And Saskia?"

"More restrained. But she was pleased. She met Hy last summer when she was in town for a bar association meeting, and they really hit it off."

"You call Elwood?" Elwood Farmer, my birth father, an artist who lived on the Flathead Indian Reservation in Montana.

"Yes. He was . . . just Elwood."

"Meaning he didn't say much and now he's thinking over the deeper meaning of it all."

"Right."

"Must be complicated, having all those relatives. Sometimes I'm glad I've got no family left."

"What d'you mean? You're a stepmother six times over."

"That's different." She paused. "Shar, I need to talk to you about a potential case for the agency."

I felt a stirring of unease. Ricky had been a notorious womanizer throughout his marriage to my sister. If that had started again, and Rae wanted me to investigate, I couldn't possibly take it on. Conflict of interest on too many levels.

"I'm asking for a friend of mine," she added. "It's something that really means a lot to her, and it could be very lucrative for you."

I relaxed. "Tell me about it."

"Her name's Jennifer Aldin. She's a textile designer, works with a lot of the high-society decorators in the city. I got to know her through Ricky; her husband, Mark, is his financial manager."

"I thought Ricky managed his own money."

"No, Charlene always did that."

"Right." My younger sister hadn't finished high school because she was pregnant with Mick, but years later she'd gotten her GED and gone to college; now she possessed a PhD in finance and helped her new husband, international businessman Vic Christiansen, run his various enterprises.

"Anyway," Rae went on, "after Ricky and Charlene split and he established the new record label, he realized he was in over his head. I've got no talent whatsoever with money—you remember how my charge cards were always maxed out—so he went to Mark, who has a lot of clients in the entertainment industry. Mark keeps things on track, and makes us a small fortune from investments."

As if they needed more. Ricky made millions yearly, and Rae's career as a novelist was about to take off.

"So," I said, "Mark's wife is a friend of yours."

"Yes. At first it was one of those situations where the husbands get together over dinner for business reasons and the wives're supposed to make small talk. But neither Jen nor I is much good at polite chitchat; when we loosened up and started talking about things that really mattered, we discovered we had a lot in common. One of those things being a horror of artificial social situations. Now Mark and Ricky go sailing to talk business, and Jen and I do whatever pleases us."

I realized that I didn't know all that much about Rae's everyday life since she'd married and become a published author. We had lunch occasionally, talked on the phone every couple of weeks, and spent Christmas Eve together because that was when all six of Ricky and Charlene's kids gathered at the Seacliff-district house he and Rae shared. But

I didn't really know how she spent her time, or who her other friends were.

"What kinds of things do you and Jennifer do?" I asked.

"We take hikes." At my incredulous look, she grinned. "Yeah, I've hiked some of the toughest trails on Mount Tam. No more collapsing to rest every quarter mile."

"Better watch out—soon you'll be running the Bay to Breakers."

"I haven't reformed *that* much. Anyway, we also go antiquing, and to galleries, visit museums, or run up to the wine country and do some tasting."

"Sounds nice." And it made me feel wistful. I'd been so busy managing the agency—which was growing month by month—that I seldom saw most of my women friends. My male friends, too; I couldn't remember when I'd last spent time with Hank.

Hell, it was a wonder I'd found the time to get married!

"Okay," I added, "now tell me what Jennifer wants investigated."

Rae nibbled on a fingernail, looking out to sea. "It's a long shot, I think. Twenty-two years ago, when Jennifer was ten, her mother, Laurel Greenwood, disappeared down in San Luis Obispo County. One of those cases where it looks like the person's either disappeared voluntarily or committed suicide, but everybody says, 'She never would have done that; it must be foul play.' And in this case they may be right. There was no trouble in the Greenwood marriage. Laurel was content with her life, a good mother, as well as a successful businesswoman, and very involved in her community."

"And no body was ever found."

"No trace of her. Afterward, Jen's father became very

closed off, didn't permit her or her sister to so much as mention their mother's name. Seven months ago, when he was diagnosed with pancreatic cancer, Jen tried to talk with him about her mother, but he flat-out refused. He died two months later, and then Jen started obsessing about the disappearance. Finally she looked up the newspaper accounts of it. There was a big media flap for the first few days, then nothing. Almost as if someone had put a lid on the case."

"This was handled by the SLO County Sheriff's Department?"

"Right."

"She talk to the investigating officers?"

"The guy in charge has died. The deputy she spoke with wasn't very interested in helping her. Can't blame him; it's a cold case, and he's got better things to do with his time."

"So she came to you, since you used to be an investigator."

"Actually, no. Mark got worried about her obsessing. She was losing weight, not sleeping or eating properly, not working well. So he decided he'd bankroll a full-scale investigation into her mother's disappearance, and asked Ricky if he thought your agency would be right for the job. Of course, he said it would."

"A full-scale investigation into a cold case?"

"The works. Mark's willing to spend whatever it takes to give Jen peace of mind."

"Sounds like he loves her a lot."

"Yeah, he does."

I asked, "So why didn't Jennifer Aldin approach me directly? Why have you pave the way?"

"She only decided to go ahead with the investigation yesterday. Last night, the four of us were having dinner, and when I mentioned that Ricky and I were coming up here for the party, she asked me to speak with you. The thing is, she wants you to handle the case personally."

"Why me?"

"Because you're the best there is."

"According to . . . ?"

"Ricky and me. The man on the street. Oh, hell, Shar, will you take it on? Jen needs closure in order to get her life back on track."

I considered. Late last month I'd wrapped up a case that had been very personal and had threatened my career, as well as the existence of the agency. After having my attention taken away from normal business affairs for two weeks, I'd been trying to make up for lost time, but managing our heavy caseload and the attendant paperwork threatened even now to overwhelm me. Still, Ted could pick up some of the slack in the paperwork department, and I had a couple of new operatives who were coming along fast. . . .

I was mentally shifting priorities and assignments as I said to Rae, "Okay. I'll call Jennifer tomorrow, and maybe we can set something up for later in the week."

"If I know her, she'll want to see you soonest."

"If so, I can fit her in on Tuesday afternoon. We're flying down tomorrow night."

"What, so soon? You and Hy aren't taking any more time off?"

"Can't. He's due in La Jolla at RKI headquarters on Wednesday. Business is booming—their clients see terrorists behind every tree—and they're hiring so many people that they need to restructure their training operations."

And they've got a situation coming up. One that will require all their resources, according to Gage. I can't even ask Hy about it, because he'd be furious at Gage for mentioning it to me. For attempting to dictate the terms of our relationship. If RKI is in trouble, the last thing they need is dissension among the partners.

Rae said, "So marriage isn't going to change anything for you guys."

"We don't expect it to."

She grinned. "Wait and see."

"What's that supposed to mean?"

"Just wait and see."

Tuesday

•

AUGUST 16

Jennifer and Mark Aldin lived down the Peninsula in Atherton, an old-money, quietly rich suburb some twenty-five miles south of the city. Red Hawk Lane had a country feel, narrow and overhung with big oak trees; a high tan stucco wall surrounded the Aldin property, and behind it sprawled a matching stucco house with a red tile roof. Sprinklers threw out lazy streams of water onto an improbably green, manicured lawn, the droplets glistening in the early afternoon sun.

A uniformed maid—Latina, with a thick accent—answered the door and showed me to a living room with a beamed ceiling and terra-cotta floors covered with jute area rugs. As she urged me with hand gestures to sit on one of a U-shaped grouping of mission-style sofas in front of a fireplace, she said, "Mrs. Aldin, she will be with you in a short time."

"*Gracias*," I replied.

A smile flickered across her lips. "*De nada.*"

California: the ultimate melting pot of this already diverse country. Some fluency in Spanish is almost a necessity here—indeed, Latinos are now the fastest-growing ethnic group in our population. For people in my profession, it also helps to understand some Chinese, Japanese, and Tagalog— as well as a smattering of ghetto slang.

As I waited for Jennifer Aldin, I looked around the room. French doors opened onto a patio with a black-bottomed pool and a scattering of teak tables and lounge chairs. The air that filtered through the doors was faintly scented by chlorine and cape jasmine. Because of the walls' thickness, the living room remained cool in the afternoon's heat, and the white cushions of the spartan-looking sofa were surprisingly comfortable. I settled back and studied a framed piece of cloth that hung over the mantel—red, orange, black, and gold, woven in a complex, abstract pattern that might have been a replica of a fire in the hearth below. Jennifer Aldin's work? If so, even to my untutored eye, she had a good deal of talent.

I heard footsteps behind me, turned, and then stood. The woman was as tall as I and slender to the point of being emaciated, clad in narrow-fitting white jeans and a matching tunic, her honey-colored hair hanging dull and stringy to her shoulders. Her eyes were deeply shadowed, her skin dry. The smile she gave me was wan, the nails of the long-fingered hand she extended me bitten down to the quick. Jennifer Aldin, I saw, had once been beautiful, but five months of obsessing over her mother's disappearance had taken their toll.

"Sharon," she said, "I'm Jennifer. Thank you for coming."

In spite of her fragile appearance, Jennifer had a strong handshake, an open face with a scattering of freckles across her small nose, and direct blue eyes. A straightforward woman. I understood why she and Rae had become friends.

After the usual pleasantries—"Happy to try to help you; Rae speaks highly of your friendship." "Congratulations on your marriage. How was the party?"—we got settled on the sofas, a wide glass-topped table between us. Immediately the maid—Alicia, Jennifer called her—appeared with a tray containing a pitcher of lemonade and two glasses. After she served us and departed, I took out my voice-activated tape recorder and asked Jennifer if she'd mind if I kept a record of our conversation. She didn't.

"I've come to this meeting better prepared than at most of my new-client consultations," I said. "Rae has briefed me on your situation, and this morning I accessed the news reports of your mother's disappearance. What we need to do now is discuss what you expect of me and my agency, as well as what we can reasonably hope to provide. I take it Rae's told you she considers the investigation a long shot?"

Jennifer nodded. "She did say that. And I've reviewed every piece of information I could find about . . . that time, so I know how little there is to go on. But . . . Sharon, do you know what it's like to lose a parent?"

"Yes, I do. My father—adoptive father, actually—died of a heart attack a couple of years ago."

"And that was painful, I'm sure; I lost my own dad to cancer only a few months ago. But my mother . . . What would it have been like if your father had simply disappeared, if you never knew what had happened to him?"

"I can't imagine."

"Let me try to describe the experience. You're ten years old. Your mother comes to your bedroom one night and together you read a chapter of the current book—in this case it was *The Wind in the Willows*—as she's done nearly every night for as long as you can remember. She kisses you, reminds you she's going to the coast to paint in the morning, and she'll be back late, so you're to mind your father and look out for Terry, your little sister. The next night she *is* late, but you go to sleep, sure you'll see her in the morning. But in the morning she's still not there. You go off to school, expecting she'll be there when you return that afternoon." Jennifer paused, took a deep breath. Her face had gone pale, and she'd laced her long fingers together and thrust her hands between her knees. After a moment she went on.

"When the school bus drops you and Terry off that afternoon, there's a police car in front of the house. Lots of people are there: your dad, who's never home that early; your mom's best friend; the next-door neighbor lady; your Aunt Anna; two men in uniform. You keep asking what's happened, but they won't tell you anything, and Aunt Anna takes you and Terry to the kitchen for Coke and cookies. Aunt Anna's upset, you can tell because she won't look at you, and when you ask if something's happened to Mom, all she says is, 'She'll be back soon.' But you know she's lying, and your throat seizes up so there's no way you can eat a bite of those cookies or take a sip of the Coke."

Jennifer's voice had slipped into a higher pitch, and her eyes were focused rigidly on the cleanly swept hearth. Going back in time, reliving the incident. I felt a prickling of concern for her, but didn't interrupt.

"For two days it goes on like that," she continued. "Dad stays at home, but he's not paying much attention to you. Aunt Anna and Aunt Sally—Mom's best friend—are there most of the time, too. You and Terry are confined to the house, they won't even let you go to school. Terry's scared— she's only six—and she's afraid to ask questions, so you do. 'What's happened to Mom?' you say. 'She's away painting,' they tell you. 'She'll be back soon.' But you know she's not away painting; in all the time she's done that, she's never been gone this long. And the postcard hasn't come. When she goes someplace to paint, she always sends a postcard addressed to herself—no message, just a souvenir for her collection. Besides, why were the police at the house that first day? Why do they keep coming back to talk with Dad? And why hasn't he gone to work?"

Jennifer shrank back against the sofa's cushions, crossing her arms, hands grasping her elbows. The singsong, childlike quality in her voice had become more pronounced. She shivered.

I remained still, sensing she was coming to a critical point in the narrative.

"Then, on the third morning, your dad's acting just like he used to before your mom disappeared. He's dressed for work, and has had Aunt Anna—who came over early—get you and Terry ready for school. But he's not really the same; he's too cheerful, and he's never cheerful in the morning. He's even made oatmeal, and it's all gluey, but you choke it down to please him, because he's been so upset, and now he seems so sad under all those big smiles. When you're finished, he pushes back from the table and looks at you and Terry and says, 'I'm sorry, girls, but we have to get on with our lives. Your mother would have wanted it that way.'

"Terry starts to cry, and you ask, 'Why, Daddy? Is she dead?'

"And then his face changes—scrunches up, gets red and ugly. He says, 'Your mother is *not* dead. We don't know what happened to her, but she is not dead. You are never to suggest that again. *Never.* Someday you will understand why.'

"Terry stops crying and looks really scared, and you don't

say a word because you know better. There's that tone in his voice that you've heard before when he's warned you not to do something. It's a tone that tells you he means what he's saying, and you obey. Besides, then his expression changes, and he looks so sad that you're afraid if you say anything more, he'll start shaking and then maybe break into little pieces. And then you'll be all alone in the world, with nobody to love you—because Aunt Anna doesn't really like kids, and Aunt Sally and the neighbor lady have families of their own to look after. You'll be all alone, except for Terry, who is so little and needs such a lot of looking after. That's too much for a ten-year-old to bear, so you keep quiet, in order to save your dad and yourself.

"That night, after you've gone to bed, your dad lights a big bonfire in the backyard and throws all your mom's paintings into it. You run out, crying, and he holds you and tells you it's for the best, so you can all make a new life without missing her so badly. But after he's put you back in bed, you cry some more because you loved those paintings, especially the one of the old hotel where Mom told you she and Dad spent their honeymoon.

"Then, after a while, you realize your dad was right, because things do kind of get back to normal. You go to school and to your ballet lessons; for a while Aunt Anna fixes meals that are actually better than Mom's; then Dad learns to cook and do the laundry and takes you camping like he always did. When you mention your mom, he sounds kind of absentminded. 'She loves you,' he says at first. And then, 'She lov*ed* you.' Gradually you stop talking about her, and it goes on for years and years like that, but there's still this . . . *place* inside you where something's not right—"

"Darling?" a voice said from outside. "You okay?"

A man in tennis whites stood in the doorway. Medium height, thick gray hair, deep tan. Craggy face, nose that looked like it had been broken more than once; deep lines around his eyes and mouth. He moved quickly into the room, toward Jennifer.

"Oh, God." She put a hand to her pale face, leaned forward. "Mark, I didn't mean to—"

"It's all right, darling." He stepped between us, as if to hide her distress from me, put his arms around her.

After a bit, he straightened. Jennifer got up from the sofa, saying, "Excuse me for a minute," and hurried from the room.

Mark Aldin turned toward me, his rough features drawn into worried lines. Up close I saw that he was much older than Jennifer—at least twenty years. Perhaps she was a trophy wife? The disparity in their ages and appearances would point to that.

"Sharon," he said, "I'm Mark. I've heard good things about you from Rick and Rae. In the newspapers as well."

I smiled wryly. "Don't believe everything you read in the press." I motioned toward the archway through which his wife had fled. "Is she going to be all right?"

"For now." He sat down in the space she'd vacated. "Telling the story of her mother's disappearance has a cathartic effect on her. She'll feel better for days afterwards. Then the downward cycle begins." He ran a hand over his forehead, pushed thick fingers through his hair.

"This has been going on since her father's death?"

"Yes. Before that, she was matter-of-fact about her mother's disappearance; it was something that had happened a long time ago. But once Roy Greenwood died . . . well, you've seen her relive the events."

"Must be difficult for you."

"I don't care about me. But it's wrecking Jen's whole life. She spends hours in her studio out back, not working, just poring over old newspaper clippings and brooding about what happened. Her clients are angry with her for missing deadlines. Her friends—except for Rae—have drifted away. I'm afraid if she doesn't have some closure on this soon, she won't have much of a life to come back to."

"I have to warn you: I may not be able to provide her with that closure. This is a very old, cold case."

"I realize that, but I don't know where else to turn."

"Have you talked to Jennifer about getting professional help?"

"Of course I have. Psychotherapy is not something she wants to pursue. So . . ." He smiled, his skewed features transformed so he looked nearly handsome. "You're the professional help, Sharon. What do we need to do to get this investigation under way?"

Driving back to the city with a contract signed by Jennifer and a large retainer check from Mark in my briefcase, I was glad that I'd boned up on the events surrounding Laurel Greenwood's disappearance before I met with her daughter. The facts of the case were rendered dry and brittle by time, but hearing Jennifer speak of her experience in a voice that more resembled a bewildered ten-year-old's than an adult's had brought the events fully alive.

Twenty-two years ago, the Greenwoods had been living in Paso Robles—officially named El Paso de Robles, the Pass of the Oaks—a small town at the intersection of state highways 101 and 46, some two hundred miles south of San Francisco. The convergence of these major east-west and north-south routes makes Paso Robles a natural stopping place for travelers; I myself used to pull off there to gas up while driving between UC Berkeley and my parents' home in San Diego. About all I remembered of the place was an A&W drive-in where I occasionally stopped for a chili dog, and the Paso Robles Inn, an old-fashioned mission-style mineral-bath spa.

In December of 2003 a devastating earthquake—6.5 on the Richter scale—had shaken the town, killing two women and sending more than forty other people to area hospitals; a number of the older buildings were seriously damaged, and financial losses soared into the millions. I'd recently read somewhere that Paso Robles had recovered from the San Simeon quake and was undergoing fast growth; wineries had sprung up in the surrounding countryside and were becoming popular tourist destinations. But back when the Greenwoods lived there, it was basically a little town where people led quiet, ordinary existences.

And up until June of 1983, the family's existence had been just that. Roy Greenwood, a native of nearby Atascadero, was an oral surgeon with offices in a medical-professional building a block off the main street. His wife, Laurel, whom he had met when they were undergraduates at San Jose State, was a graphic artist who owned a company specializing in greeting cards for children; she worked out of their home. The Greenwoods were comfortably off, but by no means rich, even by the standards of a country town; Roy's practice suffered because he extended liberal credit to patients who couldn't afford necessary dental work, and Laurel's greeting cards, while popular in stores as far north as Monterey and as far south as Santa Maria, turned only a small profit. Jennifer Greenwood and her younger sister, Terry, attended public school, where they were considered exceptionally bright and well adjusted. Both parents were active in the PTA and on various committees of St. John's Lutheran Church.

Laurel Greenwood had a ritual that provided a respite from her busy life as a wife, mother, and small business owner: every so often she would take a "mental health day" and travel to some location within an easy round-trip drive of Paso Robles, to paint landscapes. During each of these getaways, she would select a postcard that she felt best represented the area and mail it to herself for inclusion in a collection she kept in a file box in her office. The collection, she would joke, would probably be the only legacy she'd leave her daughters, but at least they'd know where Mom had been.

An ordinary, uneventful, pleasant family life. Until June twenty-second, when it was forever altered.

Laurel had planned to paint seascapes at the coastal hamlet of Cayucos, some twenty-five miles southwest of Paso Robles. She was seen doing so at a coastal overlook north of town, and one man, Jacob Ziff, stopped to look at her work and chatted with her for a while. Later Ziff spotted her in the Sea Shack, a restaurant in the center of town; she was at a table on the oceanside deck, drinking wine with a long-haired man in biker's leathers. Ziff noted that the two left separately, the man walking north on the highway to a liquor store and Laurel getting into her beat-up Volkswagen bus and driving south. The bus later turned up at a waterfront park in Morro Bay, less than ten miles away. According to a pair of dogwalkers who saw Laurel arrive, she got out and walked toward the nearby shopping area. After that no one saw her—or would admit to seeing her—again.

Roy Greenwood wasn't aware that his wife didn't return that night. He'd had a busy day, including two difficult surgeries, and went to bed early. In the morning he wasn't overly concerned; occasionally if Laurel stayed away too late on one of her painting trips, she would take a motel room and drive back in the morning. But it did puzzle him that she hadn't called to tell him her plans, so he checked back at the house at noon. When he found she still wasn't there, he called the chief of police, Bruce Collingsworth, a good friend and tennis partner; Collingsworth alerted the highway patrol to be on the lookout for Laurel's van, and later sent officers to the Greenwood house to question Roy.

When the highway patrol located Laurel's bus in Morro Bay and she failed to return the second night, the search intensified; the San Luis Obispo County Sheriff's Department stepped in. Television and newspaper reportage prompted a rash of calls from people who claimed to have sighted Laurel, the most promising being those from Jacob Ziff, the staff at the Sea Shack, and the dogwalkers in Morro Bay. Descriptions of the biker she'd been seen with at the restaurant were broadcast, but they were vague at best, and he seemed to have vanished as completely as Laurel. What further alarmed Roy Greenwood was that no postcard from Cayucos appeared in his mailbox. Laurel had never failed to add to her collection before.

And then, suddenly, the case was back-burnered. Press inquiries were routinely referred to the sheriff's department's public information officer, who merely said they were pursuing "various leads." Roy Greenwood, who had been forthcoming with the media, declined to give interviews, citing the need to "return to normalcy for the sake of my little girls." A silence settled, and since the press does not feed on silence, interest in the case waned and finally disappeared entirely.

So what had happened to Laurel Greenwood? Kidnapping? There had been no attempt to collect a ransom. Foul play or suicide? Quite possible. The bodies of many victims of violent crimes—both inflicted by others or themselves—are never found. Voluntary disappearance? Again, possible. Even though the families, friends, and associates of most missing persons insist that they would never desert them, a vast majority of disappearances are just that. Family, friends, and associates aren't always privy to an individual's true feelings and inclinations. Laurel Greenwood could have had a secret life apart from them, one she'd finally decided to disappear into—or one that had claimed her life.

And what about Roy Greenwood burning his wife's paintings so soon after her disappearance? What had prompted that? His desire for a return to normalcy, as reported in the press? His determination to make a new life for the three of them without, as he'd told Jennifer, missing her so badly?

Could have been either. People have their different ways of dealing with loss and grief.

Or it could have been something else entirely.

This case fascinated me. Both the what-happened and the why-it-happened. Tomorrow I'd assemble my staff in a meeting, reshuffle assignments, and get the investigation under way.

At nine-thirty that night I was reclining on my bed, watching Hy pack for his trip to La Jolla. Over dinner at a favorite Cajun restaurant, I'd told him what I could about the new case without violating client confidentiality, and now I was mulling over some of his comments and planning tomorrow morning's presentation to my staff.

"Damn!" he exclaimed, startling me.

I looked over to where he stood at the chest of drawers.

"I don't have any black socks," he added.

"You just bought some."

"Yeah, but they're either at the ranch or Touchstone. I'll have to buy more."

"Well, they're not exactly a rare commodity."

He shut the drawer that was designated as his and examined the contents of his duffel, then zipped it. "McCone, does it ever strike you as ridiculous, having your possessions travel around from place to place and never knowing where they're at?"

"Sometimes. I'm always running out of underwear at the ranch, and I've never driven up to Touchstone without the trunk loaded with . . . well, stuff."

"Exactly—stuff. It goes back and forth, one place or the other, and when you want it, it's never where you are."

"It would be an expensive proposition to have enough of everything at each place."

"Exactly. Three places is too many for two people. We ought to get rid of one."

"We'd never give up Touchstone, especially after all we went through having the house built there. And we need a base here in the city."

"I was thinking of my ranch."

"You love the ranch." It was a hundred acres of sheep graze in the high desert of Mono County, near Tufa Lake, on the western slope of the Sierra Nevada. Hy had inherited it decades ago from his stepfather.

"I do love it, but I'm hardly ever there. If it wasn't for Ramon Perez, the place would've gone to hell a long time ago." He paused. "Ramon's a good foreman, and he's saved practically every penny I've ever paid him. When I was up there last month, he hinted he might want to buy the place."

"What did you tell him?"

"Like I said, he only hinted. But if I did sell to him, I think I could work a deal where he'd let us come up and stay from time to time."

"It wouldn't be the same, though."

He sat on the bed, put a hand on my ankle. "Things change, and sometimes it's for the better. I was thinking if I did sell, we could use the money to buy a bigger place here in the city."

"A bigger— You mean sell this house, too?"

"Well, it *is* a little small for two people to live on a near full-time basis."

"But it's . . . my *home.*"

"I know that, and it's just a suggestion. Something to think about, is all. Now, how about we open that bottle of brandy that Mick and Charlotte gave us? Toast to us and our new beginnings."

Damn, the man certainly could drop a bombshell and just walk away while the rubble was settling. But it was a conversation I'd just as soon walk away from anyway, so I smiled and said, "Why not?"

Later that night, though, as Hy slumbered peacefully beside me, I tossed and turned and fretted. When I'd first seen the little house on the tail end of Church Street out beyond where the J-line streetcar tracks stop, it had been a pathetically shabby structure. One of the city's four thousand earthquake cottages—makeshift two- or three-room structures erected as emergency housing after the quake of '06— it had been moved from its original location, expanded to five rooms, and raised up to accomodate a garage and laundry area beneath. I was able to buy it at a very low price because of the extensive work it needed to make it reasonably habitable, and I'd had the kitchen remodeled and later contracted for three new additions: a full bathroom to replace the cold cubicle on the back porch that contained the toilet and shower, a master bedroom, and a backyard deck. I loved the house, and I loved the close-knit neighborhood.

Where else in the city could I hire a teenaged girl who was a wannabe real estate mogul to twice daily administer insulin shots to my diabetic cat, and also tend to my other cat, plants, and mail during my frequent absences? Where else would I have a doctor across the street who paid house calls? Or another neighbor who frequently dropped off care packages of homemade bread and preserves? People here cared about one another, watched out for the security of one another's homes. I supposed there were more enclaves like this in the city, but it might take years to find one, more years to develop those kinds of friendly ties.

No, I didn't want to sell my home. But I could understand Hy's rationale about it being too small. And, after all, he was willing to sell his equally beloved ranch. . . .

God, marriage was already changing things. Was this what Rae had hinted at when she'd said, "Just wait and see"?

Wednesday

·

AUGUST 17

My staff members were milling around our conference room on the second floor of Pier 24½, cups of coffee and muffins in hand. I set my briefcase on the round oak table and began taking files from it. While I arranged them, I studied my investigative team.

Ted was clad in chinos and a vintage Hawaiian shirt, his latest fashion statement. His black goatee was trimmed very short because, he'd told me, it had begun to show more gray than the hair on his head. Beside him stood Kendra Williams, his latest candidate for the position of "paragon of the paper clips." Dozens of young men and women, all of them eager to become Ted's assistant, had been paraded before my eyes in the past few months, but none had worked out. So far Kendra, whom I'd met the previous afternoon, seemed the most promising. A tiny woman of twenty-five, with a chocolate-brown complexion and cornrows, she had greeted me cheerfully and hadn't so much as winced when a great crash echoed up from the floor of the pier—two deliverymen dropping a crate destined for the architectural firm off the opposite catwalk. An ability to remain calm in chaotic circumstances was often required here at the pier, and apparently Kendra possessed it.

God, I hoped she proved equal to the challenge of the job! I would need to rely heavily on Ted's efficiency in the days ahead, and it would be good if he also had someone competent to fall back on.

Mick, who headed our computer forensics department, was leaning against one of the bookcases that lined the room, talking with his new assistant, Derek Ford. While both were tall, the resemblance stopped there. My nephew's blond good looks came from the Scotch-Irish side of our family; Derek was a handsome, dark-haired Eurasian. Mick showed evidence of putting on weight, a consequence of his and Charlotte's fondness for trying whatever new restaurant came along; Derek was very lean and had told me he followed a strict vegan diet. Mick dressed casually, with little concern for style; Derek was a devotee of urban chic, a tattoo of linked scorpions encircling his neck. But the two men had instantly bonded over their fascination with the endless possibilities of computer technology. Together they were working on developing investigative tools that I failed to understand. Of course, I didn't understand the tools they now possessed, even though Mick would dismiss them as rudimentary. I did know that one day they'd be able to retrieve just about any piece of information I'd ask for. And they'd retrieve it within the bounds of the law. Or else.

Charlotte and Mick also shared a love of technology, but her expertise was in business and finance: give her a credit card number, and she'd run a subject to earth in no time; present her with evidence of corporate chicanery, and she'd build a case that would stand up in any court. She stood by the door with her new assistant, Patrick Neilan. Charlotte was telling him a joke, one that involved a lot of hand gestures and shaking of her brown curls. When she finished, Patrick blushed to the roots of his red hair before his wide mouth twitched and he snorted. Charlotte threw her head back and let fly one of her bawdy laughs. A risqué joke, no doubt about that.

Only two staff members had yet to put in an appearance: Julia Rafael and Craig Morland. I'd decided to call the meeting to order without them when they rushed in, practically knocking each other over. Julia, a tall Latina with haughty features, moving stiffly as a result of having been shot in the chest by a sniper last month, immediately looked mortified. She was a relatively new hire; minor faux pas that wouldn't have fazed the rest of us severely discomforted her, and it didn't help that during our last investigation she'd unwittingly become embroiled in a situation that had almost cost me my private investigator's license. Craig, who shared an office with her, sensed her discomfort, and threw his arm around her shoulders, leaning on her and miming great pain. After a moment Julia smiled wryly. Craig, in his running clothes, his longish brown hair tousled, barely resembled the tightly wound FBI field agent whom I'd met a few years before. Over the time he'd worked for me, I'd found him to be a surprisingly perceptive and sensitive man—just the kind of person Julia needed as a friend.

Once they got their coffee and muffins, I called, "Let's get settled, folks. We've got a lot of ground to cover."

For an hour I went over every case on the assignment sheet, finding out its exact status from the person who was handling it. Then I called a fifteen-minute break while I did some further reshuffling. Finally I was ready to get to the Laurel Greenwood disappearance. I'd had Ted make up packets containing all the background information on the case, as well as a transcript of my tape of yesterday's meeting with Jennifer Aldin. While they glanced through the packets, I summarized the situation.

"Normally," I concluded, "I wouldn't be briefing everyone on this. But the case is high pay and thus high priority; and it promises to be a difficult one. Any cop will tell you that if you don't solve a missing person case—no matter if it's foul play, kidnapping, or deliberate disappearance—within the first twenty-four hours, chances are you'll never solve it. And what we've got here is a twenty-two-year-old case. Nearly impossible."

"Not for *this* agency."

"I said *nearly*, Mick." I looked around the table. "I'm going to need to count on all of you. Those who aren't assigned to the investigation this morning will keep their individual caseloads, and pick up the slack from others. As the investigation progresses, it may be necessary to pull some people off and make reassignments. So you'll need to familiarize yourselves with the information in your packets, and of course, you'll be briefed on what's happening during our regularly scheduled conferences."

"You'll be in the field, Shar?" Craig asked.

"Yes. Ted'll be holding things together here in the office, and Kendra—you've all met Kendra, right?—she'll be holding *him* together."

"About time somebody did," Charlotte said.

"Wait till you turn in your next expense report," Ted warned her.

I said, "Okay—assignments. I'll be personally talking to everyone we can locate who is mentioned in the accounts of Laurel Greenwood's disappearance, as well as anyone else

Jennifer Aldin suggests. Derek—you'll locate and background those people, starting immediately. I'd also appreciate it if you'd make yourself available to conduct
spur-of-the-moment searches for me while I'm in the field."

Mick was frowning, hurt at being left out.

I said to him, "You—the genius, as Derek calls you—need
to concentrate on running your department." There was a
growing corporate demand for computer forensics—the sci-
ence of recovering files that had been inadvertently or deliberately deleted. Mick had originally suggested we offer the
service to our existing clients, and once we'd announced it,
the work had poured in, both from them and other compa-
nies they'd referred to us.

"Shar," he said, "I can handle both."

"Not and have a life, you can't. And I think Charlotte
would agree that you having a life outside the agency is a
good thing."

"Amen to that!" Charlotte exclaimed.

"Don't get excited," I told her. "You may end up being the
one in your household who needs coddling and cosseting."

"Say what?"

"Needing TLC after a hard day at the office. You'll retain
your caseload, but I may have to call on you if any tricky financial angles come up. Plus I'm temporarily taking Patrick
away from you. Patrick," I added to Neilan, "you'll be assisting me full-time."

His eyes widened, and then his freckled face glowed with
pleasure.

Patrick Neilan was my newest operative, and I suspected
most of the staff regarded him as a sympathy hire. When I'd
first encountered him—as a witness during last month's
major investigation—I'd learned that he was also the subject

of a search we had undertaken for his ex-wife the year before. My regret at the fact that the information we'd provided her had resulted in his financial downfall had prompted me to hire him temporarily, and he'd shown the potential to be a good investigator. Now that I'd hired him full-time, I wanted to give him the chance to prove himself to his coworkers.

I added, "Let's get back to work, everybody. Patrick and Derek—I want to see you in my office."

My office was at the far end of the pier, a large space with a high arching window overlooking the bay and the East Bay cities and hills. One side wall rose toward the roof, a strip of multipaned windows at its top letting in soft northern light; the other was an eight-foot-high partition with a door that opened onto the catwalk. The furnishings—desk and clients' chairs; file cabinets; armoire that served as a coat closet; easy chair beneath a schefflera plant, in which to do serious thinking—seemed dwarfed by their spacious surroundings. When we'd moved in, the rent set by the Port Commission had barely seemed affordable, even though it was low by waterfront standards because of the pier's unfortunate location under the western span of the Bay Bridge and next door to the SFFD fireboat station. But within a couple of years, we'd taken over all the upstairs space on the northern side and were handling the increased cost easily. We'd also become inured to the fire station's siren going off, as well as the roaring and clanking of traffic on the bridge's roadbed overhead.

I dumped my files on the desk, motioning for Patrick and Derek to be seated. Then I pulled a list from on top of the pile and handed it to my computer expert.

"These are the people we need to locate and background,"

I said. "Whatever information we have on them appears in
your packet. E-mail the files to me, copy Patrick, and also
print it out for Ted to copy and distribute to everybody. Any
questions?"

Derek studied the list. "You want me to search in the order
you've got them listed?"

"Yes, but don't waste too much time on those that're difficult to locate, just move ahead."

"Will do." He stood.

"One more thing," I said. "Mick will want to help you.
Don't let him. He's got enough to do."

Derek nodded and gave me a little salute as he left the
office.

I turned to Patrick. "Okay, your function will be to coordinate things here in the office. I'll be messengering tapes
and e-mailing reports back from the field for you to organize and study for patterns or leads that I may have missed.
Any and all suggestions or theories will be welcome. As you
saw last month, I'm not the sort of investigator who refuses
to listen to input, so feel free to offer your two cents whenever. Right now"—I looked at my watch—"I think we
should grab some lunch. Then I want you to come with me
while I conduct a field interview with Jennifer Aldin's sister,
Terry Wyatt."

Patrick stood, looking eager. He was thirty-four, twice a
father, had a business degree from Golden Gate University,
and had been an accountant before his job was eliminated
and he'd been forced to turn to security work to make ends
meet. His wife leaving him for another man, her frequent re-
fusals to allow him to see their children, her garnishing of his
small wages—all that should have left him a broken man.
But Patrick had somehow maintained a balance, and now, as

he began a new career, he exhibited both optimism and an almost childlike pleasure in life.

We walked down the Embarcadero and had burgers at Miranda's, my favorite waterfront diner, then headed east over the Bay Bridge in the agency van, our destination Davis, the university town west of Sacramento. On the way I conducted an informal training session on the art of the field interview: how to structure it; when to press for answers; when to sit back and wait for the answers to come; what body language to watch for; what tones of voice, inflections, and hidden meanings to listen to.

"Even when a person has nothing to hide, there will be details they'll deliberately omit or that will slip through the cracks," I told him. "A bad memory, a rewriting of history, an aversion to a certain subject, or simply the idea that something isn't important—they all can contribute to your getting an incomplete picture."

"You say 'picture,' rather than 'answers' or 'set of facts.' What exactly d'you mean?"

"What do the facts a given individual provides you with add up to? How do they relate to the facts others have given you? Do they agree? Contradict? Where do they fit within the framework of the investigation? What other avenues of investigation do they point to?"

Patrick shook his head. "Conducting and analyzing an interview's more complicated than I thought. You study this in school?"

"Nope. I was a sociology major at Berkeley—which was interesting enough, but not very practical. Some of this stuff I learned from my first boss, the man whose investigator's license I trained under. But most of it came from trial and error. A lot of error. When I started training people myself, I realized I'd have to articulate the process, or they'd make the same mistakes I did. That meant I had to do a lot of thinking about what it is I actually do, whereas before I was just winging it."

"I'll bet you could write a textbook."

"I was asked to, after I gave a talk at a symposium last year, but it's not going to happen. I spend too much time at my desk as it is."

I took the central Davis exit and followed Terry Wyatt's instructions to a quiet, tree-shaded block of Twelfth Street, lined with ranch-style homes that I judged to have been built in the 1950s. The uniform size of the lots indicated the area was an older subdivision, and all the houses probably had once been alike, but over the years they'd been remodeled and embellished with decorative touches so now no two looked the same. Terry Wyatt's was the exception; its clean, simple lines were in the classic suburban style of fifty years ago.

As Patrick and I approached the front door, a dog began barking, and I heard the scrabbling of toenails on hardwood. Then a second canine voice joined in, and a woman called, "Augie, Freddie—stop that!"

The dogs quieted instantly.

"Well trained," Patrick murmured.

The door opened partway, and a tall woman with dark blonde hair who bore an unmistakable resemblance to Jennifer Aldin looked out. She was holding fast to the collar of a black dog of indeterminate breed; the dog's eyes were lively and inquisitive.

"Ms. McCone?" the woman said. "I'm Terry Wyatt. Just give me a minute to put the dogs outside." She closed the door and went away, calling, "Come on, I don't want you bothering my company." After a moment she returned, admitting us to an entryway.

"They sound like watchdogs," she told us, "but actually they're just overly enthusiastic about visitors." She glanced questioningly at Patrick, and I introduced him as my assistant. After they'd shaken hands, she said, "Would you mind sitting in the dining area? I'm making some jam, and I need to keep an eye on it."

Terry Wyatt led us through a roomy kitchen to an area containing a baker's table and invited us to sit. Behind us was a living room with a fireplace and built-in bookcases, and beyond it a glass door overlooking the backyard. The dog I'd glimpsed earlier and another tan one stood outside, noses pressed to the glass.

"Ignore them," Terry said, noticing the direction of my gaze. "They'll get bored and go play."

Up close, Terry's resemblance to Jennifer was even more striking; while her hair was darker and cropped short, she had the same high cheekbones and scattering of freckles, the same direct gaze. Her movements were similar, too—quick and economical—but I sensed an absence of the tension that was present in her sister; in fact, Terry radiated calm well-being.

She brought us soft drinks, then went back to check a big pot on the stove. A tantalizing odor rose from it as she raised the lid. "Pluots," she explained, taking a seat at the table. "My favorite produce guy at the farmer's market insisted I take an entire box. You can only eat so many Pluots—hence jam."

"Are you going to put it up in jars?" I asked, taking out my tape recorder.

"Sure."

"I've always been afraid to do that."

"Botulism, you mean?" She grinned. "Maybe, if you were putting up green beans and really didn't know what you were doing. I have a degree in home ec from UC and teach at a cooking school. Haven't killed anybody yet." She glanced at the recorder.

"You mind if I tape our conversation?" I asked. "It makes for greater accuracy."

"Not at all. It's just that seeing the recorder brought me back to the point of your visit. Jen's really serious about finding out what happened to our mother, isn't she?"

"Yes. How do you feel about that?"

She shrugged. "Ambivalent, I guess."

I glanced at Patrick. He'd taken out a notebook and was uncapping a pen.

"In what ways?"

"Well, it's important to Jen's peace of mind, and that means it's important to me. We're closer than most sisters; we had to be. After our mother disappeared, we had kind of a weird upbringing."

"In what way?"

"Our father became very distant, wrapped up in his own grief, I suppose. Our Aunt Anna assumed the mother's role in our lives, but she made it clear she resented the responsibility. And Mom's best friend, Aunt Sally, whom both of us loved and would gladly have gone to live with, was more or less banished. Dad and Aunt Anna were really strict with us; we weren't allowed to hang out with friends or date, and they always wanted to know exactly where we were at any given time. If we were delayed at school or something like that and didn't call, we were grounded. Which was ridiculous, really, since the way we lived was like being grounded anyway."

"Perhaps they were afraid you'd vanish like your mother did."

"I suppose. But in a way, their overprotectiveness *did* make us vanish, because once we left for college, we seldom went home."

"All this started when you were four years younger than Jennifer, at a very impressionable age," I said, "but your father's recent death doesn't seem to have triggered any need in you to find out what happened to your mother."

"I think that's precisely because I was so young. To tell the truth, I don't remember Mom all that well, and I never missed her the way Jen did. Besides, I have a feeling . . ."

"Yes?"

"A feeling that we may be opening up a Pandora's box here. I mean, whatever you find out, it's not going to be good, is it?"

"Why do you say that?"

"Well, odds are Mom's dead, has been dead the whole time. Once we know for sure, we'll have to grieve for her all over again. And if she's alive, it'll mean she went away of her own volition, or was taken away and didn't try to come back to us. Her being alive is the absolute worst I can imagine, because it means that she was just acting the role of loving mother. It means she never cared for Jen or our father or me at all."

"I understand how you feel."

"Do you?"

"Yes. A while back, I found out I was adopted, and decided to locate my birth parents. I did, and it turned out they're good people, and I've established a relationship with both of them. But every now and then—even though I understand the circumstances that led to them giving me up—this anger just comes out of nowhere. On some level I feel that they didn't love me enough and should have tried harder to keep me."

Terry nodded. "If you get angry, even though your parents had good reason for what they did, imagine how angry Jen and I will feel if our mother's alive. Because I can't imagine any reason that would justify her abandoning us."

"Yet you didn't try to talk Jen out of going ahead with the investigation."

"No, and I'm willing to help any way I can. As I said before, if it's important to her well-being, it's important to me."

"Then let's get started."

For the next hour we went over Terry's memories of when her mother disappeared. Her recollections were much the same as her sister's, although less detailed and insightful, which was natural, given her age at the time. Some details conflicted: Terry remembered being brought home from school the day after the disappearance by the neighbor woman, while Jennifer had said the school bus dropped them off; Terry didn't think their Aunt Anna had been particularly upset that afternoon, while Jennifer had taken specific note of it; Terry remembered their father telling them at the dinner table never to say their mother was dead, while Jennifer had said it was at breakfast. Understandable discrepancies, given her youth and the passage of time.

But one of Terry's memories was puzzling, a new memory that had only surfaced after their father's death, when Jennifer had begun calling four or five times a week, often late at night, to talk about their mother and speculate on what had happened to her. Terry remembered waking on the morning of her seventh birthday, some nine months after her mother's disappearance, to the smell of Laurel's perfume in her room, and finding a fuzzy toy lamb tucked into bed beside her. Excited, she'd shown it to her father, saying it must be from her mother. But he said he'd put it there, and that she must have imagined the perfume.

"He was lying, though," she told me. "Kids can tell when adults lie. I don't know who put that lamb there, but it wasn't Dad. Besides, it was one of those promotional items they spin off successful children's book series, in this case the Littlest Lamb. The book that my mother was reading to me at the time she disappeared was *The Littlest Lamb and the Biggest Gnu*. Big coincidence, wouldn't you say?"

I asked, "Did you tell Jennifer what you remembered?"

"God, no! Do you think I want to make her any more crazy than she already is?"

"So what d'you think?" Patrick asked as we drove back to the city. "The mother sneaked back into the house to leave Terry a birthday present? Or Terry just thought her father was lying about putting the toy there? Or somebody else left it?"

"Any and all of the above. I wonder if Jennifer has a similar recollection of her own birthday? Laurel was reading her *The Wind in the Willows*. Maybe Jennifer received a Mr. Toad."

"You'll have to ask her."

"I intend to."

When we got back to the pier, I told Patrick I wouldn't be needing him anymore that day. Then I went to my office and called Jennifer Aldin.

"How are you feeling?" I asked her.

"Much better. I'm sorry I got so emotional yesterday."

"No apology necessary; we were discussing an emotional issue. I met with your sister this afternoon, and we went over her recollections of your mother's disappearance; tomorrow I'll be heading down to Paso Robles to talk with your aunt and any of the other people involved in the case who are still in the area. I have a couple of additional questions for you before I go. Do you know what became of your mother's postcard collection?"

"I think Aunt Anna has it. She took a lot of Mom's stuff. Why?"

"I'm interested in seeing it, and anything else of hers. It may help me to understand what kind of a woman she was. Another thing: do you remember the first birthday you celebrated after your mother disappeared?"

"My eleventh? Not really. I blanked out a lot of that year."

"You don't remember anything unusual happening that day? A special present, maybe?"

". . . No. I don't even remember if I had a party. I doubt I did. Mom organized great birthday parties, but I can't imagine Dad or Aunt Anna doing that. But my birthday was ten months later. Why are you interested in it?"

"I'm trying to put events in context." Vague replies involving words such as "context" and "nuance" and "subtext" have stood me in good stead over the years.

Quickly I ended the conversation and went down the catwalk to Derek and Mick's office. Mick had gone home—it was after six—but Derek remained at his desk, hands poised over his keyboard. As I stepped through the door, he hit the print command with a flourish and swiveled around.

"Shar!" he exclaimed, looking startled. "I just e-mailed you my file, and it's printing out."

I sat down on Mick's chair and propped my feet on the bottom shelf of the workstation. "How many people were you able to find current addresses for?"

"Most of them. A few have died, a few are untraceable, but the others aren't far from where they were twenty-two years ago. I backgrounded all but two of them and can finish up tonight if you need me to."

"Let me look at the list first."

The printer clicked and whirred and clattered on, sliding out pages. When it shut off, Derek put them in order and handed them to me.

Mary Givens, the neighbor who had been close to the Greenwood family, had died five years ago, but Laurel's best friend, Sally Timmerman, was still at the same Paso Robles address, as were Roy Greenwood's dental assistant, the pastor of St. John's Lutheran Church, and the printer who had produced Laurel's greeting cards. Jennifer and Terry's regular babysitter had married and moved to nearby Templeton. Bruce Collingsworth, chief of the Paso Robles Police Department at the time, was deceased, but the detective who had handled the case was still on the force. Jacob Ziff, the Cayucos man who had stopped to chat with Laurel at the overlook where she was painting, was listed at an address on Studio Drive in that town, but the Sea Shack restaurant had gone out of business in the early nineties, and its staff had scattered. One of the dogwalkers who had spotted Laurel in Morro Bay was still living there; the other was untraceable. Derek had backgrounded all the individuals except for Jacob Ziff and the Morro Bay man.

Not bad, given the length of time that had passed. Tomorrow I'd fly down to Paso Robles—fortunately, Hy had taken a commercial flight to San Diego so the Cessna was free—

and start with the maternal aunt, Anna Yardley, then talk to the other people there. They would probably suggest still others I might interview. I like to think of the initial inquiries in this type of investigation as pebbles dropped into a pool of water: concentric circles spread out around them, each bringing you into contact with people who knew the subject in different ways and bring different perspectives to the case.

Tomorrow afternoon, I'd drop the first pebble.

Thursday

·

AUGUST 18

I put the Cessna into a descending turn and looked out its left window at the lower Salinas Valley. Narrow, as California valleys go, it was bordered to the east by the stark Gavilan Mountains and to the west by the more verdant Santa Lucias. Highway 101 ran more or less straight through it, paralleled by the Salinas River, its waters winking through the trees that lined its banks. King City, which I'd passed over some minutes before, spread to the north along a maze of railroad tracks, and below me the little farm town of San Ardo nestled among well-cultivated fields and vineyards.

To the south, however, the landscape changed abruptly. Oil wells peppered the pockmarked terrain and barren hills rose around them, crowned by holding tanks. I spiraled closer, saw the rocker arms of the wells moving up and down, like the heads of giant insects boring into the earth's core. An image of its essence being sucked dry put a chill on me. Quickly I pulled up into a wide climbing turn, then headed south again. The Paso Robles Municipal Airport lay only a few miles away; with any luck, the rental car that I'd reserved would be ready for me.

*　　*　　*

The town hadn't changed much since those pit stops I'd made during college. The drive-in wasn't an A&W anymore, but it was still in operation. The Paso Robles Inn looked as if it hadn't changed since it was built in the late 1800s. I saw no evidence of earthquake damage, other than scaffolding around a couple of boarded-up storefronts. To familiarize myself, I drove the length of Spring Street, the main arterial, then turned back toward the central business district, where I found a coffee shop and ate lunch while pinpointing addresses on a local map.

My first stop was on Chestnut Street, which paralleled Spring three blocks to the west. In the middle of a row of California-style bungalows shaded by tall trees, I found the Greenwoods' former home: beige stucco with green wicker furniture crowding its small porch and wind chimes suspended from the eaves. I pulled to the curb and idled there, trying to get a sense of the lives that had gone on in this place twenty-two years ago. But too much time had passed; the house was probably not even the same color now, and who knew what other alterations had been made. When a curtain moved in a front window and a woman looked out, I took my foot off the brake and pulled away.

It was time for my interview with Anna Yardley. As I drove to Olive and Tenth streets, I reviewed what Jennifer Aldin and Terry Wyatt had told me about their maternal aunt. A retired insurance broker, Anna Yardley was unmarried and lived in the home where she and her sister Laurel had grown up. She'd spent little time with Jennifer and Terry prior to their mother's disappearance, but afterward assumed a stern presence in their lives. "Warm and fuzzy was not Aunt Anna's thing," Terry had commented. "Her big sentimental gesture toward each of us was the gift of a thousand-dollar whole life policy—on which she probably collected the commission—when we graduated from high school."

The Yardley house was white clapboard surrounded by a picket fence with an arched gate, on a corner lot. An oak tree—oaks, on Olive Street!—took up most of the front yard, and an old rope swing hung from one of its massive limbs. Anna Yardley came to the door before I could ring the bell.

She was a big woman, tall and heavy, with iron gray hair pulled back from her face and coiled at the nape of her neck. Her features were severe, her jaw strong, her lips drawn into an uncompromising line. Although the temperature must have been in the low nineties, she wore a long-sleeved black dress of a heavy fabric whose folds rustled as she led me to a formal front parlor.

At her suggestion I sat on a settee upholstered in pale green brocade. While she settled herself on a matching chair, I placed my briefcase beside me and took out my recorder.

"You can put that away," Anna Yardley said. "Anything I tell you is to remain in strict confidence."

"The tape is only for accuracy's sake."

"Take notes instead. I have no guarantee where that tape might end up."

I wasn't about to argue with her, so I put the recorder back in my case and took out a legal pad. After noting the date, time, and her name I began, "Ms. Yardley—"

"Before you get to your questions, I want you to know that I'm only talking to you as a favor to my niece Jennifer. Quite frankly, I think this investigation is a horrible idea. She should have made her peace with what happened years ago. There are some things we're not meant to know, and my sister Laurel's fate is one of them."

Odd way of putting it. I wrote down the word "fate" and circled it.

Anna Yardley squinted at the legal pad. Before she could ask what I'd written, I said, "What about you—have you made your peace?"

"Well, certainly. It's been nearly a quarter of a century."

"Tell me—what kind of a person was Laurel?"

Anna Yardley's thin lips curved downward. "A very impractical woman. A dreamer. Always reading. Painting. Dabbling in those silly greeting cards."

"I had the impression that she was a successful business-woman, and the greeting card business looked promising."

"I admit that the cards were beginning to sell, and she was making a small profit. But she could have earned much more if she'd kept up with her nursing."

"Laurel had a nursing degree from San Jose State, right?"

"Yes. She worked at a hospital in Los Angeles for a few years while Roy studied dentistry at USC. But after they moved back here and the girls were born, she gave it up. Frankly, I was surprised that she chose to have children; Laurel possessed no more maternal instinct than I."

"Her daughters remember her as a good mother."

"No doubt she was. She had the children, and they deserved a proper raising. It was her responsibility to provide that. We Yardley women live up to our responsibilities."

"But in the end Laurel *didn't* live up to it."

"She would have, had she not died."

"You're convinced she's dead?"

"What else? Laurel must have been a victim of random violence; that's the only possibility. She never would have left her girls. Until she disappeared she was never separated from them for more than a night or two, except when Cousin Josie was dying of cancer. Then she went to stay in San Francisco for a while, but she called home twice a day, sometimes more often."

I made a couple of notes, then asked, "What about the Greenwoods' marriage? Was it a good one?"

"Of course. They had the girls, and Roy had his dental practice. They were active in their church and had a nice group of friends. There was no trouble in that marriage."

Interesting that she thought I was implying there had been trouble; the way she'd jutted out her chin when she spoke raised a red flag for me. I hesitated, framing my next words carefully.

"But every marriage has its strains from time to time, when one partner is unhappy for reasons unrelated to the other. Or when there's a difference of opinion about something major."

"Well, I've never married, so I wouldn't know about that, now would I?"

"You were close to the family; you might've picked up on something—"

"I was not all that close to them before my sister disappeared. Laurel was nearly ten years younger than I, and she'd spent years away from home. When she returned to Paso Robles, her time was devoted to her children, and I was busy with a highly demanding career. My parents and I got together with them for the holidays and family birthdays, but I didn't really know Laurel or Roy or the children. After my mother and father passed away I saw even less of them." Anna Yardley's mouth pulled taut. "Of course, that changed afterwards. Roy needed me to help raise Jennifer and Terry. I wasn't happy about the responsibility, but it was my duty. No one else was going to do it."

No, warm and fuzzy wasn't Aunt Anna's thing.

I said, "Jennifer tells me you might have some of Laurel's belongings."

"A few, yes. Some mementos, her postcard collection, some letters. I took them when Roy . . . started getting rid of her things. I've never looked at any of them, but I thought the girls might want them someday. They've never asked, though."

"You say Roy started getting rid of Laurel's things. I understand from Jennifer that he burned her paintings only days after she disappeared."

". . . Well, yes, he did. The man was distraught, not himself at all. Afterward, he regretted his actions."

"Did he tell you that?"

"Not in so many words. As I said, we weren't close. But I could sense his regret."

"Do you have any idea why he destroyed the paintings so soon after Laurel's disappearance? What might have triggered it?"

"Roy had been . . . drinking a good deal that day. I suppose in his inebriated state he resented the paintings. After all, it was Laurel's going off to paint that proved to be her undoing."

"I wonder if I might see the items you saved."

"They're in the attic. I'll have to hunt for them. If I drag them down, they're not going back; you can take them to Jennifer and let her dispose of them if she wants."

"I'm sure she'd like to have them."

"Well, I can't get to it today. How long will you be here?"

"At least till tomorrow night. Why don't I call you?"

Anna Yardley nodded and stood, looking pointedly toward the front door. The interview was over.

*   *   *

Three hours later I was sitting on the balcony of my room at the Oaks Lodge, a newish, rambling resort hotel at the north end of town, with a main building containing a bar and restaurant and several guest wings set on large, lushly landscaped grounds. The temperature was still in the high eighties, and I'd changed to shorts and a tee and had a glass of cool white wine at hand. Spread on the small table in front of me were the notes I'd taken after playing the tapes of my interviews with Laurel Greenwood's pastor and the man who had printed her greeting cards, as well as Roy Greenwood's former dental assistant. They'd added little to the picture I'd already formed of Laurel.

The pastor, Bill Price of St. John's Lutheran Church, had spoken of Laurel with enthusiasm undimmed by the passage of time. He remembered that she had contributed much of her time and energy to the church's youth committees and had done the artwork for posters for various fund-raising events. "She no longer practiced nursing," he told me, "but she often made herself available to accompany our older members to medical appointments and aided them in communicating with their doctors. It was a great tragedy when we lost her." What did he think had happened to Laurel? "I suspect she is in God's hands."

Dean Sherman, owner of Sherman's Printing, had enjoyed working with Laurel. Her illustrations were top quality, and she was open to technical suggestions about printing the cards. "She wasn't like most artists; didn't have a temperamental bone in her body. Had a nice little business going, and if she hadn't died, it would've continued to grow. She wasn't going to be another Hallmark, but she'd've made a nice living." So he thought she was dead? "Of course. I know there were a lot of theories going around after she disappeared, but that's all they were—theories."

Lana Overland, the former dental assistant, had liked Laurel. "I liked her a lot, in fact. In some professional offices, you get these wives who're always calling up, always dropping by to check on things. Not Laurel. She had her own career, was very self-sufficient. Didn't bother Roy with the little stuff, like problems at home or with the kids." How had Roy dealt with Laurel's disappearance? "He was very sad for a long time. Angry, too. You can understand that; he'd had this great life, and all of a sudden it was taken from him. After a while he kind of evened out, but then he was like this empty shell, and nothing could fill it, ever." What did she think had happened to Laurel? "Foul play, most definitely, and a shame it happened to such a great wife and mother."

Impossibly perfect, that was the consensus on Laurel. But hadn't she ever been derelict in her duties for the church? Missed a committee meeting? Forgotten some elderly parishioner who needed a ride to the medical clinic? Hadn't she ever argued with the printer about the weight of the card stock or the quality of the ink? Failed to pay her bill on time? Hadn't she ever interrupted one of Roy's surgeries to tell him the washing machine was broken? Called at an awkward time to ask him to bring home a quart of milk? Apparently not.

But then, memories are colored by the passage of time, especially if someone has met with a tragedy. Little annoyances fade, quarrels are forgotten, minor lapses are forgiven. The last three people I'd spoken with were really very peripheral to Laurel's life; perhaps her best friend, Sally Timmerman, whom I was later meeting for dinner at the lodge's restaurant, could reveal more of the woman behind the perfect facade.

*   *   *

"Laurel a saint? You're kidding, of course," Sally Timmerman said.

"That's more or less how most people I've talked with have described her."

"I guess an untimely demise confers a sort of sanctity upon one, although I've never known why."

Timmerman was a short, plump woman in her mid-fifties, with close-cropped white-blonde hair and a round, smooth-skinned face that belied her years. From my background information on her, I knew that she was an English teacher at Paso Robles High School and had known Laurel Greenwood nearly her whole life. The two had met in second grade when Sally's family had moved south from Salinas, and had quickly become inseparable. Together they'd gone off to college at San Jose State, and when Laurel married Roy upon graduation, Sally was her maid of honor. Two years later, Laurel stood up for Sally at her marriage to her high school sweetheart, Jim Timmerman. The couples socialized frequently, and Sally and Laurel apparently had remained close until the day Laurel disappeared.

I waited as our server poured a Zinfandel from a local winery that Timmerman had recommended, then said, "How would you describe her, since you knew her better than anyone?"

"Human. Clever. Generous. And she had her wild side." Someone caught Sally's eye from across the inn's spacious dining room, and she waved before turning her attention back to me. "The parents of one of my students," she explained. "You can't go anywhere in this town without running into someone you know. Now, where was I?"

"Laurel had her wild side."

"I'll say she did. But Josie and I did, too."

"Josie—that was her cousin?"

"Yes, Josie Smith. The three of us were best buddies in high school and college. The Terrible Three, they used to call us, because of all the trouble we'd get into. Sneaking out at night to meet boys, parties when the folks weren't home, smoking dope behind the gym. Then we went off to San Jose State—Laurel and Josie to study nursing and me to get my teaching certificate—and really partied hearty. We rented this dilapidated house together, and there was a little old Airstream trailer that somebody had abandoned in the backyard. We called it our 'bordello' because that's where we'd take guys when we wanted privacy."

Timmerman smiled wryly. "We thought we were really something, spearheading the sexual revolution, but it all seems so tame compared to what the kids are doing now. And, of course, we eventually settled down. Laurel fell in love with Roy. I reconnected with my high school boyfriend. Josie dropped out to marry her first husband and moved to San Francisco."

"But the three of you remained close?"

"Laurel and I did. I kind of lost touch with Josie except for Christmas cards and what Laurel told me about her life. But they still saw each other frequently. Laurel helped Josie survive both of her divorces, and she was with her when she died. Brain cancer, at thirty-four. So young." Sally shook her head.

"When the two of them got together, was it here or in San Francisco?"

"There, usually. Roy didn't approve of Josie; he thought she was a bad influence on Laurel."

"Because of their wild past?"

"Right."

"But he approved of you."

"Because by the time he and Laurel moved back here from L.A. I was a respectable wife, mother, and teacher. It also helped that I'd put on so much weight I wasn't exactly turning heads anymore. But Josie was a divorcée, drop-dead gorgeous with all that bright red hair. Roy didn't want his wife around somebody like that."

"Did he try to stop Laurel from seeing Josie?"

"Well, they had a lot of disagreements about it, but she went anyway." Sally grinned. "I've always suspected that while Laurel was visiting she and Josie lived it up some. Not," she added quickly, "that she was ever unfaithful to Roy. But she liked a good time, and Roy wasn't exactly a live wire."

"Anna Yardley claims Laurel was seldom away from her children for more than one or two nights, except for when Josie died."

Timmerman rolled her eyes. "What would Anna know about Laurel's life? She was hardly ever around till she disappeared. But it's true that Laurel kept her visits and her painting trips short."

"Anna also said she was surprised that Laurel had the children, that she wasn't the maternal type."

"Now, there her instincts are correct. Laurel never wanted kids. In fact, she had an abortion during our junior year of college. It was Roy who wanted a family, and she finally caved in to the pressure. But once she had the girls she loved them and became a very good parent."

The waiter arrived with our dinners—prime rib; how could either of us resist the Thursday night special?—and we turned our attention to them for a few minutes. When I got back to my line of questioning, I said, "What about the Greenwoods' marriage? Was it a good one?"

". . . As marriages between very different types of people go, I suppose it was. They made their accomodations. Roy was kind of rigid and very traditional; Laurel was easygoing and a free spirit. He could be overbearing and demanding, and her way of coping was to stand pat on the things that were important to her, while bending on the things that didn't matter so much."

"Obviously her visits to Josie were one of the important things. What else?"

"Her mental health days, as she called them. The religion the girls were raised in; Roy was Catholic, but she insisted they attend the Lutheran church."

"And the things she gave in on?"

Sally considered. "Well, where they went on their vacations. She would've preferred to go to a resort, but Roy liked to camp, so they went camping. Where they lived; she wanted to be in the country, but he wanted to be in town near the clinic. One time, a couple of years before she disappeared, she got into this Arts in Correction program at the California Men's Colony, the prison down at San Luis Obispo. They had local artists come in and teach the inmates all sorts of stuff, from filmmaking to painting to fiction writing. Laurel was really excited about it, taught there for maybe six months, but then Roy pressured her into quitting. Said it was taking too much of her time away from the family, but I think he really didn't want her associating with the criminal element. She was disappointed, but she turned around and devoted more time to the greeting card business instead."

Now, that was interesting. Nowhere in my files had there been a mention of Laurel teaching at the prison.

"Was Laurel friendly with any of the inmates she taught?"

"She was a friendly person. But if you mean, did she have any contact with any of them outside the classes, I'd guess not."

"And she never mentioned having trouble with any of them?"

"All she ever said was that they were a well-motivated group, and that a couple showed real talent. She would've liked to've gone on teaching, but she wanted to keep peace in her marriage."

The marriage didn't sound very good to me. Although Hy and I had been married less than a week, we'd been together for years; neither of us had ever told the other what to do or not to do, and in our disagreements we'd always been straightforward. The Greenwoods' relationship, on the other hand, seemed both controlling and manipulative. But was the situation sufficiently difficult to make Laurel walk away from her husband and children? That wasn't a move a woman who took her responsibilities seriously could easily make. There would have had to be some sort of trigger. . . .

"Sally," I said, "this may sound like a strange question, but do you know what kind of perfume Laurel wore?"

"Why on earth do you ask that?"

"Someone said something to me about her perfume. It probably doesn't have any bearing on her disappearance, but I'm curious."

"Well, I do happen to know because we both wore it. Passionelle. They stopped making it around the time Laurel disappeared."

"Speaking of that time, did anything unusual happen to Laurel in, say, the six months before she disappeared?"

Timmerman frowned, looking down and swirling the wine in her glass. "Things were pretty much on an even keel, at least as far as I know. I'd say the most unusual thing was Josie's death, but that was a full year before."

"You were at the house when Jennifer and Terry came home from school the day after Laurel disappeared. Did Roy ask you to come over?"

"Actually, Bruce Collingsworth, the police chief, suggested it. He was sending a couple of officers over to talk with Roy, and he thought I might have some insight into where Laurel had gone."

"Did you tell the police your impressions of the Greenwoods' marriage?"

"No. They didn't ask, and I didn't think it was my place to volunteer."

"Anna Yardley was there that day, too. Did Roy call her?"

"I assumed so. Although it struck me as strange at the time. I mean, Anna was hardly ever there. She and Laurel didn't get along."

"How come?"

"Have you met Anna?"

"Yes, earlier today."

"Then you know what she's like—cold, disapproving. Laurel didn't want her negativity influencing the girls. It's a shame that afterwards she took such a hand in their upbringing. Laurel would not have wanted that. In fact, it was a role she'd asked me to assume if anything ever happened to her."

"Why didn't you?"

"Roy made it plain I wasn't welcome to. Oh, he didn't come right out and say 'You're not wanted here,' but he did say things like, 'You have enough to do raising your own kids,' and, 'After all, Anna is their flesh and blood.' It hurt me to be pushed out of their lives that way, but what could I do?

The agreement between Laurel and me was only a verbal one."

"This agreement—when did you make it?"

"A few months before Josie died. Laurel was facing her own mortality. So was I, for that matter. If I'd've died, Laurel would have helped bring up my kids—with my husband's blessing."

"You say 'died.' How certain are you that Laurel's dead?"

"I'm certain."

"Could she have committed suicide?"

"I doubt it. No one who knew her considered that a serious possibility. It had to be foul play."

"You sound almost as if you want Laurel to be dead."

Sally's eyes clouded. "I suppose in a way I do. Because if she's not, if she's been someplace else living some other life all these years, it would mean I never knew her at all. It would negate our friendship and everything we ever shared during all those years."

After I said good-bye to Sally Timmerman in the inn's lobby, I walked back to my room across the tree-shaded central courtyard. The night air was warm and fragrant from the flowering plants that grew in profusion there; I could hear people splashing in the nearby swimming pool. By contrast, my room was chill from the air-conditioning I'd left on when I went to dinner; I turned it off and opened the balcony doors to take advantage of the summer night. Then I sat down with my files and called Derek at his Marina-district apartment in San Francisco.

He said, "I sent you files on Jacob Ziff in Cayucos and the guy in Morro Bay, Ira Lighthill."

"Good, I'll take a look at them tonight. Tomorrow I'm

talking with the Paso Robles police officer who worked the case, then heading down to the coast. I'll try to talk with the Greenwood girls' babysitter tomorrow night. In the meantime, I've come up with a couple of lines of inquiry I'd like you to look into: first, Josie Smith, a cousin of Greenwood's, deceased twenty-three years, lived up there in the city."

"Josie Smith. Got it. You looking for anything specific?"

"Just fishing. Now, second: about a year before Smith died, Greenwood taught art classes for around six months at the California Men's Colony at San Luis Obispo. Contact them and see if they have any record of it. Try to get names of inmates enrolled in the classes, and their whereabouts at the time she disappeared. If they don't want to give out information—and I suspect they won't—Craig has a contact at the state department of corrections who can help."

"Will do. How soon d'you need this?"

"Tomorrow afternoon will be fine."

My next call was to Patrick, who was still at the office. We went over my day's activities, and I told him I'd be faxing him my notes, e-mailing a report, and messengering the tapes of my interviews in the morning. Then I made a call to the RKI condominium where Hy stayed while in La Jolla, got the machine, and left the number here at the inn. I considered calling his cellular, but if he wasn't at the condo it meant he was probably tied up in a meeting or at a business dinner.

It had been a long day, so I decided to take a shower and go to bed early, saving Derek's information on the two witnesses till the morning. But first I rummaged in my briefcase, took out my copies of the newspaper accounts of Laurel Greenwood's disappearance, and once again contemplated the head-and-shoulders photograph that had been published with the stories. It showed a woman with a delicate heart-shaped face, large, wide-set eyes, and long, softly permed dark hair; she was posed in front of a rosebush, smiling radiantly into the camera, one hand raised to cup a blossom to her cheek.

I studied the photograph a long time, hoping for some hint of her secrets in the tilt of her head or the curve of her mouth. But they were well concealed—both from me and from whoever had looked through the lens at her.

Friday

•

AUGUST 19

As I headed west on Highway 46 to the coast, I drove out of the sunlight and into the fog. It billowed toward the car, rushed past, and closed behind me. Suddenly I was enveloped in a grayish-white world where ordinary objects took on unfamiliar shapes and headlights of approaching vehicles appeared out of nowhere. I slowed, wishing there were taillights in front of me to show the way. Of course, I reminded myself, there was no guarantee that another driver would know the road any better than I did.

Early that morning, Rob Traverso, the Paso Robles police detective, had called to postpone our ten o'clock meeting to four in the afternoon; fortunately I'd been able to reschedule my one o'clock appointment with Jacob Ziff for eleven. I hadn't yet reached Ira Lighthill in Morro Bay, but I'd try again after I finished in Cayucos.

Ziff, according to Derek's report, was an architect with offices in his home. He'd been thirty-four on the day he'd stopped at the overlook to speak with Laurel, which would make him fifty-six now. He was twice divorced, had an excellent credit rating, and owned both the house in Cayucos and a condo on Maui. No arrest record; the closest he'd come to entanglement with the law was giving a statement as to his conversation with Laurel and his later sighting of her at the Sea Shack.

The fog had thinned by the time the road intersected with Highway 1. The tourist town of Cambria and San Simeon, home of Hearst Castle, were to the right, Cayucos and Morro Bay to the left. I drove south between richly cultivated farmland and the flat, gray sea, past a tiny settlement called Harmony. After some ten miles, the highway split to form a bypass around Cayucos, and I spotted a narrow lane leading to an overlook on the cliffs. I turned in there, parked near the edge, and got out. Looked along the curve of the shore that Laurel had painted that day. Her easel, a finished canvas, and supplies had been neatly stowed in her Volkswagen bus, indicating an unhasty and untroubled departure from the overlook. I wondered if that final painting had remained in police custody or had been burned by Roy Greenwood, and made a mental note to ask Detective Traverso.

The wind blew off the water, strong but not cold. Already the fog was burning off above the coastal range, promising a clear afternoon. Like yesterday when I'd sat in the car in front of Laurel's former home, I tried to capture some sense of what had gone on here twenty-two years before, but this was merely another roadside stopping place, through which thousands of people had passed since then. I checked my watch, saw it was nearly time for my appointment with Ziff, and got back in the car.

Studio Drive was at the lower end of town, a long residential strip that parallelled the main street to the west. The buildings there were a mixture: shingled cottages, Spanish-style villas, stucco bungalows, modernistic mini-mansions. Ziff's was one of the latter, all sharp angles and redwood and glass, on the ocean side. I parked close to its high fence, went through a gate that opened into a tiny courtyard, and rang the bell. A voice called out for me to come around the side, and I followed a flagstone path to a door where a tall man in chinos and a polo shirt was waiting. He introduced himself as Ziff and took me inside to a large room with floor-to-ceiling windows that faced the sea. A computer workstation and storage cabinets took up the rear wall, and two drafting tables were positioned under a skylight. Ziff motioned at a grouping of leather chairs near the windows and said, "I'll be right with you. Coffee?"

"Yes, please."

He crossed to one of the drafting tables, picked up a pencil, and made a few notations on a set of plans that lay there. Then he poured mugs full of coffee from an urn that sat on a cabinet by the workstation.

"Cream or sugar?"

"Neither, thanks."

He brought the mugs over and set them on a low table between two of the chairs. As we sat I studied him. He had curly silver hair, a bony, tanned face, and penetrating blue eyes that regarded me with frank interest.

"I've never met a private detective before," he said. "You're from San Francisco?"

"Right." I handed him one of my cards.

He looked it over, then placed it on the table. "And you said on the phone that Laurel Greenwood's daughter has hired you to look into her disappearance. It's been a long time. I don't know how I can help you."

I set my recorder on the table. "I'd like to go over what you remember."

"Wouldn't it be better if you read the statement I made to the sheriff's department?"

"Eventually I hope to. But first I'd prefer hearing about that day in your own words; it's possible you may remember something that you didn't tell the police."

Ziff smiled, the lines at the corners of his eyes crinkling. "That's the first time anyone's suggested that my memory's gotten better with age. But I'll give it a try."

"Thanks. According to the news reports, you were driving south on the coast highway that morning."

"Right. Around eleven. I'd been up to Cambria to look over a building site. Had a one o'clock lunch with a client here in town, so I wasn't in a hurry. There was an old VW bus parked at the overlook, and this woman had set up an easel beside it and was painting. I don't know exactly why I stopped; it's not like me to approach strangers. But there was something compelling about the way she was working."

"Can you describe it?"

Ziff leaned foward, hands on his knees, staring out the window at the sea. "You know, I haven't thought about that day in years, but now it's all coming back. The weather—it was exactly the same as today. Well, maybe a little warmer. The fog was just beginning to burn off, and there were occasional flashes of sun on the water."

I looked in the direction of his gaze, where faint glints of light had begun to dapple the gray waves.

"The woman," Ziff went on, "she was so intense. Her posture, her motions. As if she was working on something very important. She didn't seem to hear my car, didn't look up till I was standing right beside her. And when she did she acted as if . . . as if she were waking up from a dream, or maybe as if I were pulling her back from some other world she'd been inhabiting. She wasn't at all intimidated about a strange man coming up to her, just said hello."

"And then you talked about what?"

"Her painting. It wasn't bad. Representational, but something more, too; she'd captured the emotional feel of the coastline. I complimented her on her technique, and we discussed that for a while. She told me where she was from, and that she was a greeting card designer. That was about it. Two hours later I went to the Sea Shack to meet with my client, and she was on the oceanside deck, drinking wine and talking with this biker type."

"Did you speak to her?"

"No. I don't think she even saw me. My client arrived, and we went into the dining room. When we left the restaurant an hour later, they were both gone."

"Can you describe the biker?"

Ziff thought for a moment. "Long dark hair. Leathers. No club logo or anything like that. He might've had an earring, but I can't say for sure. I only saw him for a few seconds. But he stuck in my mind because I wouldn't have expected a woman like that to be hanging around with someone like him."

"A woman like what?"

"Well-spoken. Obviously talented. And she was quite lovely. If I hadn't had the appointment with my client, I might've considered asking her to lunch." He turned from the window, his eyes troubled. "I wish I had. Maybe it would've prevented whatever happened to her. But probably not. She seemed . . ."

"Yes?"

"You know, the passage of all these years is putting a new spin on what happened; I've never articulated this before. She seemed as if something was ending for her."

"What?"

"It had to do with the painting. When I complimented her on it, she said, 'Thank you. But it's done. That's all over now.' And she sighed. There was a regretful quality in her voice. It was as if she was saying good-bye."

"To what, do you suppose?"

Ziff shrugged. "Maybe to her art. Maybe even to her life."

After I left Ziff, I drove north along the main street of town. Cayucos was an old-fashioned beach community, and in spite of the proliferation of antique and tourist shops, it felt as if it hadn't changed much since the day Laurel drove away in her VW bus. The space where the Sea Shack had been was now a gourmet-foods shop, but the liquor store where Laurel's biker companion had been headed was still there. I parked and wandered along until I came to the municipal pier, turned, and walked halfway out, where I leaned against the railing and regarded the beach. The sky had cleared, and people were setting up umbrellas and speading blankets for picnics. Children ran eagerly toward the water's edge. Had Laurel witnessed a similar scene from the deck at the Sea Shack? Commented to the biker on what a nice a day it had turned into? Or had they been too involved in their discussion to notice? A discussion that had to do with the regret Jacob Ziff had heard in her voice?

It was as if she was saying good-bye. . . . Maybe even to her life.

Ziff's words had once again suggested that the reason for Laurel's disappearance might be suicide. I understood why no one had thought it a serious possibility at the time: by all accounts Laurel had been content, if not wildly happy with her existence. And her personality was hardly consistent with that of a person who would be prone to take her own life. Also, no suicide note or body had ever been found. Still, it was one more possibility I'd have to consider.

Morro Bay is a working fishing village, with a sheltered harbor whose entrance is dominated by a huge rock that looms like an offshore sentry. The Spanish word *morro* means, among other things, "snout," and the rock must have looked like a giant sea creature rising from the water to the sixteenth-century explorer Juan Rodriguez Cabrillo when he sailed into the harbor and christened it. In addition to the fishing industry, the local economy receives a significant boost from tourism, and as I drove along the waterfront street toward the park where Laurel had abandoned her bus, visitors were everywhere—wandering in and out of the restaurants and shops, snapping photographs, blocking the sidewalks while consulting maps or eating ice-cream cones, crossing the street without looking.

I confess to being irritated by tourists unless I'm one myself. Then anybody who gets between me and my souvenirs had better watch out!

The street dead-ended at the parking lot where Laurel had last been sighted. I left my car near the restrooms and walked along one of the paths to a bench facing the water, sat, and took out the sandwich and Coke that I'd bought at a deli in Cayucos. It was peaceful there; the only sounds were the cries of children from a nearby play area and the sloshing of the wake from a boat that motored past in the channel between the shore and a long sandbar. After I ate, I walked back to the parking lot where Ira Lighthill had agreed to meet me at two-thirty. Lighthill, a seventy-three-year-old former civil engineer, lived on the slope above the park.

At exactly two-thirty, a slight bald-headed man in jeans and a blue windbreaker came toward me, walking a black dog whose fur hung in cords that reminded me of dreadlocks. The cords on its head were gathered up in a yellow band, presumably to keep them out of its eyes, and it trotted along at its master's side, matching its speed to his.

"Ms. McCone?" the man said.

"Yes. You're Mr. Lighthill?"

"I am. And this"—he motioned to the dog—"is Csoda. That's spelled C-s-o-d-a. Hungarian for 'wonder.'"

"Unusual dog. What kind is it?"

"She's a puli, a herding dog. My wife and I breed them for a small and select clientele. Shall we walk?"

Lighthill turned toward the path leading to the water, and I fell into step beside him. Csoda moved ahead of us on her lead, keening the air and stopping here and there to sniff at objects of interest.

"So you're investigating the disappearance of that young woman, Laurel Greenwood," Lighthill said. "Of course, she wouldn't be a young woman anymore, but when someone vanishes like that, I suppose they're frozen in time. A high school friend of mine was murdered; I remained close to the family for many years, and every time I visited them there would be Jon in the photographs on the mantel, forever sixteen, while I became twenty and twenty-five and thirty. It must be much the same for that poor woman's daughters."

"I suppose so. Will you tell me about seeing her that afternoon?"

"Well, I'd been walking my then dog, Kiro, along with my friend Bryan Taft and his standard poodle, Dewey. We were coming back toward the parking lot when one of those old VW buses pulled in. I took particular note of it because I'd owned one of the same color. I remember saying something to Bryan about being surprised the thing still ran. Mine was a dreadful vehicle—underpowered, and in the end it got so bad I'd actually have to put it in reverse and back up the hills. Anyway, the bus pulled into a space at the far side of the lot, and the woman got out. She locked the bus and came straight toward us, so we got a good look at her."

We'd reached the water's edge by now. Lighthill motioned to the right and we took a path leading toward the commercial district along the shore.

"How did she seem?" I asked. "Nervous? Upset? Business as usual?"

He considered. "I'd say purposeful. She knew where she was going and she was going to get there as quickly as possible. But first she made a detour to the ladies' room."

"That wasn't in any of the newspaper accounts."

"Possibly because Bryan didn't think to mention it. And I—well, a rest stop seemed irrelevant, and really nobody's business but the woman's."

"Did you see her come out of the restroom?"

"Yes. She wasn't in there long. Bryan and I were still in the parking lot, standing next to his car and discussing plans to go to a regional AKC show in Los Angeles the next weekend. I only glimpsed her from behind, but it was the same woman. I recognized her by the sweater she wore—I guess they're called 'hoodies' now. It was tan, and she'd pulled the hood up over her head, even though it was a warm day."

Red flag.

"You didn't see her face? Or her hair?"

"No. But it had to be the same woman. No one else had gone into the restrooms."

That you know of.

Lighthill was frowning, as if he too had spotted the error in his logic. "It was the same jeans, the same sweater," he said defensively.

"And she walked off toward town, without turning around?"

"Yes. She cut across the grass to this very path and went the same way we're walking."

"How long did you stay in the parking lot after that?"

"Only a few minutes. Bryan and I firmed up our plans. He left in his car, and Kiro and I walked home."

"Your friend Bryan—I wasn't able to locate a current address for him. Do you have one?"

"Sorry, I don't. His wife died ten years ago, and he moved to Mexico. After a couple of years my letters were returned as undeliverable. I can provide you with that address, if you like."

Just in case all my other leads came to dead ends, I gave him my card and said, "I'd appreciate it if you'd phone it in to my office, collect, when it's convenient."

We reached the end of the path and turned onto the main street, passing a row of small run-down cottages that perched above the water. Like many of the buildings I'd seen in Cayucos, they harked back to another, more gentle era.

I said, "No one here in the business district ever came forward about seeing Laurel Greenwood. Where could she have gone, that she would've escaped notice?"

"Hard to say. But it's not unusual that nobody took note of her; even in those days we had a lot of tourists."

"The town must've been quite different then."

"Well, yes. Businesses have changed hands. Old buildings have been torn down and replaced with new ones."

"D'you recall what was here? Can you describe it?"

"These cottages, they've been here as long as I remember, and I've lived here thirty years. That restaurant"—he pointed—"is relatively new; a marine supply used to be there. The shops—owners come and go, merchandise changes. Farther uphill there're new antiques stores and boutiques of all kinds. A big wine and gourmet-food emporium is on the lot where the mini-storage and equipment-rentals place was. Like any tourist town, they take away the things that're for the residents—I used to keep my camper in one of the little garages at the storage company—and put up things for the out-of-towners. But the lay of the land, that hasn't changed. You can alter what's on it, but as Morro Rock stands up to erosion, the land stands up to man."

I hesitated. "Can you think of anyone in the immediate area who would have been here that day? Who might have noticed Laurel Greenwood and for some reason not come forward?"

Lighthill stopped walking, allowing Csoda to sniff around a sidewalk trash receptacle. "Well, I always did wonder about Herm Magruder. He was the local gossip columnist, wrote a weekly piece—'Doings About Town'—for the little paper. Called himself 'Mr. Morro Bay.' Gathered most of his information in the bars or from the front porch of his house. It stood right across the street, where that shell shop is now. He was on the porch with a drink in his hand when I went by earlier that day, so he must've been there when the Greenwood woman came out of the park. Once Herm sat down with his drink, you couldn't pry him off that porch."

Magruder hadn't been mentioned in any of the news reports. "D'you know if the police questioned him?"

"Should have. He was right there, and he was the eyes and

ears of the town, but he had such a reputation as a drunk that they might not've bothered."

"Where can I find him?"

"He and his wife, Amy, moved to a condo at Pacific View, a complex on the bluff south of town, after they sold the old house."

"He still write his column?"

"No, the paper closed down about five years ago. Must be hard on Herm, having no excuse to sit in the bars and poke into people's business. He'd probably be glad to have a visitor."

After Ira Lighthill and I parted—he and Csoda heading up the hill toward home—I got the Magruders' number from information and called it. No one answered. I retraced my steps to the main street and had a cup of coffee at a café, then called again. Still no answer. In response to the high temperatures inland, the fog was creeping back; Morro Bay looked bleak and inhospitable. I decided to pack it in, drive back to Paso Robles, and phone the office.

"So that's where things stand," I said to Patrick. "Rob Traverso at the Paso Robles PD is letting me go over their files on the case tomorrow morning. He couldn't help me with Laurel's final painting; it was returned to Roy years ago, and I assume he destroyed it like the others. Traverso's putting me in touch with a Deputy Selma Barker at the county sheriff's department. After I go over the PRPD casefile, I'll meet with her and try to talk with the Magruders. And the babysitter has agreed to see me in the late afternoon."

I was sitting at the desk in my room at the lodge, the airconditioning cranked up to maximum. Today the inland temperature was in the high nineties, and showed no signs of cooling, even though it was after five o'clock.

"You want me to ask Derek to background the Magruders?" Patrick asked. "He said he'll be working late tonight."

"I'd better talk with him personally. Will you transfer me? And why don't you take your files on the case home and review them over the weekend. That is, if you don't have plans."

"No plans. My ex is taking the kids to Disneyland, so I won't have them this week."

I waited for Derek to pick up, asked him to run checks on both Amy and Herm Magruder. Then I said, "I haven't checked my e-mail yet; did you find anything on Josie Smith or the inmates who attended Laurel's art class at the Men's Colony?"

"The prison wouldn't give out information, so I'm trying to get in touch with Craig's contact at DOC. Probably I won't be able to get you anything on that till Monday. I've got basic background on Josie Smith: date of birth, marriages and divorces, date of death." He read them off to me. "Smith went by her husbands' names during her marriages—Dunn and Bernstein—but took back her birth name after the second marriage failed."

"Any children?"

"None. Smith studied nursing at San Jose State. Dropped out to get married after her junior year, then went back and finished the course after the first divorce. Worked at SF General for three years, did private-duty nursing after that. Otherwise I couldn't turn up anything. You want me to dig further?"

"I don't know as it's necessary. We'll talk when I come back up there next week."

"You staying over the weekend?"

"Yes. My plate's pretty full for tomorrow, and Sunday I have to fly down to my mother's place near San Diego. She's giving Hy and me what she calls 'a little wedding reception.' Lots of family, and my birth mother and her son and daughter are coming from Boise."

"You don't sound too happy about it."

"I'm not. McCone family parties are always horrible, and this wedding reception is a disaster waiting to happen."

Saturday

•

AUGUST 20

My room-service breakfast tray arrived at eight, a copy of the *San Luis Obispo Tribune* neatly folded next to the croissants and coffee. I took it to the little table on the balcony and began to eat, scanning the paper. A headline below the fold on the front page made me set my coffee cup back in its saucer.

NEW INQUIRY INTO LAUREL GREENWOOD DISAPPEARANCE
Information on Missing Paso Robles
Woman Sought by Private Investigator

· I picked up the paper and skimmed the article. It identified me by name, and as a "San Francisco investigator who in recent years has been involved in a number of high-profile cases," and quoted a "source who wishes to remain anonymous" as saying that I had been hired by one of the Greenwood daughters to search for new leads in the twenty-two-year-old disappearance. "McCone," it said, "is in the area to interview friends and relatives of the missing woman, as well as reinterview witnesses who gave statements to the authorities in the original investigation." It added that my offices would not confirm or deny the source's information. The remainder of the story was a history of the case, complete with photographs on an inside page of Laurel, Roy, and their daughters.

Ted, or Kendra Williams, had been right in protecting client confidentiality, but why hadn't I been told that a reporter was asking about the case? Probably Kendra had taken the call and, in her inexperience, hadn't thought it significant. Too bad, and also too bad that the newspaperman—Mike Rosenfeld, the byline read—hadn't thought to check area motels, locate me, and ask for a personal interview. I might have been able to deflect, or at least delay, this publicity.

For a moment I considered phoning the office to ask who had taken the call from Rosenfeld, but it was Saturday, and chances were I'd just get the machine. Even my workaholic employees ignored taped messages after regular business hours.

I set the paper aside. Sipped coffee and buttered a croissant as I contemplated the turn of events. It hadn't occurred to me that any of the people I'd spoken with might go to the press, but the source had to be one of them. Why had he or she done so? And why the condition of anonymity? More important, what effect would the story have on my investigation?

Possibly it could help me, prompt someone whose existence I wasn't aware of to come forward with fresh information. But more likely it could frighten off someone with something to hide. Or—if Laurel was alive and the story was picked up by the wire services—it could drive her deeper underground.

Which of those had been the person's intention?

I could call the reporter and ask where he'd gotten his information, but he'd most certainly insist on his right to protect his source's identity. I could ask each of the persons I'd interviewed if they'd talked with the press, but that seemed even more unlikely to elicit a straight answer. A better use of my time would be to proceed with my day's plans unaltered.

I didn't like the idea that the people I'd be talking with—assuming they read the *Tribune,* which called itself the "newspaper of the central coast"—would anticipate and possibly prepare themselves for my questions. A good interview always contains some element of spontaneity, and it would be a shame to lose that. Besides, press coverage always made me feel exposed and vulnerable; for some reason this story made me particularly edgy.

In spite of my edginess, the day proceeded without significant incident. From the Paso Robles police files I learned that three days after Laurel's disappearance Roy Greenwood had asked Chief Collingsworth to instruct the department's press liaison officer to give out as little information as possible on their investigation. He wanted his daughters' lives to return to normalcy as soon as possible, he said, and that would only happen if the story dropped off the front pages. The files provided by Deputy Selma Barker at the county sheriff's department headquarters in San Luis Obispo confirmed that Collingsworth had passed on Roy's request to them.

Despite Greenwood's explanation for asking that the investigation be downplayed, it seemed odd to me; in most missing persons cases, family and friends go to great lengths to keep the story in the public eye. They distribute flyers and photographs, make impassioned appeals on TV, offer rewards. But so far as I knew, none of those things had been undertaken by Roy Greenwood.

Otherwise the files contained no surprises. The statements by Jacob Ziff and Ira Lighthill were substantially the same as what they'd told me. Lighthill's friend Bryan Taft had confirmed the circumstances under which they'd seen Laurel at the park. The waitress and bartender at the Sea Shack could provide no more detailed descriptions of the biker than Ziff had, and a busboy who had seen Laurel and him leave was unsure as to whether the biker actually entered the liquor store down the street. The liquor store clerk had no recollection of him.

By two that afternoon I was on my way back from San Luis. Derek's information on the Magruders had been on my laptop before I left the inn that morning: Herm and Amy Magruder were both natives of Morro Bay, and his gossip column for the local shopping paper had been only a hobby; Herm's real work was operating a self-storage and equipment-rentals company, probably the same one that Ira Lighthill had mentioned as being replaced by a gourmet-foods and wine emporium. Herm and Amy, who had managed the office there, had retired five years ago and moved to the Pacific View condominium complex. They had a son, daughter-in-law, and two grandchildren living in a suburb of Chicago. I tried the number I'd gotten from information yesterday before leaving San Luis, but no one answered.

Although Morro Bay was a significant detour on my way to Templeton, where the Greenwoods' former babysitter lived, I had a few hours before our appointment, so I headed up the coast. Derek had supplied an address for the Magruders' condo, but when I arrived there no one was at home. I drove around town, periodically checking at the condo

without results, until I found a neighbor who said the Magruders were on vacation until sometime next week. I left my
card in their mailbox, asking that Herm call me, and drove
to Templeton, a short distance south of Paso Robles.

And then I got lost. In a country town whose population
couldn't have been more than a few thousand, I couldn't find
Edie Everett's house—at least not from the directions she'd
given me over the phone. After stopping at a deli to ask, I finally located it—the directions were curiously dyslexic, and
I suspected it was my fault—but by that time she and her
husband, Joe, were on their way out to dinner. Fortunately
they were gracious about my tardiness and invited me along
to a small café called Mr. Mom's that served excellent burgers and microbrews.

The only new light Edie could shed on Laurel was that she
took a lot of mental health days during the year before her
disappearance. "She was constantly calling me up to look
after the kids," Edie said. "I doubt her husband was aware of
it, because she always came home before he did. And I'm
pretty sure that if he had known, he'd've raised hell. I didn't
charge much, but I could tell he didn't like shelling out for
child care."

Not a great deal of information, but the Everetts were
pleasant people and good dinner companions. For the rest of
the meal we talked about their business—they owned an antiques shop in Paso Robles—and the nature of some of the
"high-profile cases" the *Tribune* had mentioned I'd been involved in. By the time we parted, my frustration over the
largely unproductive day had faded.

The white facade of the Oaks Lodge was bathed in multi-
colored lights and the parking lot was jammed with cars.

Obviously a popular place on Saturday night. I found a space near my room between two oversize SUVs, edged my rental between them. It was hot inside—I'd remembered to turn the air-conditioning off before I left that morning—so I decided to take a swim to cool off. I'd just changed into my suit when the phone rang. Probably Hy, confirming our plans for tomorrow. I was to fly down to San Diego, attend the reception at my mother's with him, and then we'd spend the night at RKI's condo in La Jolla.

"Ms. McCone?" an unfamiliar male voice said. "This is John at the front desk. We have a Federal Express package for you."

"Will you have someone bring it up to my room, please?"

"Sorry, I can't at the moment. We're shorthanded tonight, and I can't leave the desk."

"All right, I'll be down for it in a few minutes." I threw on shorts and a tee over my suit, took a shortcut across the courtyard to the lobby. Music from a live band drifted from the bar, and a group of people waited at the restaurant's hostess stand. A young Asian woman sat behind the desk, reading a magazine.

"I'm Sharon McCone," I said to her. "John called about a FedEx package that's arrived for me."

"John went off duty an hour ago."

I frowned. "Well, could you check for the package?"

She got up, looked under the counter. "There's nothing here. I could see if he put it in the office."

"No, don't bother."

There was no package. Someone had used it as a ruse to get me out of my room. Had the door automatically locked behind me? I couldn't remember. I hurried out to the courtyard and took the path toward my wing. It led me across a bridge over the little stream that fed a koi pond, then into a grove of exotic plantings—

A sudden whining and thud close by. Sounds I knew all too well.

I was on the ground before the echo of the shot died out, heart pounding, facedown in a flowerbed. I inhaled damp soil, sucked a leaf into my mouth, and began coughing; rolled away from a spotlight that shone up on the branches of a nearby tree and crouched in the shadows.

There were no more shots. All I heard were doors opening and alarmed voices in the courtyard.

"What happened?"

"That was a shot!"

"Where'd it come from?"

"Stay back, folks. Please stay back!"

"What's going on?"

"Is somebody hurt?"

"Go inside, people, please! Let us check this out."

Hotel security, getting things under control. The shooter would be far away by now. Shakily I got to my feet and moved onto the path.

How close to me had that bullet passed? Not very. And it wasn't all that dark out here—not dark enough for the shooter to miss accidentally. Whoever had lured me out of my room hadn't intended to kill me, just scare me.

Footsteps came from the direction of the main wing, and then I spotted a guard coming toward me. A second guard followed him, sweeping the shrubbery with a flashlight.

I raised my hands so they could see I wasn't armed. Called out, "Someone fired into the courtyard. It sounded like a handgun, small-caliber, and it came from over there." I motioned to the right.

The first guard hurried up to me. "Are you all right, miss?"

"Just shaken up, that's all."

He turned to the other guard. "Better get the police over here. And you, miss, come with me. They'll want to talk with you."

Detective Rob Traverso of the PRPD was the officer who had given me access to the Greenwood files. A stocky man with curly brown hair and a neatly trimmed mustache, he had an air of calmness and deliberation. When he entered the manager's office at the inn, he looked me over and said, "Well, Ms. McCone, what can you tell me about this shooting incident?"

I described what had happened, including the direction from which I thought the shot had come.

Traverso sat down on the corner of the desk and nodded thoughtfully. "We've got our people questioning the guests in all the wings. Not that anybody's going to admit to discharging a weapon in a public place. You have any reason to think the shot was meant for you?"

"Well, there's been some newspaper publicity on my investigation and someone may be trying to warn me off."

"I saw the article in the *Tribune*. You think someone you've spoken with here has a vested interest in you not finding out what happened to Laurel Greenwood?"

"It's possible."

"Who?"

"I haven't a clue."

"Who have you interviewed?"

I named them.

Traverso smiled. "Well, I haven't met Mr. Ziff or Mr. Lighthill, but the others I've known most of my life. I can question them if you'd like, but I very much doubt any of them is responsible. Maybe you were just in the wrong place at the wrong time. There's a bit of the frontier mentality in the countryside around here; it could've been some cowboy who'd had too much Saturday night in the bar."

"I suppose so." I was perfectly willing to let the matter drop. Both Ziff and Lighthill had seemed straightforward enough and, as Traverso said, he knew the others.

The detective handed me his card. "If there are any further incidents—"

"Of course."

When I went out into the lobby, the first person I spotted was Jacob Ziff. He was standing by the entrance to the bar with a slight, handsome man whose long dark hair was pulled back in a neat ponytail. Ziff frowned when he saw me come around the front desk from the manager's office, said something to his companion, and moved toward me.

"Sharon," he asked, "what's going on? I was standing at the bar when three squad cars came roaring up."

"Somebody discharged a handgun in the courtyard. I almost got in the way."

"My God!" The other man came up beside him, and Ziff repeated what I'd said.

The man said, "So that's what it was. I was just getting out of my car when the police got here, and they wouldn't tell me anything."

Ziff said to me, "This is Kev Daniel. Kev, Sharon McCone, the private investigator I was telling you about."

Daniel shook my hand. His was smooth and immaculately manicured. He wore a heavy turquoise-and-silver ring, and his silk shirt and well-tailored slacks looked expensive. I considered the conversation over and started to move away from the two.

"Why don't you join us for a drink?" Daniel said.

Although I'd cleaned up some in the restroom while waiting for Detective Traverso, my shorts and tee were stained with dirt from the flowerbed. "I don't think—"

"We can get a table on the patio," Ziff said. "It's quiet there, and no one will care how you're dressed. You look like you could use a drink."

I certainly could. I nodded and accompanied them through the crowded, noisy bar to a side door that led to a fenced patio; Daniel found us a table in a shadowy corner, while Ziff went to place our order.

When we were seated Daniel said, "Jacob was telling me about you after we finished going over the plans for my winery's tasting room this afternoon. Little did we know when we arranged to meet for a drink later on that we'd find you here—and under such circumstances."

"You're a vintner?"

"Yes, but on the marketing end of things. My two partners take care of the winemaking. The winery's called Daniel Kane—after my last name, and that of my partners, who're brothers. Jacob's designed a terrific building, and we'll be breaking ground later this month."

Ziff appeared with three glasses of wine and set them down on the table. To Daniel he said, "Daniel Kane Private Reserve Zin."

"One of our best. Cheers." He raised his glass.

I sipped. They made a good wine—if the opinion of one who only in recent years had begun buying bottles with corks in them held any weight.

Ziff said, "So what happened out there in the courtyard?"

"Someone fired a handgun. I don't know what they were shooting at, but they came close to hitting me."

"Did the police catch the person?"

"He or she is long gone. Easy to conceal a small-caliber handgun and slip away; there're exits leading to the parking lots between the wings."

Daniel said, "How do you know it was a handgun? And small-caliber?"

"I've been around guns for years, have owned several. I could tell by the sound of the shot."

"Must be scary to be shot at."

"As I said, I don't know that the shooter was aiming at me. But, yes, it's scary."

"Enough to make a woman pee in her pants, I'll bet."

I was beginning to regret having taken him up on the offer of a drink. "My being a woman has nothing to do with it. And I didn't pee in my pants."

Ziff cleared his throat, probably hearing the irritation in my voice and attempting to warn off his client.

If he noticed, Daniel didn't care. "You've been shot at before?"

"Yes." I'd also been shot once—in the ass, to my great embarrassment—but I wasn't about to bring that up.

"Shot anyone?"

"Yes."

"Under what circumstances?"

"I don't care to talk about them."

Ziff said, "Let's change the subject, Kev."

Daniel's eyes had gone hot and flat with curiosity. "No, I want to hear about this. You kill anybody?"

"She said she doesn't want to talk—"

"Because that's what I'd do. Shoot to kill, it's the only way."

Unfortunately he was right: in a situation where guns are drawn, you shoot to kill; I'd learned that when I became firearms qualified, and doing so had once saved my life, twice saved the lives of people I cared about.

I stood and said, "Jacob, thank you for the drink. I have to be going now." As I moved toward the door, I heard Ziff's chair scrape on the floor and his footsteps follow me.

He caught up with me in the lobby. "Sharon, please excuse my client. He's a spoiled rich kid, came down here from San Francisco four years ago with a lot of money and romantic notions about himself as a vintner, bought his way into a winery that badly needed a cash infusion."

"He's got to be in his forties—no kid. And apparently he romanticizes the concept of shooting someone to death."

"Yeah." Ziff looked troubled. "Under that smooth exterior, I sense he's something of a loose cannon. Not that he hasn't done wonders for Daniel Kane; he's got a good head on his shoulders." Ziff smiled crookedly. "Anyway, I apologize for his behavior."

"Not your fault." I moved toward the door to the courtyard.

Ziff wasn't content to let the matter drop. "I guess I shouldn't have told him about you and your investigation, but I had no way of knowing we'd meet up with you—or under what circumstances."

"No harm done. But let me ask you this: did you tell anyone else?"

"No."

"Do you know a reporter on the San Luis paper named Mike Rosenfeld?"

"I know of him."

"But you haven't spoken to him about my investigation?"

"No, of course not. What's this about, Sharon?"

I sighed, suddenly feeling weary. "Nothing, really. The shooting incident's made me a little paranoid, that's all. I'd better go now; tomorrow's going to be a very long day."

But the sensor that an attorney friend in San Francisco called his "shit detector" had kicked in. Immediately before closing time I returned to the lounge and spoke with the bartender. Did he know Jacob Ziff and Kev Daniel? Yes, they were both good customers. Had Mr. Ziff been standing at the bar when the police arrived earlier? No, he had been at the bar about two hours earlier, but had left and returned later with Mr. Daniel and me. And when had Mr. Daniel arrived? The man looked puzzled, then said, "I'm not sure. He was at a table in the patio when I came on shift at eight."

Seemed like I'd had a drink with a pair of liars.

Sunday

·

AUGUST 21

Ma's "little wedding reception" turned out to be quite the event.

The spacious home north of San Diego that she shared with her husband, Melvin Hunt, was filled with their friends and neighbors, most of whom I didn't know. A full bar was set up in the living room, waiters circulated with trays of canapés, and a string quartet played softly in the garden gazebo. All this she'd organized in a little over a week, and, knowing Ma, if she'd had a couple more days' notice she'd'd've had the house redecorated—something she did with great regularity. It was a far cry from the family barbecues she used to throw in the backyard of our old rambling house in San Diego proper, and I was hoping the genteel atmosphere and presence of strangers would stave off the contretemps that usually erupted when the clan gathered.

If any of them ever arrived.

Hy, in a beige summer suit, circulated through the crowd, beer in hand, charming the women and discussing with the men the stock market, the price of real estate, and golf handicaps—even though, so far as I knew, he'd never so much as picked up a club. Tall and lean, with curly dark blond hair, a hawk nose, and a swooping mustache, he wasn't handsome in the conventional sense, but he had a presence that turned heads. When he smiled and winked at me across the room, I felt a rush of warmth. This man was my husband.

Then he was swallowed up in the crowd. I clutched my wineglass with tense fingers, looked around for a familiar face, but saw none. No one was paying attention to me, and even in my most becoming pale green silk tunic and flowing pants, I felt more like a wallflower than the guest of honor.

Where the hell were my relatives, anyway?

About three minutes later the front door opened and my older brother John entered, accompanied by his teenaged boys, Nate and Matt. Nate, blond and clean-cut like his father, was carrying a large, silver-wrapped package and looked around expectantly. His brother slouched, a sullen expression on his face, which appeared to have fallen victim to recent piercings—a gold ring dangled from one nostril and his right eyebrow sported a silver one. His hair, a peculiar shade of orange, looked as if it had engaged in a hostile encounter with an eggbeater. Nate and John came toward me, but Matt slunk off toward the door to the garden. Probably planning to go behind the gazebo and smoke some dope.

John enveloped me in a bear hug, lifted me off the ground, and twirled me around. "Hot damn, you finally did it! Where's the lucky man?"

"I think Ma's friends have co-opted him."

"We'll have to make a gallant rescue." He raised his head, listening to the faint strains of the music. "What the hell's *that*?"

"Vivaldi," Nate said. "*The Four Seasons.*"

"What a drag."

"Maybe you expected Grandma to ask John Fogerty to perform?"

"Kid's a snob," John said to me, ruffling Nate's longish hair. "Thinks I'm stuck in an outdated and musically crude era."

"No, my tastes are just more eclectic than yours." Nate smiled shyly at me and extended the package. "This is for you and Hy from all three of us."

"Thank you! Should I open it now?"

They exchanged glances. "Uh, I don't think so," John said. "Not in this crowd."

"Ah-hah! Well, I'll put it with the others and open it later."

A table was set up nearby, and it was already loaded with presents. A nice thought on the part of those who had brought them, but I couldn't help but entertain the image of more stuff riding up and down the coast highway in the trunk of my MG. People who get married in their forties, particularly people with three houses between them, really shouldn't qualify for wedding gifts.

"I'll take it over there for you," Nate told me, "and then I'm gonna find some food. I'm starving."

John snagged a glass of wine off a passing waiter's tray, said, "Where're Ma and Melvin?"

"Circulating. I think she gave this party more for them than for Hy and me."

"No, I think she gave it to impress someone."

"Who?"

"Your birth mother. From conversations we've had, I gather Ma's intimidated by Saskia Blackhawk—or at least the idea of her. Lawyer, champion of her people's rights, has argued before the Supreme Court. You know."

"Saskia is a very down-to-earth person, and she doesn't care about social trappings."

"That may very well be. But you know Ma."

I sighed. "Yeah, I do. And I'm sure Saskia and my half sister Robin will like her and handle the situation beautifully."

"What about Darcy?"

Darcy, my half brother. I smiled. "I don't know how he'll feel about Ma, but I know he's going to hit it off with Matt."

"Matt doesn't get along with anybody these days."

"Neither does Darcy."

My Aunt Susan and Uncle Jim McCone, down from Jackson in the Gold Country, were the next family members to arrive, followed by Charlene and Vic and my nieces Jamie, Molly, and Lisa. Charlene looked wonderful—slender, her blonde hair streaked by the sun, her skin glowing. Obviously this second marriage was agreeing with her. But her eyes clouded for a moment as she held my hands.

"What?" I asked.

"Oh, I was just thinking of Pa. How happy he would've been. And Joey—I wish he could be here."

Our other, sadly troubled brother had died a suicide last spring. "Me too, but you know he wouldn't've come. He avoided family parties for years." I didn't mention that Charlene and Ricky's youngest son wasn't attending either. His parents' much-publicized divorce had been hard on Brian, and he was currently at a camp for troubled teens in Arizona.

"True." She squeezed my hands, then released them. "Vic and I have a gift for you guys, but we didn't think it appropriate to bring it inside." She smiled at her tall, distinguished-looking husband, and he grinned wickedly.

"Oh?" I asked. "What?"

"Later, Shar. Later."

Charlene, Vic, John, Molly, and Lisa went off to say hello to Ma and Melvin. Eighteen-year-old Jamie stayed behind. "How's Derek?" she asked. She'd developed a major crush on Derek Ford at a party she'd attended at my house last month.

"He's fine."

"Does he ever ask about me?"

Jamie was the most sensitive of Ricky's four daughters; I wasn't about to tell her that last weekend Derek had brought her older sister, Chris, an undergrad at UC Berkeley, to the party at Touchstone. "He says hello."

"Oh! Tell him I say hello, too." Her big smile immediately made me regret the lie, but I told myself it was a harmless one. Derek dated a new woman every week, and Chris was not known for sustaining long-term relationships. Even so, when Jamie didn't ask any more questions and headed off to find Ma and Melvin, I felt a certain relief.

Moments later Hy appeared at my elbow. "How're you holding up?" he asked.

"Better, now that there's family here. All these people . . . well, they're very nice, but I didn't picture this big a gathering."

"Big gatherings don't usually intimidate you. Are you still upset about that shooting incident?"

"More concerned that somebody in the Paso Robles area seems intent on derailing my investigation." We'd gone over the incident in detail when I'd arrived in San Diego that morning, and Hy's professional instincts confirmed mine: the shot had been intended to warn me off.

"To tell the truth," I said, "I'm glad to be going back home tomorrow. I picked up a bunch of Laurel's papers and her postcard collection from her sister before I flew down this morning, and I want to study them before proceeding."

I paused, thinking back on my last conversation with Anna Yardley. "You know, when I picked up the stuff I mentioned that I'd met with Sally Timmerman, Laurel's best friend. The sister, Anna Yardley, said she was surprised I'd bothered, since Laurel and Sally had fought over something and weren't speaking the year before Laurel disappeared. But Sally was called to the Greenwood house by the chief of police after Roy reported Laurel missing, and she never mentioned anything about a falling-out to me. I'm going to call her and do a little probing."

Hy nodded. "Good idea. And I can understand why you're preoccupied with the case, but that's not all that's bothering you."

I'd never been able to hide anything from him. "Okay. Saskia's plane landed an hour ago. She, Robin, and Darcy should be here any minute."

"The great maternal face-off."

"Well, I doubt it'll come to that. But it'll be awkward. Why Ma felt compelled to invite them, and why they accepted . . . I don't get it. Did you know Ma actually called Elwood and invited him?"

"I'd've loved to be party to that conversation."

"Yeah, I can just hear it: 'I'm giving a little wedding reception for our daughter on Sunday. Can you attend it?' 'Daughter. Yes. Sharon and I are working on coming to terms with our relationship.' 'But would you like to come to the reception?' 'Ask me again after I've had time to assemble my thoughts.' 'Do you think you can assemble them by Sunday afternoon?' 'I don't know. The mind works in strange ways.'"

Hy laughed. "I guess Elwood didn't assemble in time."

"No, thank God, and—"

The doorbell rang. I stiffened.

No one seemed to have heard it.

It rang again.

Hy nudged me toward the entryway. "Showtime, Mc-Cone," he whispered dramatically.

Opening the door to Robin and Saskia was, at once, like catching a glimpse of my past and future selves. Robin, with her high cheekbones and almond-shaped eyes, looked much as I had in my twenties, except that she'd recently cropped her black hair, while all my life I'd worn mine on the longish side. In the lines that bracketed Saskia's full lips and the furrows on her forehead, I could envision how I would look when I reached my sixties. We three shared the same oval facial shape, tilt of nose, medium height, and slender body type; our eyebrows were slightly mismatched, one set a fraction of an inch higher than the other. No one could have missed the fact that we were related, even though Robin and I had different fathers.

As she stepped into the entryway, Saskia smiled at me and placed her hands on my shoulders. Looking into my eyes she said, "I'm so happy for you." Then she turned to Hy and hugged him.

Robin embraced both of us, and I heard her whisper to Hy, "Thank God I've finally got a normal brother—even if you are kind of removed." Then she turned, frowning, to Darcy, who seemed to have shaved his head for the occasion. He hung back on the doorstep, arms folded across his loose black tee, which was emblazoned in red with the word "Roog." Whatever that was.

"Well?" Robin said.

"Uh, hi, Sharon," he mumbled. "Congratulations."

Robin made a clicking sound with her tongue. Although

fiercely protective of her emotionally damaged brother, she often ran out of patience.

I said, "Thanks, Darce."

He nodded stiffly, his one long silver earring bobbing. In addition to shaving off the hair that had been purple the last time I'd seen him, he'd also removed all of his facial jewelry except for a small stud in his nose. An effort to appear normal to my family, or merely a change of fashion?

Hy stepped forward and I introduced them.

"Darcy," Hy said, "I've been looking forward to meeting you. Come with me. You look like you could use a beer."

As they walked away, Robin said, "And he *wanted* to come. Can you imagine how he'd've behaved if we'd forced him?"

"Robin, dear—" Saskia began, but then her gaze was drawn away from her to the archway to the living room.

Ma stood there, her rigid social smile frozen on her lips. She held herself very erect, her blonde head at an angle that would have seemed haughty had her eyes not been so afraid. I started toward her, but Saskia—recognizing Ma from pictures I'd shown her—moved around me, reaching her in two strides and clasping both her hands.

"Kay," she said, "I'm so glad to meet you. You've raised such a lovely daughter."

Ma's cheeks went pink, and her eyes showed relief. Her fears, I realized, were not of Saskia's learning or professional stature, but that she would make a claim on me other than the one that had already been established. But by her words my birth mother—wise woman—had made it clear that she had no such intention. For a moment Ma seemed at an unaccustomed loss for words; then the social smile was replaced by a genuine one and she regained her poise.

"Thank you, Saskia," she said. "I think *our* daughter has

turned out quite nicely. Even though," she added with a dark glance at me, "I often despaired of ever seeing this day."

"I understand perfectly. Robin has a very nice young man, but apparently she prefers studying the law to him." My half sister was transferring from law school at the University of Idaho to Berkeley this fall; she'd be going straight from San Diego to her new apartment there.

Ma said, "Maybe when Robin does decide to get married she'll have a proper wedding, rather than running off to Nevada like Sharon."

The bonding of the mothers. God help me!

Robin elbowed me in the ribs and whispered, "The two of them in cahoots is not a pretty sight."

Saskia smiled tolerantly at both of us and introduced Ma to Robin. Then they linked arms and went off into the crowd, leaving us in the foyer.

An hour later Ma found Hy and me in the gazebo—he had left Darcy behind it with Matt, and denied knowledge of any controlled substances being used there—and told us it was time to cut the cake. I squared my shoulders and followed her to the dining room, glad to dispatch what must surely be the last of my bridely duties. Just what I needed to round out my day—a sickly sweet white confection with the consistency of cardboard. I only hoped it wouldn't be topped by a miniature bride and groom.

When we entered the room, a woman in a white pastry chef's coat was carefully placing a red rose on the top tier of an enormous cake covered in the the richest-looking chocolate I'd ever laid eyes on. She turned, motioned to it with a flourish, and I recognized my youngest sister, Patsy.

"What are you doing here?" I demanded. "You told me you

couldn't take time to attend the reception." Patsy and her husband, Evans Newhouse, ran three restaurants, and the newest one, in the wine country town of Sonoma, had proved problematical and time-consuming.

"It was the God's truth," she said. "I couldn't take time because I was back there"—she motioned toward the kitchen— "creating this damn thing. You don't serve store-bought wedding cake when you've got a master chef in the family."

At close to midnight, Hy and I had finished unwrapping our three gifts from John and his boys, Charlene and Vic, and Patsy and Evans. Identical baskets full of exotic bath toys from LuvYou.com sat plundered and pillaged on the floor of RKI's condo.

"Makes you wonder if they sit around speculating about our sex life," Hy said, contemplating a package of organic body paints.

"It makes me wonder about *theirs*." The Love Mermaid leered up at me as I tried to figure out what one did with her.

"Three sets." Hy looked thoughtful.

"One for the ranch, one for San Francisco, one for Touchstone. No riding up and down the highways for these babies. Good thing, too. What if we got in an accident?"

"Yes. As your mother would say, what on earth would the highway patrol think?"

"Not mother—mother*s*."

"And what would those mothers think about us experimenting with this stuff?" He winked and motioned toward the bathroom, where there was a Jacuzzi tub.

But before we could try out the new toys, real life intruded: Mark Aldin called to tell me that Jennifer had gone missing.

Monday

•

AUGUST 22

I left the Cessna in its place in the tiedowns at Oakland's North Field and walked to where I'd parked my MG, lugging my travel bag and a cardboard carton filled with Laurel Greenwood's few surviving possessions. From there I drove directly to Atherton, where Mark Aldin was waiting at home for me. Alicia, the maid, took me to the same room where I'd spoken with Jennifer and Mark last week, and he joined me a few minutes later. Red-eyed and unshaven, dressed in a rumpled shirt and chinos that looked as if he'd slept in them—if he'd slept at all—he was clearly distraught.

"Any word from Jennifer?" I asked.

"Nothing."

"Let's go over what you told me on the phone last night." I sat down on one of the sofas, but he remained standing, pacing in a continuous, jerky motion in front of the French doors.

"She left around noon. Said she was meeting Rae at SFMOMA, and that she thought it would do her good to get out of the house. I didn't want her to go; she'd slept very badly the night before, and I wasn't sure she should be driving in her condition, but she insisted. When she didn't come back by eight, I tried to reach Rae at home, but only got the machine there, and neither she nor Rick answered their cellulars. By the time Rae returned my call, it was after ten. She said they'd been in Carmel for the weekend, and that she hadn't heard from Jen since Friday. Then I started calling around to Jen's other friends, thinking I'd misunderstood who she said she was meeting. None of them had talked with her in weeks."

"And Terry hadn't heard from her either."

"Not since yesterday afternoon, around three. Jen called her from her cellular, complained that we hadn't had a report from you and that you must be having difficulty with the investigation. You'd emphasized to her that it might take a while, but Jen . . . patience has never been her long suit." He ran his fingers through his disheveled hair, flopped onto the sofa opposite me.

"Sharon, I'm afraid for Jen. I thought launching an investigation would give her some peace of mind, but instead it's made her even more disturbed. It's as if she's become caught up in her mother's insanity."

"I've found nothing to indicate that Laurel Greenwood was insane."

"Isn't it crazy behavior to lie about where you're going, run off God knows where to do God knows what, and leave the people who love you in limbo?"

"Laurel didn't lie; she went exactly where she said she was going. After that, we don't know what happened to her. And Jennifer hasn't been gone all that long. There may be a reasonable explanation why you haven't heard from her."

"Nevertheless, I'm afraid that Jen is replicating her mother's behavior for some skewed reason that only she can understand."

With a chill I thought of the possibility that had occurred

to me on Friday: that Laurel Greenwood had killed herself. Had that possibility also occurred to her daughter?

Mark added, "I think you'll agree that for the time being you should drop your investigation into Laurel's disappearance and concentrate on looking for Jen. We need to get her professional help."

"I'm not sure that's the best course of action."

"Why not?"

"Because I think it would be better if I work both cases concurrently. Like you, I have the feeling that Jennifer's disappearance is bound up with whatever happened to her mother."

"So that's where we're at," I said to my employees. It was two in the afternoon, and they were all assembled around the table in our conference room, casefiles in front of them. "And it means even more overtime for us."

No one protested. They all loved a challenge, even if it meant canceling personal plans.

"The key here is to prioritize," I added. "Do all you can for clients with urgent work, shift the non-urgent jobs to our usual subcontractors."

Charlotte said, "I tried to give the Ames job to Tamara Corbin, but her agency is swamped, too."

Tamara Corbin. The young, enterprising woman had recently become a full partner in my friend Wolf's firm, and already it seemed natural to think of it as hers.

"Dunlap and Dunlap are very good," I told Charlotte, "and there's also the Newell Agency. Now," I went on, "Mark Aldin doesn't want his wife's disappearance to become public knowledge yet. She hasn't been gone long, and there may be a perfectly good explanation for her absence. He's contacted the police in Atherton, and while they—and most other official agencies—are bound by the seventy-two-hours rule for missing persons, they've asked the highway patrol to put out a BOLO on Jennifer. I've talked with my various contacts at other departments in the Bay Area, and their people will also unofficially be on the lookout. But those of us in this room are going to have a head start on any official investigation. Something triggered Jennifer Aldin lying to her husband and her unexplained absence. It's up to us to find that trigger."

While I was handing out assignments and Kendra was passing around copies of the photograph of Jennifer that her husband had provided me, Rae slipped into the conference room and sat on an extra chair by the wall. I finished with Charlotte, asking her to get a list of Jennifer Aldin's bank accounts and credit card numbers and check for activity on them, and then ended the meeting.

Rae stood up and came over to the table. The fog had swept in around noon, enveloping the city in cold and damp, and she was bundled against it in a blue sweater that matched her eyes, her red curls disheveled by the wind off the bay. The sweater fit loosely, and I realized that she'd lost the five pounds of extra padding she'd always complained about. All that hiking, I supposed.

I asked, "What're you doing here?"

"I want to help you look for Jen."

"You're supposed to be home writing your novel." She'd told me she had an October deadline.

"It's not going well. In fact, I'm blocked. They say that happens with second books sometimes. Ricky's down in L.A. for a couple of days, and I need a distraction. Better to be doing something to find Jen, rather than sitting around worrying about her."

I considered. Rae had been a damn good investigator, and I could use all the help I could get. "Let's sit down and kick some ideas around, then. From what Mark tells me, you're one of the few people Jennifer's remained in touch with."

"I am. Her other friends . . . well, I guess they just got tired of hearing about her obsession with her mother."

"But you've stuck by her."

"I don't give up when a friend's in trouble. You know that."

"Yes, I do. The two of you talked on Friday?"

"Yes. She called in the morning, concerned because she hadn't heard from you. I told her that the investigation would probably take time, assured her that you'd be in touch when you had something to report. But frankly, I don't think she listened to me."

"How did she seem?"

"Frustrated. Overly emotional."

"I've got Patrick, Craig, and Julia interviewing her other friends and clients. Charlotte's checking on her credit cards and bank accounts. But this doesn't feel like one of those situations where she's just checked into a motel to brood. You have any idea where she might've gone? A special place, maybe?"

"She and Mark have a second home near Tahoe—"

"He asked a neighbor who has a key to check it; she hasn't been there."

"His sailboat? It's berthed at the St. Francis Yacht Club."

"One of the first things he thought of. No."

An uneasy look crossed Rae's face.

"What?" I said.

"Well, there's the flat. But I called there last night and went by first thing this morning and again before I came over here. No sign of her."

"What flat?"

"Jen has this place that Mark doesn't know about, here in the city, where she sometimes goes to be alone. It's in one of those big old Victorians on Fell Street, across from the Panhandle."

The narrow wooded strip that extends some eight blocks from the eastern edge of Golden Gate Park. "She goes there to be alone?"

"Yes," Rae said firmly. "To be alone. Not to meet men, if that's what you're thinking."

"I wasn't. But can't she find space to be alone in that big house in Atherton? Or at their Tahoe place?"

"Shar, to understand her, you've got to understand Jen and Mark's relationship. He's a nice guy and he loves her, but he has a big ego, big needs. Sometimes it gets to be too much for her and she has to escape."

"Explain these big needs."

"Nothing unusual for a high-powered guy. He just wants her to be there for him twenty-four seven. Ricky can be like that, but it's okay for us because the record-company business and his performing keep him away from home a lot of the time, and I can work then. But Mark does most of his work out of his home office, and Jen has her studio on the property; when Mark wants attention, he feels free to interrupt her whether she's working or not, and she feels she has to drop everything. They also have a busy social life— exhausting, I'd call it. So, once a week she tells him she's taking a class or meeting a friend or a client, and goes to the flat to work on her textile designs in peace."

Just as her mother had gone on day trips to paint.

"And she told you about this place that she keeps secret from her husband. Why? So you could cover for her?"

Rae frowned. "You sound so judgmental."

I guessed I did. I liked Mark Aldin, and the idea of Jennifer deceiving him that way bothered me. But I'd learned long ago that you shouldn't attempt to judge a relationship that you don't live inside of. "Sorry," I said. "But *does* she ask you to cover for her?"

"No. I found out about the flat by accident two months ago—one of those odd coincidences. I'd parked right in front of the building and walked a few blocks to the DMV—naturally, their lot was full—to renew my driver's license. When I got back to my car, Jen was coming down the steps, and I called out to her. She was so shocked at running into me that she couldn't come up with an excuse for being there, so she invited me inside and explained."

"And you believe her story?"

"I have no reason not to."

"Well," I said, standing, "I think we'd better go have a look at this flat."

The block of Fell Street where Jennifer Aldin rented her flat was lined with tall, narrow Italianate Victorians, most of which were broken up into three units. Across from them the forested Panhandle was cloaked in mist, and in between traffic rushed by on the busy crosstown route.

Rae parked her new BMW sports car in front of the building and motioned at the second story. "That's Jen's, the one with the blinds drawn."

I got out of the car and looked up at the bay window. Maybe it was some trick of the light, but even from this distance it looked as if the place were empty, perhaps abandoned. When Rae joined me on the sidewalk I asked, "Does she have garage space, or park on the street?"

"The day I ran into her, her car was out front. Both times when I was here today I drove around, but didn't spot it."

I studied the entrance, up a steep flight of steps from the street level. Three doors, each with an iron security gate across it. "Well, let's ring the bell and see if she answers now."

We climbed the steps. Rae indicated the door in the middle, and I pressed the buzzer. The bell rang above, a hollow sound. I pressed again, and again. No response.

I said, "I don't suppose she keeps a spare key hidden out here."

"I don't know."

"Well, let's look."

A large rubberized doormat covered much of the marble floor. I lifted it, peered underneath. Nothing. I then turned my attention to the big potted jade plants to either side, went over and tipped one. Nothing under it. I felt around in the pot, but came up with only fallen leaves and dirt.

"Check the other," I said to Rae.

She tipped it. Beneath lay a key.

I picked it up and slid it into the gate's lock and it turned. One chance in three, and we were in. I hesitated, debating the situation. Even though Jennifer was our client and her husband had asked us to locate her, we'd be committing criminal trespass.

Rae pushed my hand away from the key. "Jen gave me this spare so I could keep an eye on the place."

"Oh yeah? And what if she's hiding out in there and decides to contradict that statement—to the police?"

"She's not there. I can feel it." She turned the key and opened the gate. Unlocked the inner door and stepped inside.

Ahead of us a steep staircase rose to the second floor. Musty air came to my nostrils, smelling of old carpet and dry rot. I followed Rae, shutting the door, and we climbed to a long hallway that ran the length of the building. Off it were several closed doors and an archway that opened into the front room. Rae called out to Jennifer, but there was no reply.

I went through the archway, found a living room with a small gas fireplace and an armchair with stuffing leaking from tears in its maroon upholstery. Nothing else.

Rae said, "That chair must've been here when she rented the place; Jen would never own anything that shabby. The time I ran into her, she took me directly back to the kitchen and dining area at the rear, where she had a drawing board set up."

I backed out of the room and went to the first door off the hallway. A bedroom, empty. The next led to a bathroom with a claw-footed tub and pedestal sink, the one after that to a smaller room containing only a toilet—standard arrangement in flats of this vintage and type. Another empty bedroom, and the hallway ended at the kitchen. It was old-fashioned, with outdated fixtures and high wooden cabinets whose top shelves even a tall person would need a ladder to reach. It looked as if a wall had been knocked out between it and the space where the drawing board sat. That, a stool, and a blue canvas chair were the room's only furnishings.

I said, "Why would she rent a place this big, if she only planned to come here to work?"

Rae shrugged. "The building's old and in poor repair; maybe the rent was cheap."

"No rent's cheap in San Francisco, and I doubt that would've been a consideration, anyway."

"Well, she did say something about the light being good in this room."

I moved around the kitchen, examining its few contents: a tumbler and a wineglass in the sink, a couple of plates in one cabinet, a few pieces of cutlery in a drawer, a corkscrew on the countertop. The stove was old, its oven encrusted. The fridge held nothing but a half-full bottle of Sauvignon Blanc and a carton of milk with a two-week-old sell-by date. The remaining cabinets were empty of anything but mouse droppings.

Why had a woman of Jennifer Aldin's means rented such a dismal, depressing flat? How could she possibly stand to spend time here? Why, if she needed a quiet place to work, hadn't she rented a light-filled loft in SoMa? Or an attractive apartment in one of the city's many new high-rise buildings?

Rae was standing at the drawing board. I went over, and she pointed to the large sheet of paper spread there. It was a charcoal drawing: arcs that formed a series of parabolas that flowed one into the other. In the large, central one was a woman's face, and when I leaned closer I recognized it as identical to the newspaper photograph I had of Laurel Greenwood. And at each corner of the sheet, in smaller parabolas, were figures: two little girls and two men. The faces of the girls and one of the men were well drawn, but the other was a question mark.

Jennifer, Terry, and Roy. And another unidentified man.

Whatever her reasons for renting this particular flat, Jennifer didn't come here to work on designs. She came to try to make sense out of what had happened to her mother.

"Jesus," Rae said, "she's worse off than any of us suspected."

"Apparently. How long ago did she rent the flat?"

"She said six months, but now I'm wondering how truthful she was with me."

"We'll have to find out who owns the building, get the details."

We were on our way back across town to the pier. Rae, always a fast driver, was working the gears as if she wanted to punish the little car for her friend's possible betrayal.

"Take it easy," I said. "You don't want to get a speeding ticket because you suspect Jennifer wasn't completely candid with you."

She eased off on the accelerator. "I just don't get it, Shar. Maybe she's really gone crazy, like Mark keeps saying."

"Maybe." But my thoughts were taking another tack. "You know Mark pretty well, right?"

"Well enough. He and Ricky are close. Sometimes I tease him—Ricky—about how two such enormous egos can possibly fit on Mark's little sailboat. Ricky says he has to leave his on the dock, otherwise they'd sink."

"How did Mark and Jennifer meet?"

"Through a mutual friend, I think. Why?"

"I'm just wondering about the marriage. He's a good bit older than her, and they really don't seem to have much in common."

"Well, I suppose there is an element of the trophy-wife syndrome there. Mark likes to show her off, and she *is* an asset in his business socializing."

"Mark handles a lot of money. Is in a position where he needs to maintain the trust of his clients."

"Yes. I'd say he handles billions. And is worth millions himself."

"What about Jennifer? Is her business successful?"

"She does pretty well, charges big fees for her designs, but she's not in Mark's league."

"So he wouldn't stand to benefit financially if something happened to her."

"Well, I suppose there might be a substantial life insurance policy on her, but it would be nothing compared to— What are you getting at, Shar?"

"Okay, Mark would not benefit in a major financial way from her death, but if the clients who place their trust in him were to hear that his wife was behaving irrationally, that he couldn't control her, it might have a negative effect on his professional life."

Rae almost ran the red light at Seventh and Howard. She slammed on the brakes, throwing both of us forward against the seat belts, and turned to me, blue eyes wide. "You think that Mark engineered this disappearance?"

"I don't *think* anything. I'm just tossing out a possibility. You've got to admit it's an interesting scenario: wife's mother disappears years ago under suspicious circumstances; wife begins obsessing over mother, becomes a liability. Wife disappears, probably because—and these are Mark's own words—she's caught up in her mother's insanity; husband no longer has to contend with her obsession and its possible negative effects."

Someone beeped behind us. Slowly Rae put the car in gear. "Mark loves Jen," she said.

"According to whom? Jen? Ricky? You? How well does anybody know what anybody else really feels?"

Rae was silent.

My phone buzzed. I pulled it from my bag, answered. Terry Wyatt, calling from her sister's house in Atherton.

"Any progress on locating Jen?" she asked.

"I'll know more after my staff meeting at five. You're staying at the Aldins'?"

"Yes, but my husband's at home, in case Jen tries to contact me there. I don't think that's likely, however; we argued when we spoke yesterday."

"About . . . ?"

"This obsession of hers, of course. She was carrying on about Mom's cousin who died when we were little, Josie Smith. Said she thought Josie had something to do with Mom's disappearance. When I told her it was a ridiculous notion, reminded her that Josie died a full year before Mom left, she got very dramatic and secretive. Said there were things I couldn't understand because I hadn't been there."

"Been where?"

"That's exactly what I asked her. When she wouldn't explain, I kind of—no, I *did* lose it. I told her she'd better grow up and get some professional help for her problem."

I tried to recall the death date for Josie Smith that Derek had supplied me. It had indeed been a full year before Laurel's disappearance. "Maybe Jennifer meant that the shock of losing Josie prompted your mother to disappear."

"Realize life is too short, dump everything and everyone, start over, you mean? I don't know; I was too young to gauge how much or how little Josie's death affected her. But if it was traumatic enough to make her want to bail on us, why would she have waited a year? And why all the drama on Jennifer's part?"

Good questions, both of them. I told Terry I'd phone her after the staff meeting and ended the call.

Rae had been glancing anxiously at me as I'd been talking. She said, "That was the sister?"

"Yes. Apparently Jennifer has concocted a conspiracy theory involving a dead woman."

Nearly ten that evening. I was on the couch in my sitting room, the box of Laurel Greenwood's possessions open at my feet. I had a fire going against the chill of the fog and a cat slumbering on either side of me. Ralph and Alice, happy to have me home. A vase of orange gladiolas, a card reading "Congratulations!" propped against it, sat on the cedar chest I used as a coffee table. Michelle Curley, teenaged neighbor and guardian of the pets and premises in my absence, knew how to win points with her clients—even if her mother was going to give her hell about picking the flowers from her carefully tended garden.

I sighed and closed my eyes. They felt dry, tired. Maybe I should try some of those drugstore reading glasses for close work. . . .

The staff meeting I'd called for five o'clock had run over two hours. Charlotte had come up with no activity on Jennifer's credit cards and bank accounts. The field interviews with her friends and clients had proved inconclusive; all they really accomplished was to confirm that Jennifer had been out of touch with everyone except Rae. As I listened to the verbal reports, I was struck by the similarities between what people had said about Jennifer and her mother: both were described as talented, professional, reliable, a good friend, and by all appearances as having an excellent marriage.

After I'd shifted some assignments and adjourned the meeting, Patrick, Rae, and I called out for a pizza and held a brainstorming session. We concluded that Rae should look into the particulars of Jennifer's renting the flat on Fell Street and Patrick should continue coordinating our findings.

I called Derek at home and asked him to dig further into the backgrounds of the two men who had lied to me in Paso Robles, Jacob Ziff and Kev Daniel. I would continue to delve into Laurel's past, flying back to the central coast for follow-up interviews with Ziff and Daniel later in the week, and also try to see the Magruders upon their return to Morro Bay.

Tonight I'd begun looking through Laurel's possessions: handmade birthday, Valentine's Day, and Mother's Day cards from Jennifer and Terry; a fifth-wedding-anniversary note from Roy, saying it was redeemable for "one hot screw" at the bearer's request; Laurel's diploma from San Jose State and other professional certificates; a framed photograph of Laurel, Sally Timmerman, and an attractive redhead who must be Josie Smith, all in their late teens and posed in front of a small Airstream trailer—the infamous "bordello." There were dozens of letters from people whose names had not come up in the background on Laurel, but which seemed innocuous and had made for uninteresting reading. She'd saved programs from church and PTA events she'd helped organize. A newspaper picture of the Greenwoods on the occasion of the tenth-wedding-anniversary party Sally and Jim Timmerman had given them at the Paso Robles Inn showed a handsome couple; Roy was very lean, with chiseled cheekbones and wavy brown hair and a brilliantly white smile—a good advertisement for a dentist. And then there were the usual souvenirs: playbills and ticket stubs from productions that had run here in the city over twenty years ago; programs from sports events; a map of Yosemite National Park with a Tuolomne Meadows campground circled in red; mementos of various family-oriented tourist destinations. And photographs, dozens of them, of the four Greenwoods on those vacations.

What was interesting to me was what was *not* there. Personal letters of the intimate kind I remembered exchanging with distant friends in the age before e-mail. A diary or journal. Mementos of her parents or sister, Anna. Her own school papers or report cards. Any evidence of any man before Roy came into her life.

Well, maybe Laurel hadn't been a letter writer. Or kept a diary or journal. Maybe Anna had held back the family and school mementos. Maybe, as he had her paintings, Roy had destroyed anything from her former lovers.

Or maybe, if Laurel had deliberately disappeared, she had

taken the important things with her, leaving behind what didn't matter.

Cards from her children and family photographs didn't matter?

Cold, extremely cold.

Of course, if she'd deliberately disappeared, she *was* cold.

I made a note to ask Anna Yardley if there were any more things of Laurel's in existence, and then turned my attention to the last item in the carton, her postcard collection.

It was contained in a small wooden file box, the kind that women with more domestic inclinations than me use to store recipes. A bundle of cards nearly three inches thick. I took out the first, saw it was addressed to Laurel in a bold, slanting hand at the Greenwoods' home in Paso Robles. Just an address, no message. Its postmark was five years before her disappearance, roughly a year after Terry was born. I checked the postmark on the last card: two weeks before her disappearance; they must be arranged in chronological order. Then I began examining them from front to rear.

First mental health day: Cayucos. Ironic that it was the same as her final destination. Second: San Simeon. Third: Cambria. Fourth: Morro Bay. Then she'd ventured inland: to Santa Margarita Lake, San Miguel, and Guadalupe. And on it went, with no seeming pattern, the destinations ranging farther and farther away. After four years the mental health days came closer together, from once or twice a month to once a week. I wondered if Roy had noticed the increased frequency; certainly the girls' babysitter had. And I wondered why Laurel hadn't sent postcards from here in the city when she came to visit her cousin Josie. Maybe the cards were only allowed on her solitary getaways.

Pismo Beach, Orcutt, Oceano.

Lompoc, Lake Nacimiento, San Luis Obispo.

Shell Beach, Sisquoc—

And then a card with a message. A photograph of the pier in Cayucos and a postmark a day after the disappearance.

Roy—
Please don't notify the police that I'm missing, or look for me. It's no use. I ask only that you and the girls remember me as I was, not as I have become.
Laurel

Deliberate disappearance, then.

In spite of the fact that I'd suspected it all along, I felt shaken and saddened. Angry, too. Laurel Greenwood, loving wife, mother, and friend, had abandoned everyone she'd supposedly loved.

Given the circumstances of her marriage, I'd felt a certain empathy for Laurel Greenwood, but now it was gone. It wasn't in my nature to connect with someone who could so calculatedly abandon all the people who cared about and depended on her—particularly her young children. What Laurel had done to her family and friends raised echoes of what my brother Joey had done to ours: gone off, infrequently maintaining contact by postcard, and then committing suicide.

Laurel's actions, in my eyes, were worse than Joey's, because they were so clearly planned. And because of the uncertainty of her fate, they had created an even more widespread and damaging ripple effect of pain and grief.

Suicide is the absolutely worst thing a human being can do to those who love him or her. It is unforgivable. The second worst is a coolly calculated disappearance.

So here was the trigger that had caused Roy to burn Laurel's paintings. And to call off the police investigation.

The evidence had existed in this box for twenty-two years, undiscovered by Anna Yardley because, as she'd told me, she'd never looked through Laurel's things. Placed there by Roy, out of chronological order where no one would find it. I pictured him taking the card from the mailbox, reading her words, and—once the shock wore off—slipping the card into the collection.

But why keep it? Why not destroy it along with the paintings, rather than hide it in Laurel's "legacy" to Jennifer and Terry?

Simple—he'd wanted them to eventually know the truth.

My own father had done a similar thing: collaborated with Ma in keeping the fact of my adoption from me, but stored the official documents in a box of papers he'd known I would be responsible for going through upon his death. The discovery had shocked me, sent me on a wild quest that, fortunately, had culminated in new, rewarding relationships. But nothing rewarding would come of Roy's bequest to his children.

Nothing but disillusionment and devastation.

Tuesday

·

AUGUST 23

"So are you going to tell Mark Aldin and Terry Wyatt about the postcard?" Patrick asked.

"Not yet. They've got enough on their minds. I won't mention it until we locate Jennifer, and maybe not then."

It was ten in the morning, and we were seated on the floor of my office, files strewn around us, a big flowchart that Patrick had constructed spread between us. The chart impressed me: each line of investigation was delineated in a different color of ink, and it looked as if he hadn't omitted a single piece of information. Questions and theories were jotted and circled in the margins. If only my mind were that orderly. . . .

He said, "Don't you have to make periodic progress reports to the clients?"

"Only if they request them. Even then, I don't share everything—too much danger of discouraging them or raising false hopes. When I wrap up a case, I make a verbal report, and present them with a copy of the written."

"Clients ever get pissed at you if the news is bad? Want to kill the messenger?"

"Sometimes. Goes with the territory. So let's see what you've got there." I motioned at the chart.

"Okay. This is the Laurel case. And this"—he moved the paper aside to reveal a second chart—"is the Jennifer case. Since we're acting on the assumption that Jennifer's disappearance is linked to—or maybe it would be better to say caused by—what happened to her mother, we should go over the Laurel chart first."

"Right."

"Basic lines of inquiry: Laurel's last moves. You've interviewed Jennifer and Terry, Anna Yardley, Sally Timmerman, and all the official witnesses who could be located except for Bryan Taft, the second dogwalker in Morro Bay. Those lead to secondary lines: Herm Magruder; Jacob Ziff, because he lied to you; Kev Daniel, another liar; Josie Smith, the deceased cousin, because Jennifer seems to think she was posthumously connected with the disappearance. And then there's the question of the biker."

"Ira Lighthill, the other dogwalker, phoned to say he couldn't find Taft's last known address in Mexico, so that's a dead end, at least for now. Magruder's not due to return from vacation till later in the week. I've got Derek doing deep background on Ziff and Josie Smith, and starting to background Daniel. The biker could conceivably be someone who was in Laurel's art class at the Men's Colony, but we're having difficulty getting information from DOC."

Patrick was silent, drawing a circle in pencil around Josie Smith's name. "I agree with you about Smith. You take a discontented woman like Laurel apparently was, and when a contemporary dies, it makes her question why she's leading the kind of life she is."

"The postcard she sent pretty much confirms it. Let's look at Jennifer now."

He moved the Laurel chart aside. "Basic lines: bank accounts and credit cards. Haven't been used. Second home and boat at yacht club. Unoccupied, and the husband's continuing to have them monitored. Flat on Fell Street. Rae's looking into that." Patrick paused. "Why'd she decide to work on this? I mean, she's got a book to write, and her husband has millions." When I didn't respond immediately, he added, "I don't mean to pry."

"You're not. Rae admits she's blocked on this second book and is looking for a distraction. Plus she genuinely cares about Jennifer. But I see another factor: Rae really loved investigative work; she probably misses it."

"Then why'd she quit?"

"She'd always wanted to write, and once she and Ricky married, he encouraged her to try. Now she just needs a vacation from it."

Patrick's freckled face relaxed some.

"You weren't afraid she was going to come back permanently and take your job?" I asked.

"A little."

"Well, you shouldn't've worried. Even if she wanted to come back there's more than enough work for both of you. And when I hired you, I made a commitment; I wouldn't go back on that. Besides, I never in my life have seen anything like these charts." As I spoke, a flash of inspiration hit me: maybe I should assign Patrick to coordinate cases in this way for all the operatives. I'd have to think about that.

"Thanks." He turned his attention back to the chart. "Okay, the highway patrol's got a BOLO out on Jennifer. I've been monitoring that; no sightings. She may have ditched her own vehicle and rented another. But the husband says she doesn't carry much cash, and she'd've had to pay cash in lieu of using the credit cards and bank accounts."

"She could have borrowed a friend's car, but she's out of touch with all of them except Rae."

"Unless there's a friend we're not aware of."

"I'll put Craig onto that and I'll ask Rae if she can remember anybody we haven't contacted."

Patrick nodded. "Now we come to the subject of the husband. The theory that he may have made Jennifer disappear because she'd become a liability."

"That we have to pursue very carefully. Ricky's flying back from L.A. this afternoon and plans to visit with Mark. He may pick up on something. Frankly, I'm hoping he doesn't."

"But you're the one who came up with that angle."

"I've got a naturally suspicious mind. That doesn't mean I have to like my theories."

"My mind works that way, too." Patrick smiled wryly. "Of course, given my relationship with the Ex from Hell, that's to be expected." He consulted the chart. "I see only one question left: motive for Jennifer's disappearance?"

I thought, shook my head. "She was impatient for results from us, but that's not enough."

"The thing about the cousin's death being responsible for her mother's disappearance? The first time that came up was the day she took off."

"It sounds like a mental tic on the part of a stressed-out person. And it's not enough either."

He pushed the chart aside. "Then we're done with this. But I misspoke before—there is another question left, the biggest of all: where the hell *is* she?"

*   *   *

I spent the next two hours closeted in my office with Ted, going over agency business. Kendra Williams, he told me, was working out splendidly, in spite of her neglecting to tell him about the San Luis newspaperman's inquiry about the case.

"She apologized, and I didn't make a big deal out of it," he said. "Don't you either. I can't lose her. She is indeed a paragon of the paper clips."

"What kind of an ogre do you think I am?"

"I know exactly what kind of an ogre you can be. Make nice, please."

A while back, when I'd given Ted a raise and authorized him to hire an assistant, we'd jokingly discussed his new job title, and he'd opted to be called Grand Poobah. Now I sensed he was rapidly growing into the exalted position.

Just as Ted and I were wrapping up our session, Derek appeared in the doorway. "Got a minute, Shar?"

"I'm outta here," Ted said, gathering up his files.

I motioned for Derek to take one of the clients' chairs. "You have something for me?" Unnecessary to ask; his dark eyes shone with excitement.

"Well, nothing on Smith, and nothing more on Ziff. But Daniel's another story."

"Tell me."

"Kevin James Daniel. Born Marin County, June ten, nineteen fifty-nine. Parents James William and Janet West Daniel. Father owned a wholesale foods company which was later acquired by a conglomerate, making him a very wealthy man. Plus there was inherited money on both sides. Mother died when Kevin was only eight. He grew up in Ross, attended Catholic schools. Was expelled from high school several times for various offenses, including drug use; then the father sent him to a school for incorrigible teens in Colorado. He seemed to straighten up, so after he graduated his father rented him an apartment here in the city and he began studying business at Golden Gate University. Daniel spent more time in the bars than on the books, however, and in nineteen seventy-nine he was convicted of DUI manslaughter—motorcycle hit-and-run accident—and sentenced to prison at the California Men's Colony, San Luis Obispo. Served four years of a twelve-year sentence, with time off for good behavior. Was released on probation, and has been clean ever since."

Which put him in CMC when Laurel had been teaching her art classes there.

"What was his release date?"

"May twenty-third, nineteen eighty-three."

In time to encounter Laurel Greenwood in Cayucos.

"And where was he paroled to?"

Derek smiled triumphantly. "SLO County. The records show a Cayucos address for him."

I said, "I think we have our biker."

It all fit: Kev Daniel had been sentenced to the Men's Colony for a DUI manslaughter—involving a motorcycle. He was there at the time Laurel taught her art classes. He was released on parole the month before she disappeared. For some reason they met in Cayucos. And then . . . ?

If Daniel was responsible for Laurel's disappearance, I would need to proceed very cautiously. I already had good reason to be wary of him: he had lied about his whereabouts when the shot was fired at me in the courtyard of the Oaks Lodge.

I sat in the armchair by my office window, putting together a theory while staring at a wall of fog.

*Start with the premise that Daniel is the biker. Someone the
San Luis Obispo County Sheriff's Department searched inten-
sively for twenty-two years ago.*

Even if he was innocent of any wrongdoing in connection
with Laurel's disappearance, a recent parolee wouldn't have
wanted to come under the law's close scrutiny, so when the
call went out for information about her, he didn't volunteer.
Or if he wasn't innocent, he had even better reason to remain
silent.

Jacob Ziff had indicated to me that Daniel came down from
San Francisco four years ago, so he'd probably left SLO County
at his first opportunity. But now, because he'd returned and
bought into a winery there, he found himself in a position of
some importance in a community that would not be forgiving
were his incarceration and later involvement in the Greenwood
case—however innocent—to come out.

So far, so good.

Okay, then I showed up. Daniel found out about me from
Jacob Ziff, who thought it interesting to have met with a private investigator, and talked casually about our interview
with his client. Daniel was afraid that I would find out about
him if I went on probing, so first he tipped the reporter from
the San Luis newspaper in the hope that publicity would
hamper my investigation—

Wait, when had Ziff told him about me? Before or after
the article came out? I'd have to ask him.

The newspaper article aside, Daniel wanted to discourage
me. Ziff had referred to him as something of a loose
cannon—the kind of man who might discharge a weapon in
a public place if the stakes were high enough. From our brief

conversation over wine on the patio, I could tell that Daniel thought being shot at would scare a woman off.

Wrong assumption, Daniel.

What to do now? I couldn't take my theory to Rob Traverso at the Paso Robles PD. He struck me as a man who acted strictly upon facts, and I really didn't possess anything concrete. I'd first have to ask Ziff to explain his lie about being at the lodge's bar when the shot was fired, as well as about when he discussed me with his client. Perhaps talk with Mike Rosenfeld, the reporter, too. Only then would I go up against Daniel.

After a moment's thought I got up and went along the catwalk to Ted's office, where the agency's safe is located. He and Kendra were in the supply and copy-machine area in back, so I hurriedly worked the safe's combination and took out my .357 Magnum. Ted worried about me every time I flew and every time I removed the gun from the safe. That meant he worried often about the former, infrequently about the latter. In this busy time, it was best I kept his unease to a minimum.

When I returned to my office, the fog outside the window looked thicker. I put the gun in my bag, then called aviation weather. Socked in at Oakland; I wouldn't get off the ground in the Cessna tonight. Clear skies all the way down the Salinas Valley. Naturally.

Commercial flights from both Oakland and SFO would be delayed under these conditions, and no carriers went to Paso Robles anyway. Even if I could get a flight to Monterey or San Luis, I'd have to rent a car and drive some distance and, under the current tight security regulations, I might have difficulty taking the gun aboard, even disassembled and in a checked bag. Better to drive down in the MG—

"Shar?" Derek.

"Yes, what have you got?"

"The additional information on Kevin Daniel. He was paroled to the San Luis area, but in July of the year of his release asked for permission to serve out the rest of his probation in the San Francisco area. The request was granted, he returned to his father's home, finished his undergrad and graduate degrees—in marketing—and became a model citizen. Worked for his father until the company was sold, then stayed with the conglomerate that bought it until four years ago, when the father died and he inherited big bucks. A few months later he went down to Paso Robles and bought into what was then called the Kane Winery. Daniel has never been married, races motorcycles in area competitions, lives in a million-dollar home on winery property. I'd say he probably gets a lot of women."

An astute observation from someone who also got a lot of women. I remembered Jamie's tentative question—"Does Derek ever ask about me?"—and the way Chris had smiled up at him at the party at Touchstone. And frowned.

"Something wrong?" he asked.

Stay out of your employees' private lives, McCone.

"Uh, no. That's good stuff. Nothing else on Ziff, or Smith?"

"Ziff looks squeaky clean. Smith I haven't started on."

"Thanks, Derek. I'm heading out this afternoon for Paso Robles. You can reach me by my cell or at the Oaks Lodge."

He nodded and left the office. I reached for the phone, to buzz Ted and ask him to reserve me a room, guaranteed for late arrival, but before I could, he buzzed me.

"Rae on line two."

I picked up. "Hi, how's it going?"

"I'm at the building on Fell Street. Property records show it's owned by one Carl Dunn."

"Why is that name familiar?"

"He's Josie Smith's first husband. He says that the year she died, he was letting her live in the second-floor flat while she tried to evict the tenants from a house she'd bought out in the Avenues."

"He lives in the building?"

"Right. He occupies the same third-floor flat now that he did then. I've already confirmed that he rented the second-floor flat to Jennifer, but I think you'd better get over here so we can both interview him. I've got a feeling my skills along those lines are kind of rusty."

"I'm on my way."

"I had no idea Jennifer Aldin was Josie's niece," Carl Dunn said. "I knew her and Terry when they were children, but the last time I saw Jennifer was when she was nine or ten. Why didn't she tell me who she was?"

I said, "Perhaps she didn't remember you."

We were seated in Dunn's living room in the third-story flat of the Fell Street building, a bright comfortable space with large abstract paintings on the walls. Dunn was a big, bearded man with a mane of silver-gray hair, a real estate agent, Rae had told me.

Dunn frowned. "She might not've remembered my name or face, but I'm surprised she didn't recognize the building. She stayed here several times with her mother."

"How did Jennifer Aldin come to rent the flat from you?"

"My former tenants vacated it four months ago, and I listed it with my agency, plus posted a sign in the window. A few days later, Jennifer Aldin rang my bell, said she was driving by and saw the sign. I showed the flat to her, and she liked it. Said she would prefer a long-term lease and would be using the place as a studio only one or two days a week. The idea of a tenant who wouldn't be around much appealed to me; the last pair were noisy and disruptive. And I like long-term leases; the woman on the first floor has been here since I bought the building in nineteen seventy-nine. So I accepted a deposit, and she gave me the names of three of her clients as references. They checked out, and we signed a year's lease two days later."

"You still have those names?"

"Somewhere in my files. Let me see." He got up and went down the hallway.

I said to Rae, "Jennifer just happened to rent the same flat where Josie lived? I don't think so."

"Me either. And I now know why she lied to me about how long she'd had it; she didn't want me to realize that it was connected with her obsession over her mother's disappearance. Figure it out: her father dies five months ago, she begins to dwell on Laurel. Four months ago she rents a place that she associates with her."

"Dunn said she came to the door after she saw his sign while driving past. Maybe she was on a sentimental tour."

"Or had driven by more than once."

Dunn came back into the room, a slip of scratch paper in his hand. "Here you go. Keep it, if you like."

"Thanks." I glanced at it, saw three unfamiliar names. One of the phone numbers was familiar, however: the Aldin residence. I handed the slip to Rae, my eyebrows raised.

She examined it and said, "Home, studio, cellular."

Jennifer had supplied her own references.

"Mr. Dunn," I said, "what can you tell us about Josie?"

He smiled—gently, for a man about to discuss his former wife. "When I met Josie, I'd just graduated from San Jose State and was moving up here to take a job at Wells Fargo Bank. We had a hot and heavy romance, and the next spring she dropped out of college to marry me. The marriage was a mistake from the beginning. Not her fault, not mine either. We were just too young, too different. We split up after five years, but remained friends. We'd have lunch every few months, talk on the phone. When she met Don Bernstein, we kind of lost touch, but after he dumped her—the bastard took off with another woman, left her with a heap of credit card debt—we started seeing each other again."

Dunn paused, narrowing his eyes as if he was in pain. "Josie partied too much—one of the things that broke us up in the first place—but she was also a hard worker. She'd gotten her RN after we split, and when Bernstein took off, she started taking on private-duty nursing jobs, made very good money. Neither of us suspected she'd soon be in need of private-duty nursing herself."

Another pause, a headshake. "Anyway, she made good on the debts, invested her money, bought a house out on Thirty-third Avenue. But the tenants were putting up a fuss about moving, and until the dispute went to court, I suggested she move into my empty flat. The dispute dragged on and on—suits, countersuits—and just after it was settled she was diagnosed with brain cancer."

Dunn seemed to sink into thought, and Rae prompted, "So she stayed on here and you took care of her?"

"Of course. I wasn't going to let her move into her house alone, not in her condition. And neither was Laurel Greenwood. She came often while Josie was sick, although she could only stay a night or two at the most; then, when the insurance that paid for the nursing had run out, she came and stayed to the end."

"Did Josie die here or in the hospital?" I asked.

"Here. I wish we'd had her hospitalized."

"Why, Mr. Dunn?"

"I don't know if you're familiar with brain cancer, but with the type Josie had and at the stage she was when she died, you can be lucid one moment, totally disoriented the next. While Laurel was napping one afternoon, Josie got out of the bed in the front room where we had her and wandered into the hallway. Fell down the stairs and died."

It took a moment for my thought processes to kick in. Then I tried to remember the cause of death Derek had reported to me. Complications resulting from brain cancer.

Some complications.

I asked, "Were you here at the time?"

"No, I was out showing a property to a client. I returned just as the ambulance was taking Josie away."

"And Laurel? You said she was napping?"

He nodded. "She was exhausted. Slept right through Josie's fall. By the time Laurel found her, she was gone." He compressed his lips, his eyes moist. "We never got to say good-bye, either of us. And then I never got to say good-bye to Laurel."

On our way out of the building, I hesitated in front of the door to the first-floor flat. "Didn't Dunn say the woman down here has been his tenant as long as he's owned the building?"

"Right."

"So she would have known Josie, maybe Laurel. And probably Jennifer." I pressed the doorbell.

After a minute or so a slender, dark-haired woman in a

black tailored suit looked out at us. I introduced Rae and myself and handed her my card. "We were speaking with Mr. Dunn upstairs," I added, "and he tells us you've lived here since nineteen seventy-nine."

"Nineteen seventy-eight, actually. The year before Carl bought the building. Is there some problem?"

"Nothing concerning you, but we would like to talk to you about the tenant on the second floor."

She glanced at her watch. "I can give you half an hour before I have to change for my book group."

The woman opened the door wide and ushered us into a flat that was slightly larger than the upper ones because it lacked a staircase. The living room was to the left, darker than Dunn's or Jennifer's and furnished in what looked to be good-quality antiques. When we were seated she said, "I'm Melissa Baker, by the way. Or did Carl tell you that?"

"He didn't mention you by name, but he did say you were a good tenant."

She smiled. "And he's a good landlord. Has repairs made promptly and hasn't ever raised the rent, except for cost-of-living adjustments. He could, you know, since this building is owner-occupied and only three units, and thus isn't covered by rent control. But you said you're interested in the people who lived on the second floor. What did they do? Steal the bathroom fixtures?"

"They?"

A look of confusion passed over her features. "You're asking about the Jordans, aren't you? The people who vacated a few months ago?"

"No. We're interested in the present tenant."

"Jennifer Aldin. Lovely woman. Such a change, after the Jordans."

"Do you recall when you last saw Ms. Aldin?"

"Last weekend. Sunday. We had a cup of tea together."

Rae and I exchanged glances. "D'you recall what time that was?" I asked.

"After lunch. One, one-thirty." Melissa Baker's brows knitted together in concern. "Has something happened to Jennifer?"

"She hasn't come home since Sunday, and her husband has asked us to locate her."

"Oh no. I hope she wasn't upset by what I told her. Although she didn't seem to be."

"Perhaps you could start at the beginning."

"Well, Jennifer has been renting her flat as a studio. You probably know she's a textile designer. There was some problem with her studio at home."

"Did she tell you what?"

"I don't know exactly. I gather her husband also works at home, and there are tensions in the marriage."

"Such as?"

"She didn't mention anything specific, but I could sense she wasn't very happy. She's a successful professional woman: there was an article on her in a home-decorating magazine that I picked up at my hairstylist's; it said her career had really taken off. But whenever I ran into her she seemed depressed and distracted. And I think she drank alone upstairs. A few times when I encountered her, I smelled it on her breath."

Depressed and distracted—by her marriage, or by her obsession with her mother? Or a combination of the two?

I said, "How often did the two of you get together?"

"Only three or four times. Yes, three."

"What did you talk about?"

"Nothing special. Her work, mine. The books my group

was reading. She did display some interest in Carl and the previous tenants of her flat. I guess that was only natural; she may have been thinking about staying there on a more regular basis."

"She said that?"

"No, but at first she wasn't there more than once a week, then I noticed her quite often. I work in the building also—I'm a CPA—and the hours Jennifer put in here at her studio have escalated in, I'd say, the past two or three weeks. Almost as if she didn't want to go home."

"And when she stopped by to see you on Sunday . . . ?"

"She seemed much better, as if she'd made up her mind to make some changes. And she hadn't been drinking. We talked more about the neighborhood and the building, and I felt I had to tell her the one thing I'd been withholding because I was afraid it might upset her. You see, there was a tragedy that happened in her flat. I'll never forget it. For a while it almost made me want to move away."

"What Melissa Baker told us puts a different slant on Carl Dunn's account of Josie's death," Rae said.

"A disturbing one."

We were seated by the pit fireplace in the living room of her Seacliff home—backs to the windows, ignoring the fog that was still streaming toward the Golden Gate. Our feet were propped on the raised brickwork, and we had glasses of wine in hand.

She said, "We should be glad Baker's office window opens onto the airshaft, and that she's a bit of an eavesdropper."

"What's wrong with eavesdropping?"

"Nothing. I've always considered it a professional asset—both as an investigator and as a writer."

"Okay." I began ticking off items on my fingers. "Laurel has been staying with Josie for a week. Josie's in the terminal phase of her illness, but still lucid at times, and has the unfortunate tendency to get out of bed and wander. On the afternoon of Josie's death, Laurel receives a phone call, which Baker overhears via the airshaft. She can't make out much of it, but it upsets Laurel, because she shouts, 'You're making it up! You've always been jealous of my friendship with Josie, and now for some reason you want to hurt me.'

"Then Baker hears Josie's voice in the background. Laurel moves far enough away from the shaft that Baker can't make out their conversation—except that very soon after they start arguing. It's tax season, Baker's busy, so she closes the window in order to concentrate on the forms she's preparing. When she goes outside an hour and a half later to walk down to the corner mom-and-pop store, the police and an ambulance are in front of the building, and Josie's being taken away on a gurney. Laurel's hysterical. Carl Dunn arrives and takes charge of her, and they retreat to his flat. The next day, Laurel goes back to Paso Robles and doesn't return, except briefly for the funeral."

Rae nodded and took a handful of popcorn from a bowl on the hearth. "Easy to jump to the conclusion that Laurel and Josie were quarreling when Josie fell down the stairs."

"Quarreling for nearly an *hour and a half*?"

"That's kind of hard to believe. Maybe they quarreled, Laurel got Josie back to bed, and then took her nap. It could've happened the way Carl Dunn thinks it did."

"Or they quarreled, Josie fell, and Laurel didn't call nine-one-one till later."

"Why? Because she was in shock? I don't think so. Remember, Laurel had also been a nurse." Rae munched on the popcorn, thinking. "Accidental death? Or did Laurel push her?"

"If there was anything suspicious about Josie's death, there would've been an investigation."

"Do we know for sure that there wasn't?"

"Not yet." I went to where I'd left my purse on a side table, took out my cellular, and speed-dialed the apartment that my friend Adah Joslyn, an inspector on the SFPD homicide detail, shared with Craig Morland. She wasn't at home, but Craig told me to try the Hall of Justice. Adah was at her desk, working late, and—per usual—in no mood for idle chitchat.

"What?" she said.

"Information on a nineteen eighty-two accidental death that may have fallen under suspicion as involuntary manslaughter."

"Don't want much, do you?"

Typical Adah grumbling, but I knew she'd come through for me, because she always had. And she was more bark than bite these days, since the trouble-plagued department, and her career, was on the mend after the appointment of an intelligent, evenhanded female chief of police.

"Too much," I admitted, "but it's important to the major case we're working on."

"Yeah, Craig's told me about it. Why can't you ever come up with something minor, like a skiptrace?"

"We do our fair share of those, too."

"Okay. Particulars?"

I recited them.

"I'll get back to you. When I can."

I set the phone down, saw Rae smiling. "Adah," she said, "she's really something. D'you think she and Craig'll ever get married?"

What *was* it about married people? As Wolf, my investigator friend, was fond of saying, they all wanted to see everyone else locked up in the same institution. Of course, he was
married now and, good God, so was I!

"I don't know," I told Rae. "It could be that Adah and Craig
don't want the attendant hassles. Craig is from a WASPy,
conservative Virginia family. And you know Adah . . ."

Adah was half black, half Jewish, and her aging leftist parents
still participated in—or helped to organize—whatever radical
protest movement was currently gaining momentum. The picture of the Joslyns and the Morlands coming together at a wedding reception made Ma's gathering for Hy and me seem like a
stroll through the park on a sunny spring day.

Rae seemed to be picturing the same scene. Her lips
twitched in amusement, but then she looked up at the archway
that led to the foyer. I followed her gaze, saw Ricky standing
there. He dropped his travel bag on the floor, slung his leather
jacket over the back of a chair, and came toward us. His expression was brooding, and he moved as if he was tired.

Rae went to greet him, going up on tiptoe to plant a kiss
on his cheek. "Hey," she said, "what's wrong?"

He hugged her, forced a smile over her shoulder at me.
"I've just come from the Aldins' house, and I need a drink.
Be right with you."

Rae watched him walk toward the kitchen, turned to me,
and shrugged. Ricky returned shortly, a thick crystal tumbler
containing a dark amber liquid in hand. His chestnut hair
was tousled, and worry lines stood out on his handsome
face. He sat next to Rae, took a swallow, and said, "Something's wrong down there, other than the obvious, and I
really don't like what I'm thinking."

When he didn't go on I said, "And that is . . . ?"

"Mark's acting very upset and concerned for Jen, but that's exactly what it is—acting. I'm enough of an actor myself that I can tell it from the real thing. And after we'd been talking a while and he'd let his guard down some, he said that in a way it would be a relief if she disappeared for good like her mother did, because he wasn't sure he could take any more of her obsessing."

Rae said, "That's normal. There're times in any marriage when one partner thinks it would be a relief if the other disappeared into thin air. And Mark's had to put up with more than most spouses."

"Red, this wasn't like that. It was the first time during our conversation that I heard genuine feeling in his voice. And twice after that he referred to Jen in the past tense. Besides . . ." He shook his head, sipped his drink.

"Besides?" I prompted.

"I think he's been having an affair."

"Oh? What makes you think that?"

"Shar, as you very well know, I'm no stranger to cheating and the kind of behavior it generates. I thought it through on the way home, and there've been little signs for a few months now."

"Such as?"

"He's late a lot of the times when we get together, and never has a good explanation for it. An attractive woman walks by, I comment on her, the way guys do, and he doesn't respond, as if he's trying to avoid the subject of women entirely. He's overly complimentary in what he says about Jen and his marriage. Overly sympathetic with her obsession with her mother. Overly willing to throw money at the problem, rather than deal with it in a personal sense. Besides, the times he's been late, he's had the look."

"The well-fucked look."

"Thank you, Sister Sharon, for being so delicate."

I smiled. "Sister Sharon" had been Charlene's nickname for me—as in "Sister Sharon who is holier than thou, unless nobody's looking"—and Ricky still used it occasionally.

I said, "You're welcome, Brother Ricky, and if anybody could recognize the look, it's you."

Rae asked, "Am I gonna have to referee?"

"No," we said in unison.

I added, "I think you may be on to something, Ricky. And you"—I turned to Rae—"are going to have to pursue this line of investigation while I'm down in Paso Robles."

She frowned. "Wait a minute, Mark's the agency's client. We can't investigate our own client."

"No, Jennifer's the client. Her name's the only one on the contract."

Ricky stood. "I don't want to hear any of this. It's none of my business and, besides, I need another drink."

When he'd left the room I said, "You'll do it? Check out Mark?"

"I'll do it. If he's done anything to Jen—"

"Don't get ahead of yourself. It could be Ricky's reading more into the situation than there actually is."

"Or it could be he's right—and we've got a real disaster on our hands."

Wednesday

·

AUGUST 24

By the time Rae and I had finished on Tuesday night—mapping out our next courses of action and bringing Patrick up to speed on the new developments—it was late and I'd decided against driving to Paso Robles until morning. My alarm woke me at six, and I found the fog had receded; aviation weather confirmed good conditions all the way. So once again Two-Seven-Tango and I headed south.

When you're piloting an aircraft, your senses are heightened, even on the longest and most tedious of flights. You're checking the gauges, monitoring the radio, watching for other aircraft, maintaining your altitude, making adjustments for the wind, as well as enjoying the view of the terrain below. You experience a great feeling of freedom, having broken loose of the earth and the concerns that envelop you there. And after a while your thoughts also soar free, often in ways that they don't on the ground.

This morning as my thoughts turned to the investigations, I found I wasn't thinking of them as separate or even loosely connected entities. The parallels were simply too strong. After a while the facts melded into a decades-long continuum, and

I began to sense what had happened to Laurel and Jennifer. I felt with a growing certainty that I would find both of them and, by the time I did, I would already understand the reasons for their disappearances. It was simply a matter of putting everything into its proper place.

After I had left the Cessna in the tiedowns and claimed my rental car, I called Jacob Ziff's number but reached only a machine. Although I loathe the practice of hanging up when no one answers, I broke the connection before the beep; a certain amount of surprise would work to my advantage with Ziff. Next I dialed Herm Magruder's condominium in Morro Bay; the gravelly voiced man who answered identified himself as Magruder and told me yes, he'd found my card in his mailbox. When I said he'd been recommended to me as an authority on his town, he invited me to come over as soon as I wished.

"I've got to warn you, though," he added, "the wife and I just got back from vacation last night, and the place is a mess."

The spacious condominium *was* something of a shambles. A heap of dirty laundry sat on the living room sofa, and unpacked cartons were stacked on the floor. Beside one stack sat a terra-cotta donkey wearing a sombrero that also served as a planter—a variation on the garden gnome, perhaps?—and atop the other were two brightly colored piñatas.

"You've been to Mexico," I said. Detective work at its finest.

"Yeah." Magruder, a stocky, balding man with a hooked nose and horn-rimmed glasses, looked around as if he were surprised to find such objects in his condo. "We took the motor home down to Baja for some camping and fishing, then stopped in Tijuana to shop. Tequila for the son, the donkey for the daughter-in-law, piñatas for the grandkids. They live in the Midwest, think crap like this is exotic. Our Christmas shopping is done." Then he flashed me a quick grin. "Of course, there's the other crap we bought for ourselves."

After I'd declined his offer of a soda, Magruder took me to a small balcony overlooking a courtyard with a swimming pool and colorful plantings. The weather here on the coast was as clear as it had been inland, the air balmy. We sat at a small wrought-iron table with an umbrella tilted against the sun.

He said, "You told me on the phone that I've been recommended as an authority on Morro Bay. May I ask by whom?"

"Ira Lighthill."

He smiled. "Mr. Puli. I've called him that for years, since before I knew his true name. Breeds those ropy-haired dogs. Hear he makes good money at it."

"I suppose he does."

"And how did my name come up?"

I explained about my investigation and my conversation with Lighthill. "He said he was surprised that you hadn't noticed Laurel Greenwood when she left the park, since he'd seen you on the porch of your house earlier that afternoon."

"Drinking on the porch, he probably said. And it's a fact; that's what I did in those days. Lighthill tell you I wrote a column for the little local rag?"

"Yes."

"I studied journalism in college. Always wanted to be a reporter. But I ended up back here where I was born, running a business— Hell, you don't want to hear this."

"I do. Please, go on." I meant it; I've always been interested in how people end up doing what they do, probably because when I was in college, I never would have envisioned myself as a private investigator.

"Well, I graduated from Berkeley and I had a wife and a child on the way. There was the possibility of a job with the UPI, but before I heard on that I got a call from a friend who was starting up a self-storage business here—the standard units for people's extra crap, plus little garages for boats, RVs, or cars. He offered me a partnership, so what could I say? I came back, and when he wanted out a few years later, I had enough money saved to buy both the land and the business.

"But I wasn't happy. So I left the business in the wife's hands—Amy was the brains of the operation, anyway—and got this little job writing the column. Got full of myself, too, thinking being Mr. Morro Bay was some big deal. But underneath I knew it wasn't, so I started gathering most of my material in the bars or from my front porch with a fifth of Scotch for company. Wasn't until Amy threatened to leave me that I stopped drinking." He smiled wryly. "Of course, after that the column went to hell because I couldn't tap into my usual sources, and then the paper went belly-up."

"But you were still doing the column when Laurel Greenwood vanished?"

"Yeah. I was on the front porch that afternoon, and I wouldn't't've missed her if she'd passed the house. I was the kind of drunk who reaches a certain level of mellowness and can go on for hours—thinking as clearly as if I were stone cold sober. At least until I passed out when I went to bed."

"So you remember that afternoon?"

"Absolutely."

"Will you describe it for me?"

"Sure. It was sunny, like today—"

"Herm? Is this Ms. McCone?"

A tiny, sun-browned woman with white-blonde hair stood in the door to the balcony. Blue tank top, khaki shorts, great legs even though she must be well over sixty.

Magruder didn't immediately reply, although his lips twitched with annoyance, so the woman held out her hand to me and said, "I'm Amy Magruder."

We shook, and she took a seat at the table. "Herm, were you able to help her?"

"I'm trying." Stiffly spoken; she'd intruded. Magruder no longer experienced many situations where he was the center of attention, and he probably resented sharing.

I smiled at his wife, then turned back to him. "As you were saying . . ."

"What were you saying?" Amy asked.

"I told you that Ms. McCone is investigating the Laurel Greenwood disappearance—"

"Oh, yes, poor woman." She turned to me. "You know she was last seen at the waterfront park near our old house?"

"Yes, Amy, she knows that. As I was about to say, Ms. McCone, I saw a number of people: My barber. Several of the local fishermen leaving a little bar they used to frequent before it was torn down for a souvenir shop. Tourists, of course. Hordes of tourists, even back then."

"And there was Cindy. Don't forget Cindy."

Magruder gave his wife a long, measured look. "My wife's archenemy, leaving the bar with a man who wasn't her husband."

"And you wouldn't even mention it in your column."

"Had no place there."

"Look what she did to Dave afterwards, running off with—"

"Water under the bridge, Amy."

This was obviously an old, ongoing argument between the two of them, and I wanted no part of it.

"Anyone else, Mr. Magruder?" I asked.

"A couple of waitresses from the seafood joint. A woman who sold shell jewelry to a little shop that went out of business the next year. The paperboy and—"

"There was that customer of ours," his wife interrupted. "You mentioned her two days later when I told you she took off with a week paid up on her rent and didn't even leave a forwarding address for the refund."

"Who?"

"You know, what's-her-name. The pretty one who kept her van in number one-oh-two."

"Oh yeah, her." Magruder narrowed his eyes in thought. "Came out of the park, like they said the Greenwood woman did, walked past me, and went up the hill toward the self-storage yard. What was her name?"

Amy Magruder shook her head. "I don't remember. Don't even recall much about her, except she was pretty. A youngish woman, with red hair."

Magruder said, "I never saw her up close like Amy did." He turned to his wife. "You sure you don't remember what she looked like?"

"Well, she was tallish and slender. But her hair—it was so beautiful that it was all you really noticed. Long, silky, and bright red."

I felt a prickling at the base of my spine.

Josie Smith: *drop-dead gorgeous with all that bright red hair.*

But Josie had been dead a year—

"Mr. Magruder," I said, "is there any way you could find out the woman's name? Access old business records, for instance?"

"Is this important?"

"It could be. Very."

He looked at his wife, and she nodded.

"Well, I suppose I could. But it'll take a couple of hours. We keep the records at a self-storage unit in Cambria." He smiled. "I guess you'd call it ironic—the owner of the place is the guy who bought us out on the cheap and then sold the land for big money to a goddamn developer. Now there're tourists gobbling cheese and sucking up wine where we once had our little business."

As I was walking back to my rental car after leaving the Magruders' condo, my cell phone rang. Hy. I hadn't spoken with him since late Monday night.

"Where are you?" he asked.

"Morro Bay. You?"

"El Centro."

A desert town some seventy-five miles east of San Diego. RKI had a camp near there, where they trained their operatives in the techniques of executive protection. New employees did intensive classroom work, practiced evasionary techniques—otherwise known as car chases in clunkers— underwent rigorous practice on the firing range, engaged in paintball wars, simulated emergency field medical procedures, and held mock hostage negotiations. Since 9/11, executive protection had become one of the hottest commodities in the security field—and also the most dangerous. The possibility of death by bullet, knife, bomb, or hand-to-hand combat was a very real on-the-job hazard, and RKI made sure their operatives possessed optimal survival skills.

"Teaching a class?" I asked. Hy was RKI's top hostage negotiator and often gave seminars at the desert facility.

"More like troubleshooting." His tone precluded my asking anything more; the firm operated on a need-to-know basis, and unless they hired me as a subcontractor—which they twice had—their operations were none of my business.

I felt a prickle of unease, remembering Gage Renshaw's words to me at the party at Touchstone: *We've got a situation coming up that's gonna require all our resources. See that your man's ready for it.*

"Looks like I'll be here a couple of days," Hy added, "so I thought I'd check in with you. I'm hoping to get up to the city over the weekend. How's your case going?"

"It's coming together."

He didn't press me either; certain aspects of my investigations were also confidential, and he knew he'd hear whatever I could tell him when we saw each other. We talked a few minutes more, tentatively deciding that if he wrapped up his work there and I wrapped up my work here, I'd fly to El Centro and pick him up on Friday. Then we ended the call, and I started the car and headed for Cayucos.

Jacob Ziff was home and seemed pleased to see me. He took me to the chairs by the big windows of his office and, as before, offered me coffee, which this time I declined. When we were seated, he asked, "Did the police find out who shot at you last weekend?"

"No." I shook my head, let a silence build.

Ziff frowned. "They have no idea who did it?"

"None, but I have a couple of suspects in mind."

"Oh?"

Again I made use of silence. Ziff shifted in his chair. I took a small notepad from my bag, paged through it. My last week's grocery list, a reminder to make a dental appointment, a number of items to pick up at the hardware store, a list of supplies we needed at Touchstone, a note to add a friend's new phone number to my address book, and a couple of pages of scribbling about a potential client an acquaintance had referred to me.

"Here it is," I said. "On Saturday night, you told me that you were at the bar at the Oaks Lodge when the police arrived."

"That's right."

"That's right—that's what you told me? Or that's right—that's where you were?"

"I don't understand." But he did; a flush was spreading up from the neck of his polo shirt.

"After you left, I spoke with the bartender. He said you weren't there."

"Maybe you spoke with a different bartender. The shifts change—"

"He'd been on duty since eight."

"Well, then, he's mistaken. I was there."

"You were there two hours before the police arrived, but left. Where did you go?"

Ziff compressed his lips.

"Perhaps to the courtyard, to choose your vantage point? Or to the house phone to call me and pretend to be the desk clerk? Or to wait in the shadows with a handgun?"

"No! I had nothing to do with that!"

"I didn't think you did."

He blinked. "Then what—?"

"I just wanted to get your reaction, to make sure I hadn't misjudged you. Where were you, Jacob?"

He got up, moved to the window wall, and pressed his hand to the glass, looking out at the sea. "It's none of your business."

"Maybe not mine, but if I mention your lie to Rob Traverso at the PRPD, he'll make it *his* business."

"All right!" Ziff turned, hands balling into fists. "I was in one of the guest rooms. With a woman friend. A married woman friend who has a great deal to lose if our relationship were made public."

A simple explanation, most likely a true one. "Thank you. That information will remain confidential, but I do have a few additional questions." I looked pointedly at the chair that he had vacated.

He relaxed somewhat, went back, and sat down. "I don't know why I should continue to talk with with you," he said, but his words lacked conviction.

"I think you do. Both you and I suspect who the shooter was."

Ziff spread his hands on his thighs, looked down at them. "Kev Daniel," he said after a moment. "He told me he arrived at the lodge at the same time the cops did, but I saw him go through the bar to the patio right before I went to meet my friend. And later, when I went back to the lobby, he came in from the direction of the far guest wing."

"Where the shooter stood. Does Daniel own a handgun?"

"Maybe. He's a hunter, has a number of rifles."

"A marksman, then. When did you tell him about me?"

". . . Shortly after you left here on Friday. He called to confirm our Saturday appointment, and I was jazzed at having met a real-life private investigator, so I talked about you."

"What was his reaction?"

Ziff thought. "Quiet, at first. I thought he was focused on something else, maybe checking his calendar or his e-mail, but then he started asking a lot of questions."

"Such as . . . ?"

"What you'd asked me, what I'd told you. Where you were from, where you were staying—which you hadn't told me. Then he got off the phone really fast, said he had another call."

"That article in the San Luis paper about me reopening the Greenwood case—did you read it?"

"Yes."

"Didn't it make you wonder who the anonymous source was?"

"It did. I thought about asking Mike Rosenfeld—I know him, he did a profile on me once—but I knew he wouldn't tell me."

Now, how often does a bit of serendipity like that drop into one's lap?

I said, "Why don't you call him now? Explain that I need to know and promise him that when the Greenwood case breaks, he'll get an exclusive interview with me."

After an initial hesitation, Mike Rosenfeld caved in to the offer of an exclusive and confirmed to Ziff that it was Kev Daniel who had told him about me. Ziff put me on the phone, and Rosenfeld repeated what he'd said.

I asked, "Did Daniel say why he was giving you the information?"

"Kev and I are drinking buddies. He feeds me a lot of gossip about the winemaking crowd; sometimes I can find a good story in it. This time—well, the Greenwood disappearance has always interested me; I'm a *Cold Case* junkie—you know, the TV show. I thought if I publicized your investigation, someone might come forward with information that would help you solve it. I wanted to talk with you, but Daniel didn't know where you were staying, and your office wouldn't give out any information. It was getting close to press time, so I just filed the story. I suppose I should've waited, but . . ."

"That's all right, Mr. Rosenfeld. In a roundabout way, your story did help me. And I hope to be able to tell you how very soon."

When I broke the connection, I saw Ziff frowning at me. "Why d'you suppose Kev planted that story?" he asked.

"I'm pretty sure he was the biker Laurel Greenwood was seen with, and I recently found proof that her disappearance was voluntary. One thing that occurs to me is that Kev knows Laurel is alive and was trying to get a message to her."

"But why would Kev think he could reach her by way of the San Luis paper? If she's alive, she's not living around here; someone would've spotted her long ago."

"That's true. But a lot of people subscribe to a local paper after they leave an area, and Laurel would have a vested interest in knowing if the investigation into her disappearance were still active, or if the police and sheriff's department had developed any new leads."

"Why would he want to warn Laurel?"

"For the same reason he wanted to scare me off. Now that he's in with the winemaking crowd here, he wouldn't want his involvement in the Greenwood case to come out."

Ziff closed his eyes, brows knitting. "You know, Kev could've been the man with Laurel. Same body type and hair color, anyway. What was his relationship to her, exactly?"

"That's a little hazy right now, but you'll find out when you read Mike Rosenfeld's exclusive."

When I left Ziff's house, it was time to meet with Herm Magruder at the self-storage place in Cambria, where his old business files were kept. The facility was on the northern edge of the town, and before I reached it I drove through an area that was lined with upscale shops, restaurants, and motels, and clogged with cars, buses, and RVs. Slow-moving throngs of tourists crowded the sidewalks. The gateway to Hearst Castle was in full moneymaking mode, and the merchants must be enjoying every second of it.

Magruder was waiting for me in front of his self-storage unit, leaning on a red Jeep Cherokee and talking with a slender, sandy-haired man. When I pulled up, the man walked off, raising a hand in farewell.

"That's the son of a bitch who made a fortune off my land," Magruder called to me as I got out of the car.

The man gave him the finger over his shoulder and kept going.

"You can't help but like a guy with his chutzpah," Magruder added. "And besides, Amy and I made out okay on the deal. Money doesn't matter all that much to us, so long as we can keep the motor home in good running order and get away to fish and buy Mexican crap a few times a year."

"Sounds like you're enjoying your retirement."

"Yeah, we are." He picked up a folder that was lying on the Jeep's hood, handed it to me. "The records you wanted."

"Thanks." I opened it, examined the two sheets inside. A photocopy of a canceled check drawn on an account at the Haight-Ashbury branch of Bank of America, dated September 1982, and a rental agreement for a single-vehicle garage at Magruder's facility, dated the same. The check was for a full year's rent. The signatures on the document and the check were the same: Josephine Smith.

Josie, who by the time the agreement was signed, had been dead three months.

"I can give you the same room you had last week, Ms. McCone."

I smiled at the desk clerk and said, "I'm surprised you're letting me stay here again. That incident on Saturday night was the wrong kind of publicity for the lodge."

"Not your fault. And I guess you don't know small towns—any publicity is good. Business in the bar and restaurant is up ten percent; people all want to hear firsthand about what happened." He reached beneath the desk and pulled out a few message slips. "These came in this afternoon."

While he ran my credit card, I thumbed through them. Rae, Craig, Patrick, Adah. None of them had called my cell, but that didn't mean their business wasn't urgent; my friends and operatives knew the unit would be turned off when I was flying, and I'd often enough warned them against interrupting me when I might be conducting a field interview. Sally Timmerman. How had she known I was here? Someone named Emil Tiegs, with a number with a familiar prefix.

I took the key and my credit card from the clerk, wheeled my travel bag across the courtyard, and went upstairs to the familiar room. The maid had left the air conditioner on preparatory to my arrival, and it was frigid in there, so I turned it off. Immediately I took my .357 from my bag and locked it in the little safe in the closet, then opened the balcony door and went out there to make my calls.

Adah was out on an investigation. Patrick wasn't in the office, but Craig was there. Rae had left instructions with Ted for me to call her on her cellular. I went over some routine matters with the Grand Poobah, then asked him to put me through to Craig.

"Shar," Craig said, "my contact at DOC finally got back to me. Kevin Daniel attended Laurel Greenwood's art class the whole time she taught at the Men's Colony. He—my contact—provided the name and home number of the re-tired prison official who oversaw the educational programs, and he's expecting to hear from you." He read them to me.

"Contacts—they're wonderful, aren't they?" I said.

"This one is gonna cost me; he'll be down here next week and wants to meet for lunch at the Slanted Door—my treat, of course."

"Put it on your expense report."

"Gotcha."

I ended the conversation and looked at my watch, then di-aled the number of the former prison official, Orrin Ander-son. No answer there, but Rae picked up her cellular on the first ring.

"Interesting stuff, Shar," she said.

"I'm listening."

"I followed up on Josie Smith's estate. Guess who was her only heir and also executor?"

"Laurel."

"Right. Laurel inherited a small savings account and Josie's house on Thirty-third Avenue, which she sold two months after Josie's death for a profit of a hundred and six thousand dollars."

"Big profit, considering Josie only bought it the year before."

"From the figures I saw, I'd say it was undervalued at the

time of purchase, and nineteen eighty-two was probably a good year for San Francisco real estate."

"So Laurel would've had plenty of money to disappear on."

"Close to a hundred and ten thousand."

"Anything else?"

"Yeah, and it's not good. I did deep background on Mark Aldin. Thirteen years ago, before he met Jen, he and a partner were managing a hedge fund headquartered in Kansas City."

"Hedge fund—high-risk investment, big returns?"

"Always high risk, sometimes big returns. I got the skinny on them from Charlotte. Basically, they're lightly regulated investment pools for wealthy individuals and institutions like pension funds. Anyway, Mark was connected with a large financial planning firm, and he persuaded them to put a lot of their wealthy clients into the fund. Six months later, a routine audit showed that the assets of the fund were nearly depleted; and right after that Mark's partner disappeared. He's never been found, and neither has the money. Mark rode out the scandal, cooperated with the SEC, and then went to Los Angeles, where he started his own money-management firm. Six years ago he moved up here, where he met and married Jen."

"That *is* interesting. Raises quite a few questions."

"Yeah, like what happened to the partner? And where did Mark get the capital to set himself up in L.A.? And it raises questions of trust for Ricky and me. Mark's never disclosed any of this to us."

I considered. My initial impression of Aldin was of a loving, concerned husband, but that's what I'd been led to believe by Rae. And I'd had no reason to doubt his honesty; after all, he handled millions for Ricky. But these new revelations bore looking into.

I said, "It's definitely cause for concern. In light of Jennifer's disappearance, I should confront Mark—"

"Ricky's doing that as we speak. Both of us feel Mark should have been honest with us from the beginning."

"God, Rae! If Mark had anything to do with either Jennifer's or his partner's disappearance, confronting him could be dangerous!"

She laughed. "Ricky may present the appearance of a country boy onstage, but you and I know that's just a facade. He asked Mark to come to the house, where one of the guys from our security firm will be highly visible. And he'll tape the conversation."

"If Mark's involved in either disappearance he'll just stonewall Ricky."

"And then we'll know he is, because Ricky's going to make it plain up front that if he doesn't get some damn good answers, Mark is going to be out mega bucks in fees every year. An innocent person doesn't throw away that kind of loose change."

In spite of the seriousness of the situation, I couldn't help but smile. Ricky had come a long way from the scruffy dreamer and scribbler of unsold songs who had married my sister. And Rae had come a long way from the insecure young woman with chronic credit card debt and—as I had found out much later—a history of shoplifting whom I had hired years ago to be my assistant at All Souls Legal Cooperative.

But then, I'd come a long way, too: wine bottles with corks in them; haircuts by an in-demand stylist; my own agency; three houses; an airplane; a terrific husband—

Good God, what other wonderful surprises would life shower upon us?

It was a good thought to hold on to every morning when I had to clean out the cats' litter box.

Adah didn't pick up at any of her numbers. Patrick still hadn't returned to the office and wasn't at home. He'd yet to join the legions of us who were tethered to cell phones—even though I'd told him he could buy one at the agency's expense—so I had no way to reach him till he arrived at one place or the other. Again I tried the retired prison official, and got no answer. No one was home at the Timmerman residence, so I left a message.

Now what? Oh, yes, the remaining message—Emil Tiegs. The phone book showed his was a Cayucos prefix. I dialed, and after six rings a man picked up. He sounded as if he had respiratory problems.

"This is Sharon McCone. You left a message for me at the Oaks Lodge."

"Right. I heard about the story in the *Trib*. Got some information about the Laurel Greenwood disappearance that you'll be interested in."

From the sly way he spoke, I knew what was coming. "Would you like to set up a meeting, Mr. Tiegs?"

"Not yet. First there's money matters to settle." He coughed, then went on, "This information is valuable—"

"How valuable?"

"Five thousand dollars, in advance."

"Five thousand—! And *before* I know what the information is? I don't think so."

"Half up front, half when I tell my story."

"My client won't front that kind of money for information that may not be useful to us. Why don't you describe it—in a general way."

"I'm not givin' away no freebies here."

"I said, in a general way."

". . . Okay. Laurel Greenwood. How she disappeared. And who helped her."

"Sounds promising. But my client and I have no assurances that your information is accurate."

"It's accurate."

"I have only your word on that. Let's meet, at least, so I'll know who I'm dealing with."

"I'll agree to a meeting for fifteen hundred up front, the rest afterwards."

I considered Mark Aldin's net worth. "Five hundred up front, another five hundred if the information is useful."

Silence.

"The ball's in your court, Mr. Tiegs."

A frustrated, rasping noise. "Okay, we'll meet. You know the pier in Cayucos?"

"Yes."

"I'll see you there. Ten o'clock tonight."

Wait a minute! Was this a setup engineered, perhaps, by Kev Daniel?

"Mr. Tiegs, as I said before, I need to know who I'm dealing with. And since I don't, I'm not about to meet you at night in a deserted place."

"Christ! Okay, tomorrow. But you make sure you got the five hundred on you. I need my earnest money."

I had only about a hundred dollars with me, and I doubted that the lodge would cash that large a personal check, but I'd spotted a branch of my bank a couple of blocks away. In case this guy was offering a legitimate lead, I could withdraw the maximum daily amount from the ATM tonight and the same again in the morning.

I said, "I'll have it. How about nine o'clock tomorrow?"

"No, I got another appointment. Can't make it till noon. I'll be down near the end of the pier. A real tall, skinny guy in a black windbreaker and a Giants cap and a big Labrador retriever on a halter. Have the money, and you won't be sorry." Emil Tiegs hung up.

Quickly I dialed the office and got Derek started on a background check on Tiegs. Then I consulted the phone directory; Tiegs was listed: 30 Hillside Drive in Cayucos. I was starving, so I decided to grab a burger and then stop by the ATM before I drove over there to scope out who I'd be dealing with.

Hillside Drive was in the older part of the beach community, a narrow two-block-long strip of pavement lined with small clapboard houses that rose above the commercial district. I spotted number 30 as I drove past, continued to where the street dead-ended at a high retaining wall supporting the larger residences above, and parked. From that vantage point I could easily study Tiegs's house. It was one of the smallest— boxlike, with a flat roof and two windows overlooking the street, beige in color, except where the paint had been scoured gray by the elements or stained dark by mildew. An old-fashioned TV antenna leaned drunkenly above it, and a rusted white Toyota Tercel was parked in the driveway.

Having nothing better to do this evening, I waited for signs of activity. There were none. People walked their dogs, came and went at the other houses, but Tiegs's looked deserted. In the distance the sun sank closer to the horizon, infusing the sky with pink and gold and orange; when the purple hues of the late sunset appeared, I decided to stay till dusk, then check out the house on foot.

My cellular rang. Derek.

"Got the preliminary on Tiegs," he said. "Born San Luis, nineteen fifty-six. Parents— D'you want the boring stuff, or should I just e-mail it to you and cut to what's important?"

"Cut, please."

"Okay, Tiegs was at the Men's Colony down there at the same time Kevin Daniel was. Doing a term for forgery. Was paroled the year before Daniel got out and went to live with a sister in Cayucos. The sister died of a drug overdose five years later, and Tiegs took over the lease on her house."

"Thirty Hillside Drive."

"Yeah. And that's what I've got so far."

A forger. Maybe he'd turned his talent to art while incarcerated, taken classes from Laurel. If only I could get hold of Orrin Anderson, the former prison official who had overseen the educational programs—

"Shar?" Derek said. "You want me to continue digging on Tiegs?"

"Please. I'm supposed to give him five hundred of the client's dollars tomorrow, and I want to make sure it's a worthwhile investment. Try to find out what the specific charges against Tiegs were."

After Derek and I ended our call, I sat in the gathering darkness, thinking. Emil Tiegs, a forger who might have known Kev Daniel in prison. Who had been released a year earlier than him. Who lived in Cayucos, where Daniel had lived after his parole and where Laurel had been sighted with a biker whom I presumed was Kev. Before I went up against Daniel I needed to hear what Tiegs had to tell me. Five hundred dollars of Mark Aldin's money was a small amount to risk—especially when the risk posed to me by Daniel was so much greater.

As darkness fell, I watched one window of Emil Tiegs's house glow into a rectangle of light. Someone there, after all. I slipped from the car, pulling the black sweater I'd brought with me over my head, and walked slowly along the opposite side of the street. Through the window I could see a woman—heavyset, dark-haired—sitting on a green sofa, knitting and occasionally looking up at a TV.

Tiegs's wife? Girlfriend?

After a while a man came into the room—thin and tall, carrying a can of beer. He moved haltingly toward the sofa, as if he didn't wish to be there, and sat down. A few seconds later, a blond Lab followed, settling itself at his feet.

Okay, this was probably not some setup Kev Daniel had engineered. Tiegs was as he'd described himself, and he certainly didn't look dangerous. Tomorrow, on the pier, I'd hear his story.

Thursday

·

AUGUST 25

"I wanted to talk with you because my conscience has been troubling me," Sally Timmerman said. She sat opposite me in a booth in the lodge's restaurant, clutching a coffee cup with both hands. She'd pushed aside her plate of half-eaten French toast.

"Something you told me about Laurel that was untrue?" I asked.

She nodded, brow furrowed. The frown seemed unnatural; hers was a face made for smiles.

Timmerman had called my room fifteen minutes ago, saying she was downstairs having breakfast and working up the nerve to ask me to meet her. When I'd entered the coffee shop she was drowning her plate in syrup, but now it seemed she'd lost her appetite. I, on the other hand, was looking forward to the scrambled eggs, hash browns, and bacon strips I'd ordered. A full breakfast is a rarity for me, but when I do have the meal, I eat heartily and cast aside any guilt about cholesterol.

Sally said, "After I heard about you being shot at on Saturday night, I got scared for you. I mean, I hadn't realized looking for Laurel might put you in danger. And then I thought that because I . . . Well, I didn't exactly lie, but I withheld something from you, and I was afraid that your not having all the facts might put you in more danger. On Monday I tried to call you here, and they said you had left, so I thought, 'Okay, that's it. She's gone, let it go.' But I couldn't, so yesterday I called your office and they said you were back down here."

It looked as if she were trying to strangle the coffee cup. I put a hand on her arm and said, "I understand. Why don't you relax and tell me about it?"

"Okay." Deep breath. "You were interested in the relationship between Laurel, Josie, and me. I said I lost touch with Josie after she dropped out of college to get married, but that wasn't exactly the way it happened. I stopped dealing with her after she came down for a visit about a year later. I caught her in bed in the house Laurel and I still shared—with Laurel's fiancé, Roy Greenwood."

"Did you tell Laurel about this?"

"No. Josie threw on her clothes and left—acting like it was my fault for coming home at the wrong time—and Roy pleaded with me not to tell. Said it was a stupid mistake, they'd been drinking wine, and Josie came on to him. I told him I'd keep it to myself if he promised never to see Josie again."

I sensed there was more, waited.

"Roy kept his promise—I thought. He and Laurel married, had the girls, seemed happy. Laurel couldn't understand why he disapproved of her spending time with Josie, but I did. Or at least I thought I did until five years before Laurel disappeared, when I got together with an old friend from San Jose State who had recently run into Josie in a restaurant in San Francisco. You can imagine how I felt when she said, 'Wasn't Roy Greenwood engaged to Laurel Yardley in college? Strange that he'd end up with her cousin.'"

"So Roy had been seeing Josie all those years?"

"Maybe not all of them, but at some point they'd started up again. I confronted Roy, and at first he denied it, then he admitted he was seeing her and again begged me not to tell Laurel. The man cried, actually cried, and Roy was not a very emotional person. So once more I said I wouldn't tell, if he'd break it off with Josie."

"Did he?"

"He did not. I caught on to what was happening about a year before Josie died, when Laurel was telling me about phoning Josie and a man answering. She said, 'I could've sworn to God it was Roy, but it turned out to be Josie's new boyfriend. Isn't that the strangest coincidence, that she's dating a man who sounds exactly like my husband on the phone!' After that, I checked with Roy's office, and found out he supposedly was in San Francisco at a dental convention that weekend."

"Did you tell Laurel?"

"No, but I confided in my husband. He advised me to keep quiet, said that I didn't have actual proof, and that telling Laurel would only hurt her and the girls, possibly destroy their family. It wasn't easy, but I did as he said. Then Laurel went up to San Francisco to be with Josie when she was dying. I couldn't stand the idea of her tending to a woman who had betrayed her in the worst way anyone can. The idea of Laurel emptying Josie's bedpan and washing her and feeding her, and Josie thinking she'd gotten away with something—that was more than I could bear."

When Sally didn't go on, I said, "And?"

"And I called Laurel at Josie's. Told her everything I knew. She didn't want to believe me. Finally I yelled at her. I said, 'You may as well face it, your husband's been banging Josie ever since college.' Laurel accused me of lying. I can remember her exact words: 'You're making it up! You've always been jealous of my friendship with Josie, and now for some reason you want to hurt me.' And she hung up."

So it had been Sally whom Melissa Baker had overheard Laurel talking to through the airshaft in the Fell Street building.

Sally said, "The next day, Roy called to tell us Josie was dead. He came right out and asked me if I'd ever told Laurel about his relationship with her. I said no; I couldn't bring myself to tell him what I'd done. And he said it was best to let it go, let Laurel remember Josie as a good friend. Jim and I didn't go to the funeral, and after that I saw Laurel around town, but we never spoke. Then, a year later, she was gone."

I reconstructed what had happened: Laurel ended her phone conversation with Sally, looked up, and saw Josie. Although she had accused Sally of lying, she must have known her friend had no reason to make up such a story; she may have suspected Roy's infidelity for some time and chosen to ignore it, but she couldn't any longer. So she confronted Josie, asked if what Sally had said was true. And Josie . . . ?

A truth-telling session at the top of the stairs? An admission of an ugly betrayal? Hands raised in anger? A shove that would quickly kill a terminally ill woman?

Sally Timmerman was watching me. "I did a terrible thing, didn't I?"

"I'm amazed that you kept silent as long as you did."

"That was terrible, too. I'm an awful person."

"No, Sally, you're not. You're just human, like the rest of us."

After leaving Sally Timmerman, I went back to my room to make some phone calls. Adah was in a meeting. Patrick still wasn't available at either the agency or home, but Orrin Anderson, the retired prison official, answered his phone on the second ring.

"DOC told me you'd be in touch," he said. "I remember Mrs. Greenwood very well—and not only because she disappeared under mysterious circumstances. She was one of the best teachers we had during the time I directed the educational programs at the Men's Colony. Delightful and genuinely interested in her students. She could be warm, yet maintain the appropriate distance that was necessary for any young, attractive woman who taught there."

"Do you recall a convict named Kevin Daniel, who took her classes?"

"DOC told me you were interested in him, so I've had time to refresh my memory. He was a young man from an affluent family whose alcohol abuse had resulted in the death of an elderly woman. He adjusted well to the prison routine, and over his time there took a number of classes, mainly in the arts."

"Can you describe Mrs. Greenwood's relationship to Mr. Daniel?"

Anderson was silent for a moment. "She was closer to him than to the other students. He showed considerable artistic talent, and she took an interest in him, critiqued extra work that he brought to her. On the basis of her introduction, he actually sold two watercolors through a small gallery here in San Luis."

"And you weren't concerned about this closeness?"

"Initially I was. But after a talk with Mrs. Greenwood, I decided that she simply wanted to see talent rewarded. Kevin Daniel was excited about the sales, and told the board at the time of his parole hearing that he was grateful to Mrs.

Greenwood and hoped to continue his artistic pursuits while finishing his education."

"I see. Let me ask you this, Mr. Anderson: did an inmate named Emil Tiegs ever take one of Mrs. Greenwood's courses?"

"Emil Tiegs? No, I'd remember that name. What was he in for?"

"Forgery."

Anderson laughed. "Well, I'm surprised he didn't take Mrs. Greenwood's class. What better way to maintain his skills than by studying art?"

I thanked Anderson for his information and ended the call. Time to head for the ATM, and then the Cayucos Pier for my meeting with Emil Tiegs.

At close to noon a chill fog enveloped the pier; it was deserted except for a couple of fishermen and a tall, lone figure and a dog at its end. I walked along, my purse heavily weighted with my .357 Magnum, my footfalls echoing on the planks. A seagull wheeled overhead, then dove toward the water.

As I neared the tall man he turned. His unseeing gaze and the halter on the big blond Lab confirmed the latest on Emil Tiegs, which Derek had relayed to me by cell phone half an hour earlier: Tiegs had been blinded nine years ago in an explosion at a meth lab he and two friends were operating, and his lungs had been damaged as well. He'd plea-bargained, testifying against the friends in exchange for immunity from prosecution, and now he was living on state disability. His wife, Nina, worked as a clerk in a convenience store. No wonder Tiegs had tried to hold me up for five thousand dollars. And why he was willing to take a lot less.

"Mr. Tiegs," I said, turning on my voice-activated recorder.

"Ms. McCone. Did you bring the five hundred?"

I removed the envelope containing the cash from my bag and put it into his hand. He felt its thickness, ran his fingers over the bills, and shoved it in his pocket. "When can I have the rest?"

"If your information is useful to us, I'll have it wired to your bank account within twenty-four hours."

"It'll be useful." He stepped back, breathing raspily and leaning against the rail; the dog moved with him, sitting down protectively at his feet.

"So tell me what you know."

"In nineteen eighty-three I was living here in town with my sister. I'd gotten out of the Men's Colony at San Luis a year before after doing a stretch for forgery. Not checks, no penny-ante stuff like that. Identification, everything from driver's licenses to passports. Man, I was good, a real artist. Nobody ever questioned my work."

"Except when you got caught and sent to prison."

Tiegs shivered, pulling his thin windbreaker closer. "That was a setup. Guy I owed money to turned me in to the cops. Anyways, in eighty-three I wasn't back in business yet. You gotta be careful after you get out, move slow, you know? But then this guy I knew from down there comes to me, says he needs some ID fixed for a friend."

"The guy have a name?"

"Kev Daniel. He was just a kid at the time, in the Colony for manslaughter—ran some old lady over with his motorcycle while he was drunk. Rich kid from Marin County, but okay. Not snotty or anything like that. Not then, anyways."

"You fix the ID?"

"Yeah. It was for a woman. She had the social security and

credit cards, but the problem was with the driver's license. The name and everything else was right, but she needed her own picture on it. A snap, for me. I worked my magic, Kev paid, and there I was, back in business."

"The woman's name?"

"You must've guessed by now—Laurel Greenwood."

"And the name on the identification?"

"Josephine Smith. I remember, because it was a combination of fancy and plain."

Laurel had been executor of Josie Smith's estate. Easy enough for her to retain the credit and social security cards, as well as any other useful documentation, but picture ID would have posed a problem. So she asked her old student, Kev Daniel, to use his prison connections. Kev owed her, because of her introduction to the gallery owner who had sold his watercolors, probably was fond of her and willing to help out.

Well, now I knew the *how* of her disappearance. Other details were still unclear, but I could sort them out later. What interested me was the *why*. Specifically, why had Laurel decided to assume Josie's identity? As a convenient way of escaping a life that, after Sally's revelation, had become insupportable to her? Or had something more complex been operating there?

What had Laurel been thinking?

She took my husband from me. I took her life. Now I'll take her identity to escape both him and my crime?

No, not just her husband and her crime. In her postcard to Roy, Laurel had said that she was a dreadful person and her family would be better off without her. She'd been trying to escape from herself, and Josie naming her heir and executor had given her the out she needed.

Tiegs was uncomfortable with my silence. He shifted from

foot to foot, stooped to pat the dog. "It's the truth, Ms. Mc-
Cone, I swear it."

"I believe you. But how come you want to sell the information to me, rather than Kev Daniel? You must know he's a big
man in the area now, partner in a successful winery. He
wouldn't want his past or his connection to Laurel Greenwood's disappearance made public knowledge."

His mouth twisted bitterly. "Oh, yeah, I know about him.
Nina—my wife—read me the article from the paper when he
first bought into that winery, and we've kept tabs on him ever
since. At first I thought he had some balls coming back here,
but then I realized that when you've got money, who cares if
you're an ex-con? The only time they care is when you're hungry and need a job."

"So you haven't approached Daniel?"

"Yeah, I have. Six months ago, when Nina was out of work
and things were really rough for us. The way I figured it, even
if he didn't care about people finding out that he did time at
the Colony, he sure wouldn't want me talking to the cops
about him getting that ID for the Greenwood woman. I
wasn't being greedy, just asked for a loan. He told me to get
lost, said who was anybody going to believe about Greenwood—him or me? And then he said if I told anybody, he'd
have me taken out of the gene pool. He meant it, too—I
heard it in his voice. And Nina—she was with me, drove me
over to that winery of his—she saw it in his eyes. So when
Nina read me the article about you reopening the case, I
thought I'd give you a try. The information's worth another
five hundred, ain't it?"

I didn't like Emil Tiegs, in spite of his unfortunate circumstances. They were, after all, of his own creation. But fair market value was fair market value.

I said, "It's worth it. Give me your bank account number, and I'll have the rest wired to you."

He nodded, relieved, and took out a checkbook. Tore off a blank check and handed it to me. In return, I gave him one of my cards, telling him to call if the money didn't arrive by close of business tomorrow.

As I left the pier, I reflected that a thousand dollars was probably more than he'd expected or would have settled for. The Emil Tiegses of the world make a lot of demands, but they never expect them to be met.

After I left Cayucos a number of things came together in quick succession.

I was driving east on Highway 46, plotting my strategy for confronting Kev Daniel, when my cellular rang. Rae.

"Sorry to take so long in getting back to you," she said. "Ricky was with Mark a long time yesterday, and then we had some decisions to make. He couldn't get a handle on whether Mark had anything to do with either Jennifer's or his partner's disappearances. He did say that Mark seemed very disturbed and angry when he spoke of Jen, but I suppose that's normal under the circumstances. And he did admit to having an affair, although he wouldn't say with whom. But here's the thing: Mark was very evasive about the money that vanished from the hedge fund, said the case was still under investigation and he couldn't talk about it, even to his current clients—which is a load of bull. Ricky didn't react at all well to that. You know him: he doesn't let a lot of people get close to him, but when he does he trusts them completely."

And when one of them broke that trust, he acted swiftly and forcefully. I'd seen him in that mode more than once. "He's decided to cut Mark loose," I said.

"Yes, he called and told him after he talked it over with me and I agreed. It hurts, because of my friendship with Jen, but then, I'm also beginning to question that friendship."

"I wouldn't cross it off just yet. You know better than anyone what pressures she's been dealing with. So that's all you've got?"

"For now. Anything else you need?"

"Not at the moment. I'm going to have a surveillance run on Mark. Where are you?"

"The office. I came in to talk with Patrick, look at those charts he's made up, get an idea of the big picture. But he's not here."

"Damn! He left me a message yesterday, and I haven't been able to reach him since."

"Let me see if anybody knows where he might be." She put down the phone, returned a few minutes later. "Nobody's seen him since about three yesterday afternoon."

Around the time the clerk at the lodge had taken the message. "Well, thanks. Will you explain the situation with Mark to Craig and ask him to run the surveillance?"

"Craig's pretty busy. I could—"

"Not a good idea. Mark knows you."

"Well, what about Julia?"

I hesitated. A Latina might stand out in a wealthy enclave like the Aldins', but there were also plenty of them—legal and illegal—working for the families there. To the casual observer, Julia, in the battered old car she'd recently bought, would look as if she were waiting for a friend.

"She'll do fine," I said. "Talk to her and give her the information she needs. I don't have time to fill you in on everything else that's going on right now, but I'll write a report and e-mail it to everybody."

I ended the call, made another to Mark Aldin. He sounded

strained, his voice curiously flat. I skipped the pleasantries, got down to business.

"Nothing yet on Jennifer, but the various law enforcement agencies and my people're on the alert," I said. "I just talked with an informant who had important information on Laurel. The informant wanted a thousand dollars. I gave him five hundred, promised him the rest of it by wire."

"Cheap enough. But why should I pay it? You've got the information."

I thought of Emil Tiegs, alone except for his seeing-eye dog at the end of the pier, shivering in his thin windbreaker. I hadn't liked him because I'm a strong proponent of law and order, and I particularly detest people who manufacture and distribute drugs. But Mark Aldin had many millions, some of them perhaps as a result of a crime, and he'd done something else I detested: lied to Ricky and damaged his already fragile trust in his friends.

I said, "Because I gave my word, that's why you have to pay it. This is the bank and account number for you to wire it to." I read it off to him, made him repeat it. "Make sure you do it today."

"Whatever." Aldin hung up.

No questions as to what the information was. No further questions as to our search for Jennifer. Having one of his biggest clients confront him about his past and fire him had depressed Mark more than the possibility of losing his wife.

When I got back to the lodge, there were two message slips waiting for me: Adah and Patrick. They'd both come in shortly after I left that morning.

I looked at the area code on Patrick's message: 707. Well, that could be almost anywhere in the northwestern part of the state, from the Sonoma County line to the California-Oregon border. What the hell was Patrick doing out in the field? He was supposed to be in the office, coordinating our efforts. I dialed the number.

"Santa Rosa Travelodge."

The Sonoma County seat, an hour and a half north of the city. Why had Patrick stayed the night there?

"Patrick Neilan, please."

"I'm sorry, he's checked out."

"This is his employer. Did he indicate where he was going next?"

"No ma'am, he didn't."

"Thank you." I hung up the phone hard, then felt ashamed of my show of petulence and hoped I hadn't hurt the clerk's ear.

Patrick would have had ample time to return to the office by now, if that's where he'd been headed. Since he hadn't, what the *hell* was he doing?

Next I dialed Adah. She was at her desk at SFPD, and in top form.

"You ask somebody to get you information, she puts herself out for you, and then your damn cell phone's either not on or busy. Had to call your office to find out where the hell you're staying. You want to know about this Josephine Smith's death or not?"

"Forgive me, I'm guilty of the terrible sin of being unreachable."

"Smart-ass."

"Sorry. What have you got?"

"The death was investigated as a suspicious one—normal procedure, under the circumstances. But the autopsy results showed nothing that was inconsistent with a terminally ill woman—who would have died in a matter of weeks anyway—taking a bad fall. Laurel Greenwood was a former registered nurse, a relative, and a lifelong friend of the deceased. Smith's ex-husband, who lived upstairs, confirmed that Laurel was devoted to Smith. Tragic circumstances, but accidental. Case closed."

"Thanks, Adah. I owe you."

"You *always* owe me, McCone."

I was in the middle of the report to my operatives—wishing Patrick were here to help me focus—when my cellular rang. By the time I realized what the feeble sound was, located my purse, and dragged out the unit, it had summoned me six times. I told myself that I had to get a better model than this antiquated one my staff had given me on my birthday a couple of years ago.

"Yes!" I snapped, thinking it was Patrick, and prepared to give him hell.

"Sharon? It's Mark Aldin."

"Yes?"

"My neighbor from across the street, Estee Pearson, came over a few minutes ago. She and her husband have just gotten back from a trip to Italy."

"And?"

"She wanted to know if I knew when Jen had borrowed her car. I didn't realize this, but Jen and Estee are in the habit of trading vehicles. Jen has a Mercedes SUV, which Estee likes for transporting groceries and large objects, and Estee has a Porsche Boxster, which Jen loves to drive. Estee came back and found the SUV in her garage and wondered when Jen would be bringing the Porsche back."

Now, there was a break.

"Okay, Mark, now we know what Jen is driving. You'll need to contact the highway patrol with the description and license plate number of the Porsche, as well as the other agencies who have BOLOs out on Jen's SUV—"

"Can't you do that?"

Again, his voice was curiously flat. Good God, despite his personal and professional setback with Ricky, didn't the man care anymore if his wife was found?

I said, "The information should come from you, as next of kin and the one who reported her missing."

"I don't think I can deal with—"

I sighed impatiently. "What's the color and license plate number of Estee Pearson's car?"

"I don't know."

"Well, will you find out?"

Silence

Dammit! "Is Terry there?"

"Who?"

He's losing it.

"Terry—Jennifer's sister."

"Terry went home. Yesterday evening, after— Sharon, I have to go."

I hung up before he did, and called Terry Wyatt in Davis.

"Damn right I left," Terry Wyatt said. "There's such a thing as family loyalty, but as far as I'm concerned, Mark isn't family anymore."

"What happened?"

"Yesterday afternoon he came home from an appointment in the city in a foul mood. Holed up in his office for a while, then came out, went straight to the wet bar and started sucking up Scotch. After his fourth drink, I suggested we eat the dinner the housekeeper had prepared and left in the oven. He said he wasn't hungry. I told him he needed to eat and swilling booze wasn't going to bring Jen home. And that's when he attacked me."

"*Attacked* you?"

"Threw his glass and hit me on the forehead—I've got a nasty bruise to show for it. Then he started ranting about what a bitch I was, but at least I wasn't a lying cunt like my sister. I was trying to leave the room, but he got between me and the door and shoved me so hard I fell against the back of the sofa. He trapped me there, loomed over me, and said all sorts of awful things."

"Such as?"

"That Jen was the worst thing that ever happened to him. That she was crazy and he ought to've had her committed months ago. That because of her he was ruined profession-ally, and he hoped she'd rot in hell. And then he just started cursing—some of the worst obscenities I've ever heard, and I've heard plenty. Finally I managed to get away from him. I grabbed my car keys and ran out of there without taking any of my stuff. And I'm never going back. When you find Jen, I want her to come stay with my husband and me, so we can convince her she should divorce that maniac."

"Those were his exact words—that he hoped Jennifer would rot in hell?"

"Yes. Why— Oh my God, you don't think he *killed* her?"

"I doubt it," I said quickly, with more confidence than I felt. "Mark had just suffered a major professional problem that probably wouldn't have happened if your sister hadn't disap- peared. He was taking it out on you."

"Well, he's going to suffer a major *personal* problem before I'm through with him."

"I think your anger's fully justified. But now I need you to do something for me." I explained about her sister borrowing the neighbor's car. "Mark sounded as if he was incapable of notifying the highway patrol. He couldn't even give me the color or license plate number of Estee Pearson's Porsche."

"I know Estee and her husband, and I'm sure they're listed in the directory; they're the kind of people who can't bear to miss a call, even if it's from an aluminum-siding salesman. I'll phone them and get the information, then notify the highway patrol myself."

"Thank you, Terry. Will you call in the information on the car to my office manager? He'll notify any other agencies who're cooperating."

"Will do." A pause. "Sharon, I'm scared for Jen."

"Don't be," I said—again more confidently than I felt. "Just hang in there, and we'll get through this."

So what had happened to Jennifer Aldin? Had the story Melissa Baker told her about Josie's last day triggered a breakdown? Had she then gone home to Atherton, taken her neighbor's car, and begun running on a reckless course like her mother's? No, not like her mother's. Laurel Greenwood's course had been well planned and deliberate. Emil Tiegs's story had proven that.

And what if Jennifer *hadn't* taken the neighbor's car? What if she'd gone home, quarreled with her husband, and Mark, unable to cope any longer with her obsession, had killed her? I had only his word that he wasn't aware that she and Estee Pearson possessed keys to each other's vehicles. Knowing the Pearsons were away on vacation, he could have taken the Porsche, loaded Jennifer's body into it, and left her SUV in its place. And then disposed of both the car and its burden.

When the Porsche was finally located, would it—and Jennifer—be in some remote place, such as the bottom of a ravine in the Santa Cruz Mountains, buzzards circling above?

God, McCone, get a grip on that imagination! Finish your report, e-mail it, and try to find an angle to work on Kev Daniel.

I don't do waiting very well. Once I'd finished and sent my report, time lay heavy on my hands. I tried to read, but my thoughts kept coming back to the case. I channel-surfed and found nothing of interest on TV. Finally I decided to order dinner from room service and picked up the guest information folder; a map of area wineries was tucked into one of its pockets. Daniel Kane Vineyards was on Paloma Road, some ten miles east of town.

Fifteen minutes later I was speeding along Highway 46 in my rental car. Just checking out the territory, I told myself.

The winery was farther off the highway than it looked on the map. I was beginning to think I'd turned the wrong way on Paloma Road when rows of grapevines appeared, covering the flat fields to either side; then a floodlit sign, gray with gold-and-black lettering, loomed up on the right. Stone pillars flanked the foot of a blacktop drive that snaked off under a canopy of oaks. No gate.

I drove by, doused my lights, and pulled onto the shoulder next to a drainage ditch. Got out of the car and walked back. Slipped under the protection of the trees and moved along parallel to the driveway. After about a hundred yards it divided around another stand of oaks. I kept going to the left, following an arrow with the words "Wine Tasting" lettered on it. From the top of a low rise, I spotted a collection of brightly floodlit buildings: what looked to be an old barn, and several prefab metal structures—the winery itself. One of them bore a sign indicating it was a tasting room. Temporary, until the new one Jacob Ziff was designing could be built.

After studying the layout for a moment, I backtracked to the fork and followed the drive to the right. The trees ended, and I found myself in more vineyards. Faint lights shone ahead; I crouched down and made for them, peering through the vines as I got closer.

A house: gray wood and stone, one-story and sprawling, with plenty of large windows to take advantage of the vine-yard views. The driveway ended in an oval in front of it. Floodlights illuminated the house's facade, but its windows were dark. The vines grew up to within a few feet of a wide deck that wrapped around the entire structure. I hesitated only a moment before I moved closer.

The windows' glass glinted in the moonlight. I crept through the vines toward the back, but saw nothing. Went around the entire house and was almost back to the driveway when headlights shone through the trees. I crouched down next to the side of the deck.

A low-slung car came out of the trees, going fast. For a moment I thought it would overshoot the pavement and plow into the deck, but then the driver geared down and slammed on the brakes. The car—a light-colored Jaguar—skidded and came to a stop near the house's front steps. I edged around the corner of the deck and saw the headlights go out and Kev Daniel lurch through the door. He staggered toward the house as if he was drunk. In the brightness of the floods, I could clearly see his rumpled clothing and di-sheveled hair; one shoulder of his long-sleeved shirt was nearly ripped off.

Good God, had the man been in a bar fight?

Daniel paused at the bottom of the steps to the deck, placed a hand on the railing. Leaned there and hung his head, then shook it. When he looked up again, I got a good view of his face.

He wasn't drunk. He looked sick—and terrified.

He remained there for at least thirty seconds, breathing heavily before moving up the steps. I was debating whether to go after him and confront him while his defenses were down when my cell phone rang.

Stupid to have left it on. Stupid!

I yanked the damned device from my bag, pressed the answer button, and scrambled away through the vines. Behind me Daniel bellowed, "Who's there? Whoever you are, you're trespassing!" His voice sounded more frightened than angry.

As I reached the shelter of the oak trees along the driveway, I heard a voice coming from the phone.

"Shar? *Shar?*" Charlotte Keim.

"Yes," I whispered, "I'm here."

"What?"

"I'm here." Somewhat louder.

"*What?*"

No sounds of pursuit, and I was well down the driveway by now. *"I'm here!"*

"Well, don't bite my head off!"

"Sorry. What d'you have for me?"

"The break we've been looking for on Jennifer Aldin. Her ATM card was used three hours ago—and guess where?"

I was near the road. Still no sounds of pursuit. I leaned against one of the oaks to rest. "Keim, I'm in no mood for guessing games. Where?"

Her voice was somewhat subdued when she replied, "Right down the road from you, in Morro Bay."

Friday

•

AUGUST 26

Five minutes after midnight, and Morro Bay was wrapped in mist, its streets deserted.

Earlier, while I returned to my car on Paloma Road, Keim had gone to Ted's office and found the license plate number of Estee Pearson's silver Porsche Boxster that Terry Wyatt had earlier phoned in. Armed with that and the photograph of Jennifer that Mark had provided, I started out for the coast.

On the way, I considered relaying the information on the Porsche to the SLO County Sheriff's Department, but decided against it. All the circumstances now pointed to Jennifer's disappearance being voluntary, and I wanted to spare her any unpleasant publicity, as well as give myself the opportunity to talk with her.

I thought I knew what she'd tell me; I'd begun to intuit what Jennifer was doing, and why. Given enough time, I could find her.

Now I drove along the waterfront to the park where Laurel Greenwood had last been seen, checked the few vehicles parked there. No Boxster, but I hadn't really expected to see it. Then I began a tour of lodging places: Embarcadero Inn, Bayview Lodge, Ascot Suites, the Breakers, Tradeswinds Motel, San Marcos Inn, and on and on. At each I first toured the parking lot looking for the Boxster, then went inside and showed the clerk Jennifer's photograph and asked him or her if they'd seen my missing friend. Friend, because an ordinary person in distress garners more sympathy than a private detective, who often means trouble for the individual she's seeking.

Most of the desk clerks said Jennifer hadn't checked in, and a few at the higher-end establishments claimed they couldn't give out information about guests, but I was reasonably sure Jennifer wasn't staying with them either. There were a lot of motels in the town, and by the time I'd finished with them, it was after four a.m. and I was ready for a cup of coffee and a bite to eat.

The matronly, gray-haired waitress at the all-night restaurant I found on the outskirts of town said she thought Jennifer might have been in yesterday or the day before, but she couldn't be sure. She recommended their BLT as the best on the coast, and quickly brought coffee. The place was deserted, so when my food was ready, she asked if she could join me; I agreed. She said, "I hope your friend's not in trouble," as she sat down opposite me.

"In trouble emotionally, anyway." I bit into the BLT. "She disappeared last Sunday, and only tonight I found out she was in this area. Everybody at home is worried sick about her."

"Well, of course they are, honey. And you look like you're about worn out." She reached for the photograph I'd left lying on the table. "Such a lovely young woman. Reminds me a little of my granddaughter; she's in Los Angeles now, working in advertising. I'd go crazy if I didn't hear from her every week or two. Why would your friend want to go and worry her people like that?"

"She has her reasons, I guess. Let me ask you this: if she's not registered at any of the motels here in town, where might she be staying?"

"Lots of places. Plenty of bed-and-breakfasts. Everybody with an extra room seems to've gotten into that tax-break racket lately. Or she could've gone down to San Luis or up to Cayucos or Cambria."

"No, I think she's here in Morro Bay. She has . . . a sentimental attachment to the town."

The woman frowned, drumming her fingertips on the table. "You say she doesn't want anybody to recognize her?"

"I think she's probably afraid her husband has reported her missing."

"Well, then, I have a few ideas. But I don't dare make any calls till at least six. Why don't you finish your sandwich, have a little rest, and come back after seven? Maybe I'll know something then."

I thanked her and gave her the make, color, and license plate number of the car Jennifer was driving. There was no sense in checking into a motel for only a couple of hours, so after I'd eaten and paid, I went out to the parking lot and curled up on the backseat of my rental car. It was cramped and cold, but I'd left a sweater there after my meeting with Emil Tiegs. I covered myself as best I could and fell into a fitful sleep. My dreams were so unpleasant that when they were broken by the ringing of my cellular, I was grateful for the intrusion.

"McCone, what's your ETA?"

"My . . . huh?"

"It's your husband. Remember me? You never called to say when you're picking me up this afternoon."

"Ripinsky. Oh God . . . It's so early."

"It's after eight."

"You're kidding!" I sat up, looked at my watch. "I can't imagine how I slept so long, considering how uncomfortable it is here."

"Where's that?"

"The backseat of my rental car, in Morro Bay."

"You're alone, I hope."

"Very funny."

"Very gruffly." It was our private word for grumpy, grouchy, and then some.

"Yeah. Sorry." I ran my hand over my face, pushed my hair away from where it was stuck to my cheek. Good God, had I drooled in my sleep?

Hy said, "I take it the weekend's in jeopardy."

"Yeah, there's been a break in the case." I began pulling my twisted clothing into place. It was way past time to return to the restaurant and the nice waitress whose name I hadn't even asked. Come of think of it, she hadn't asked mine. A heartening example of the kind of trust that sometimes develops between total strangers.

"Well, that's good news," Hy said. "There's more stuff I can do here, so I'll wait till I hear from you."

"I hate to wreck our plans."

"Don't worry. Your case is important, and we've got lots of weekends ahead of us. Call if you need me."

McCone, how did you get so lucky?

We broke the connection simultaneously. I got out of the car and went back into the restaurant.

The place was starting to fill up. The matronly waitress,

who looked as if she was ready to go home, motioned to me from behind the counter and took me into a hallway that led to the restrooms.

"You must've caught a nap," she said, "but you still don't look so good, honey. Better clean up some, then go on out to the Creekside Springs Resort and talk to Bud Ferris." She thrust a piece of paper into my hand. "I drew you a map, and in case you get lost, that's Bud's phone number. If you hustle, your friend might still be there."

I peered at the penciled map. "I can't thank you enough. And I don't even know your name."

"Hey, honey, I don't know yours either. But as the Bard said, 'What's in a name?' " She winked at me and started back down the hallway, then called over her shoulder, "BA in English lit, UC Santa Cruz, seventy-one. How's that for a smart career choice?"

As soon as I saw it, I recognized Creekside Springs Resort from one of the postcards in Laurel Greenwood's collection: a white clapboard main building and several small cottages nestled in a sycamore grove at the northern edge of Los Padres National Forest. Its weathered sign advertised luxury lodging, mineral baths, and fine dining, but it was obvious to me as I rumbled over the bridge that spanned the creek in front of it that the resort had seen better days. The grounds, while not completely overgrown, had an unkempt appearance, roses running rampant up trellises and onto the roof of the main building, and the cottages looked as if they could use several coats of paint.

I parked in a graveled area out front and went inside. The large common area was filled with old-fashioned rattan furniture cushioned in faded floral prints, and a stone fireplace was soot-blackened and choked with ashes. Glass-paned doors to the dining room were closed and curtained on the inside. There was no reception desk, but a sign next to a door at the rear read "Office." I knocked and waited.

After a moment the door opened and a man with unruly brown hair peered out at me. "You're the lady who's looking for her friend?"

"Yes. My name's Sharon McCone. You're Mr. Ferris?"

"That's right." He opened the door wider and motioned me into a room that was filled to overflowing with books, newspapers, and magazines. Two TVs, three VCRs, two DVD players, and numerous tapes and discs sat on shelving that took up an entire wall, and a computer with two oversize screens, two scanners, and two printers covered a nearby desk. Ferris saw me looking at them and said, "Backups. You never know when one of the damn things'll die on you. Now, about this friend of yours—I understand you have a photograph of her."

I produced it and he looked it over carefully before he handed it back to me. "Your friend's run out on her family?"

"Yes. Everyone's frantic with worry. We need to know if she's all right."

"Well, that would depend on your definition of 'all right.' Have a seat, why don't you?"

I glanced at the chair he motioned to, removed a stack of *Newsweek*s, and sat.

"The term 'all right' covers a lot of ground," Ferris went on. "Mrs. Greenwood shows no evidence of alcohol or drug abuse, but something about the lady feels wrong."

"Excuse me—Mrs. Greenwood? Jennifer Greenwood?"

"No. Laurel. Isn't that correct?"

"Her name is Jennifer Aldin. Laurel Greenwood was her mother."

Ferris frowned. "Some sort of neurotic identification, perhaps."

"What makes you say that?"

"She told me her mother and father stayed here on their honeymoon, and that her mother had painted a picture of the place. I wouldn't know about that; I only bought the resort nine years ago. At the time I'd just sold my commercial real estate holdings in San Jose, and my wife and I were looking for a business that would pay the bills and allow us to live comfortably on our savings. We came down here and operated profitably for a time, but then business dropped off. Four years ago, my wife died suddenly, and since then I haven't put much effort into the place. I don't get a lot of guests, just older people who have been coming year after year, but I like it that way." Momentarily his gaze turned inward.

I said, "Is my friend here now?"

"No. She's out on her appointed rounds."

"And they are . . . ?"

He spread his hands. "I have no way of knowing. She leaves in the morning around eight. Returns around four, always with a bag of groceries—I've installed microwaves and little refrigerators in the cottages since I no longer operate the restaurant—and she always has her sketchbook in hand. One time I asked her what she was drawing, and she gave me a strange smile and said, 'The past.' Then she looked embarrassed and said she was something of a historian."

"And she's staying in one of the cottages?"

"Yes. I've closed up the rooms in this building. She's in cottage three." His gaze shifted to his watch. "You'll have to excuse me now; there's a film I want to watch."

I stood. "You won't tell her I've been here? I think it's best if she's not expecting me when I come back this afternoon."

"Of course I won't." He began searching for the remote control to whatever TV he planned to use. "When you come back you can wait for her in the cottage—they're never locked."

I hurried along flagstone steps that scaled a small rise toward cottage three. It was fronted by a small deck with an old redwood hot tub and a couple of plastic chairs. Inside, I found the same kind of furnishings as in the main building—outdated rattan, shabby but comfortable-looking. The double bed was unmade, but the rest of the unit was tidy. On the glass-topped dining table that sat next to the tiny galley kitchen photographs and charcoal drawings lay scattered.

The photographs: informal shots of Laurel, Roy, Jennifer, and Terry; a formal portrait of the entire family. Candids of Laurel with Sally Timmerman, Josie Smith, and other people whom I didn't recognize. A studio portrait of Mark Aldin.

The drawings: the Greenwoods' former home in Paso Robles, as seen from four different perspectives; four scenes that I vaguely recognized as lying along Highway 46 between Paso Robles and the coast; four sea views that resembled the ones from the overlook where Laurel had made her final oil painting; the Cayucos pier, the beach adjoining it, a liquor store with a mailbox in front of it, and a biker astride a motorcycle, his face obscured by his helmet; four different views of the waterfront park in Morro Bay.

And one drawing that didn't fit with the others, done over and over again in dark, angry slashes of charcoal: the building on Fell Street in San Francisco. Not so much a representational portrait of an ordinary building as an expression of rage.

I hurried from the cottage, down the steps, and along the path to the parking area.

If my intuition was correct—and it was, it had to be—I knew where I would find Jennifer.

She was at the overlook north of Cayucos: a slender figure dressed all in black, sitting on an aluminum folding chair, one foot propped on the low retaining wall, the sketch pad supported by her knee. Her neighbor's silver Porsche was parked a short distance away. She didn't look around as I drove in, but she wasn't immersed in her drawing. Instead she stared out to sea.

I parked and got out of the car. The weather was the same as it had been when I'd first come here—fog burning off above the hills. The same as it had been when Jacob Ziff had stopped here to speak with Jennifer's mother all those years ago.

I crossed toward her, gravel crunching under my feet. Still she didn't seem to notice me. Finally, when I was beside her, she looked up. For a moment her gaze didn't focus on me. How had Ziff described the look on Laurel's face when he'd approached her?

As if she were waking up from a dream, or maybe as if I were pulling her back from some other world she'd been inhabiting.

After a moment Jennifer recognized me. "Sharon. How did you know I was here?" Her tone was curiously unsurprised.

"I guessed where you would be." I glanced down at the sketch pad. Blank, although she held a stick of charcoal in her hand. "The work's not going so well today?"

"Work? Oh, this." She flipped the pad shut, dropped the charcoal on the ground. "It's not work, it's just . . ."

"Just?"

"Craziness." She stood, handed me the pad, began folding the chair. "I suppose Mark asked you to drag me back home."

"I can't make you go home if you don't want to."

"I don't know what I want."

"Shall we talk about it? Maybe I can help you decide."

"Yes. Maybe."

"Why don't we go back to Creekside Springs? We can take my car, come back for yours later."

She hesitated. "It's not my car. I don't feel right about leaving it here."

"Okay, then we'll take it. But I think I should drive. You look . . . tired."

To my surprise, Jennifer smiled. "I'm not so crazy that I can't drive, but if it will make you feel better, go ahead."

When we got back to her cottage, Jennifer went into the bathroom to freshen up, and I again studied the photographs on the table. Laurel: a nice small-town girl with her college friends. The Greenwoods: a nice small-town family. And then it had all gone wrong. . . .

"Aunt Anna salvaged those," Jennifer said from behind me.

"When?"

"Right after my father burned my mother's paintings. Anna went over to the house while he was at the clinic and saved the photographs and other mementos. She wouldn't give them to Terry and me, though. She said she was afraid if Dad found out we had them, he'd destroy them, too."

"Then how did you get these?"

She sat down in one of the chairs at the table and fingered a photo of Laurel and Terry. "I knew where Anna kept them in her attic. When I was about to go away to college, I sneaked up there and took the ones I wanted. I never planned to live at home again, so they'd be safe with me. And Anna wouldn't miss them; as far as I know she never so much as looked at them after Mom disappeared."

I sat down opposite her, picked up the studio portrait of Mark. "And why's he here?"

"He's part of the puzzle."

"The puzzle?"

"Why this is happening to me, and how can I survive it."

"You mean what you call the craziness."

"The current craziness, yes." She hesitated, then drew a deep breath. "Sharon, am I your client, or is Mark?"

"You're the one who signed the contract, and Mark wrote the retainer check on your joint account. When he asked me to find you after you disappeared last Sunday, there was no new contract or addendum to the existing one. So, yes, you're the client."

"Then you're on my side?"

"I'm always on my clients' sides—so long as they're truthful with me."

"Okay, then, I'll tell you what happened. Sunday morning I overheard a conversation between Mark and his attorney. They have a regular date to play tennis on our court, and they'd come into the house afterwards, were talking in his office and didn't realize I was coming down the hall to ask if they wanted coffee or juice. Mark was quizzing him about how he could get me committed for psychiatric observation. I thought, since he'd agreed to fund your investigation, that he was fully supportive of me. He said more than once that he understood the pressures I was under, and would let me work through them in my own way. I was very upset by what I heard, so later I made up an excuse about meeting Rae in the city and got out of there."

"And went to the flat you rent on Fell Street." When her eyes widened, I added, "Yes, I know about that. And about your conversation that afternoon with the downstairs tenant."

For a moment she sat very still, then she sagged and sighed—with relief, I thought. "Thank God I don't have to explain all that to you. I've been over and over what Melissa Baker told me about the day Josie died, and everything I imagine is so ugly."

"And that was what made you come down here?"

"Yes. First I called Terry, but she didn't want to listen to me, told me I needed to get help. What I needed was space and distance—so badly I could barely breathe. So I took my neighbor's car and some money that I knew she had stashed in the house. I didn't have any conscious purpose in coming here, except that I thought maybe being where Mom disappeared would help me understand things."

"And since then, you've been reliving the past through these drawings." I tapped my finger on the one of her childhood home.

"I've followed the same routine every day: up early, drive into Paso Robles. Draw the house. Drive west on Forty-six. Draw a roadside scene there. I'm at the vista point at the exact time my mother was sighted there, and I draw that. Go to Cayucos. Another drawing. Go to Morro Bay, wander around the park and the waterfront area, wondering where she went from there. Yet another drawing. I don't like what I'm doing, but I can't seem to help myself. And then, this morning at the vista point, I ran out of steam."

"Maybe because you've worked something out?"

"I doubt it. The only conclusion I've come to is that I must be worse off than either Mark or I imagine."

I hesitated, carefully framing what I would say next. "You could probably use a few sessions with a good therapist. But you've been on the right track."

"I don't understand."

"Whether you realize it or not, you've been doing detective work. On a deeper psychological level than I—but you've got a very deep psychic investment in the investigation. And I think you've come to many of the same conclusions as I have."

Long silence. Then: "My mother killed Aunt Josie, didn't she?"

"I suspect she may have."

"Because Josie was having an affair with my father?"

"Most likely."

She nodded. "There were signs that something was wrong between Mom and Dad. Little ones. Kids pick up on signs, but then they forget them until something happens to bring them to the surface again—like my conversation with Melissa Baker at Fell Street last Sunday."

"Do you think your mother confronted your father about the affair?"

"I doubt it. It wasn't her style. But I do remember that my dad was gone a lot for a few years before Josie died. And then afterward, my mother seemed cold and distant around him. But, no, even though Mom was with Josie when she died, I doubt my father would have ever suspected her of . . . murder."

Or he suspected, but chose not to open up that particular can of worms.

Jennifer said, "Earlier you said that you think I've come to the same conclusions you have. What else?"

"Well, consider what you've been doing—following your mother's trail over and over, and never coming to its end."

For a moment her gaze held mine, then it dropped, and she leaned forward until her forehead touched a photograph of Laurel that lay on the table in front of her.

"Because it has no end," she said. "Because my mother—damn her to hell!—ran out on us and is still alive somewhere." She raised her head, looking me straight in the eyes. An odd mixture of fury and sadness twisted her features.

"I hope you find her," she said, "but I also hope you don't. Because if I ever come face-to-face with her again, I don't know what I'll do."

Jennifer didn't want to go home or to Fell Street, so I suggested she stay with her sister in Davis. She liked the idea and felt she was okay to drive there. After calling Terry to tell her she was coming, she called her neighbor in Atherton to apologize for taking her Porsche and cash. When she got off the phone she was smiling.

"Your neighbor's not angry?" I asked.

"No. Estee understands I've been going through a very rough patch. I'm going to miss her when I move away."

"You're leaving Mark, then?"

"I'm ninety-nine percent certain I am. For about six months now I've suspected he's been having an affair, and what I overheard him telling his lawyer last Sunday pretty much confirmed it. He said that I had become an inconvenient burden and an obstacle to his future happiness. I think now that when he agreed to pay for your investigation, he was looking at it as a way to distract me from the trouble in our marriage until he could hide most of our assets."

She grimaced bitterly. "It's hard to face the fact that your marriage was only a balance sheet to your husband. I see now that Mark married me because I was an asset—

attractive, reasonably well-spoken, with an interesting career. And he wanted me gone because I was a liability. Hard to face, but I'll have to."

When she heard what Terry had to tell her about Mark's recent behavior, she would be a hundred percent certain about a divorce. I decided not to reveal what Rae had uncovered about Mark's past and how it had precipitated the break between Ricky and him; Jennifer would find out soon enough.

I helped her pack her things and load them into the Porsche. She was smiling when she dropped me off at the overlook north of Cayucos.

Jennifer had asked me to call Mark and tell him she was okay, so I tried his office, cellular, and home numbers as soon as I reached the Oaks Lodge. A machine picked up each time. I had a fourth number, for an office in San Francisco where he met with some of his clients and where a majority of his support staff worked, but the receptionist said he had called in this morning to say he was taking a long weekend.

I dialed Julia's cellular. "Aldin's on his sailboat at the yacht club," she told me. "Just sitting on deck, drinking beer."

"Alone?"

"As far as I can tell."

"Okay, I've found his wife, so I'm pulling you off the surveillance. Will you please go down there and tell him the news, ask him to call me? And then take the rest of the day off."

"Gladly. Tonio's coming home from summer camp today, and it'll be a nice surprise if I'm there to greet him." Tonio was Julia's young son. A single mother, she shared an apartment with her older sister, and together they looked after him. Still, an aunt waiting to hear about summer-camp adventures was no substitute for a mother.

"Must be nice," Julia added, "sitting around on your boat in the sun while everybody else is working."

"I don't think Aldin's enjoying himself. Be careful when you talk with him; turns out he's got a temper."

"I can take care of myself."

"I know you can, but be careful anyway." I broke the connection, picturing Mark soaking up alcohol while he pondered what could be the first of a series of professional reverses. Word got around around fast in the kind of circles he and Ricky traveled in, and I was certain my former brother-in-law would have no qualms about spreading it.

It was now after three in the afternoon, and I should also let Rae know her friend was okay and on her way to Terry's. There had been no message from Patrick when I'd returned; I was beginning to worry about him. He was relatively inexperienced and shouldn't be wandering around God knew where doing God knew what.

And then there was Hy, who was waiting in El Centro to hear from me. This was ridiculous! We'd been married less than two weeks, and had barely spent any time together—

A knock at the door. Who would show up here? Hy? He had friends at virtually every small airport in the state—perhaps in the country—and often caught rides with them. Just like him to get somebody to drop him off at Paso Robles and surprise me. Eagerly I crossed the room.

But it wasn't Hy standing there. It was Rob Traverso of the PRPD and another heavyset, balding man whom I didn't know. "Ms. McCone," Traverso said, "this is Detective Jim Whitmore of the SLO County Sheriff's Department. We'd like to ask you a few questions."

*   *   *

"The dead man's name is Emil Tiegs," Jim Whitmore said. "He was found under the Cayucos pier by a fisherman at five-thirty this morning. Your business card was in his wallet."

"How did he die?" I asked.

Whitmore ignored the question. "What kind of dealings did you have with Mr. Tiegs?"

We were seated at the table in my room, Whitmore across from me, Traverso to my right. I glanced at the police detective; his face was impassive, and he didn't meet my eyes.

I said, "Mr. Tiegs offered to sell me information on the Laurel Greenwood case. When I met with him, I gave him my card."

"When was that?"

"Yesterday around noon."

"And what did he tell you?"

I considered. Tiegs's information had implicated Kev Daniel in a minor crime upon which the statute of limitations had run out. Revealing it and sending the county sheriff after him would destroy any leverage I might have to force him to reveal where Laurel had gone after she received the new identification from him, or her present whereabouts. However, I'd seen Daniel returning to his home late last night, disheveled and terrified—

"Ms. McCone?" Whitmore prompted.

I opted for shading the truth. "As you probably know, Emil Tiegs had a criminal record. He struck me as unreliable. Also, he was asking for a good deal of money. I wanted to ask my client whether she was willing to pay."

"And was she?"

"I wasn't able to reach her. May I ask how Tiegs died?"

Whitmore glanced at Traverso, then shrugged. "Autopsy

hasn't been performed yet, but Tiegs's neck was broken. He could have fallen from the pier, or been pushed."

"What about his seeing-eye dog?"

"It hasn't been found."

I pictured the dog, the way it had protectively moved with Tiegs. An animal like that would fight to the death for the man it guided.

I asked, "Did you talk with Tiegs's wife?"

Whitmore turned keen eyes on me. "How do you know he had a wife?"

"I had one of my staff background him as soon as he contacted me."

"Yes, we talked with her. She was evasive. Seemed more frightened for her own sake than concerned that her husband was dead."

Frightened. Yes, that figured. Emil Tiegs had told me about the day he and his wife went to Daniel's winery and attempted to extort money from him: *He said if I told anybody, he'd have me taken out of the gene pool. He meant it, too—I heard it in his voice. And Nina—she was with me, drove me to that winery of his—she saw it in his eyes.*

I thought I knew how Tiegs had died—and why.

I just wasn't sure what to do with the information.

Early evening on Hillside Drive in Cayucos. Number 30 was dark and again looked deserted. I knocked on the front door anyway, and after a moment it was opened by the woman I'd seen through the window on Wednesday evening. Her eyes were puffy and red, her hair dirty and unkempt.

"You're selling something, I don't want it," she said.

"I'm Sharon McCone. Your husband sold me something

the other day. Five hundred dollars' worth. There should be another five hundred in your bank account by now."

She snorted. "And that's gonna go a long way to pay for burying him."

"Maybe I can arrange for more, if you'll let me in so we can talk."

She hesitated, then motioned me inside. The room that I'd glimpsed from the street last night was dark, the TV turned off. Nina Tiegs moved to the couch and sat heavily.

"How are you holding up?" I asked as I took a seat in a rocking chair.

"How d'you think?"

"Probably not very well. I know I wouldn't be."

"You married?"

"Yes."

"Long time?"

"Long enough."

No, not long enough—no amount of time will ever be long enough.

"Then you know." Nina Tiegs sighed. "My mother used to tell me, 'Husbands, you sure miss them when they're dead.' I thought it was a peculiar thing to say, but now I understand. Of course, my dad died in bed at eighty. Emil was only—" She bent her head, began to cry.

For a few moments, the only sounds in the room were her muffled sobs; then she raised her head, pulled a Kleenex from a box on the table, blew her nose, and wiped her face.

"I keep goin' off like that," she said. "Stupid. Emil hated it when I cried."

"You've got good reason."

"Yeah, I do. You know the stupidest thing? That dog—

Blake—that's what makes me cry the hardest. Best damn dog I ever knew, loved Emil. I just know he's dead, too."

"Animals can become a big part of your life. Particularly one like Blake."

"Yeah." She blew her nose again.

"Nina, what d'you think happened to Emil?"

"I don't know. He went out, he didn't come back. What I told the cops."

"But that wasn't true, was it?"

Silence.

"Did he decide to hit Kev Daniel up for more money than I could offer?"

Even in the darkness, I could see fear flare in her eyes at the mention of Daniel's name.

I added, "You didn't tell the police because you're afraid of Daniel. And you're afraid they'll arrest you as an accessory to extortion."

"Could they do that?"

"Yes, but I doubt they would, if you were honest with them."

A long silence. "I want to see them nail that bastard Daniel, but I'm afraid if they can't make it stick, he'll come after me."

"They'll make it stick."

"I don't believe it. These rich guys, they always get off."

"Not always."

"Mostly they do." She sighed. "You know, Emil could be such an idiot sometimes. Brilliant forger and top dog in prison, according to him. But then, what was he doing screwing around with meth and getting himself half blown up, for Christ's sake? And then this Daniel thing—" She broke off, putting her fingertips to her lips.

I said, "So he *did* try to extort money from Daniel."

"You tell the cops any of this, I'll say you're lying."

"Look, Nina, the sheriff's department investigator already knows you're hiding something. He told me as much a couple of hours ago. It's only a matter of time before they come down hard on you. Why don't you talk with me, and I'll see what I can do to help you."

She bit her lip, considering. "You mean it—that you'll try to help me?"

"Yes."

"And what about more money? You said you might be able to arrange it."

"That, too."

"Okay. This is what happened: After Emil got that five hundred off of you, he was high. Said he knew what he had was worth a lot more. He called Daniel that afternoon, told him he had a five-thousand-dollar offer from you, but was willing to keep quiet for real money—fifteen. They set a meet for the pier last night, at ten-thirty. Daniel said he'd have the cash with him.

"I wanted to go along, but Emil wouldn't let me. I told him the situation would go bad. 'What kind of person keeps fifteen thou in cash just laying around?' I asked. But he wouldn't listen, he never listened to me. He went anyhow, and now he's gone and Blake's gone and I'm all alone." She bent her head and began to cry again.

I rummaged in my bag for my wallet and took out my remaining hundred dollars. Laid it on the coffee table. Nina Tiegs didn't notice; she'd pressed her face into her hands, and tears were leaking around her fingers.

Before I left I touched her shoulder and said, "Thank you for talking with me, Nina. I'll be in touch. And I'm sorry for your loss."

I'm sorry for your loss.

Conventional, empty words. They don't help anybody.

The way to help someone like Nina Tiegs is by nailing the man who killed her husband.

"Why did you withhold the fact that when you met with Tiegs you paid him for this information?" Jim Whitmore asked, pointing at my voice-activated recorder on which I'd just played him the tape of my meeting with Tiegs.

I turned it off. "Client confidentiality."

"Come on, McCone. You can do better than that. You also withheld the part about seeing Kevin Daniel returning home last night."

"Okay, I wanted to talk with Tiegs's wife first. And frankly, I was concerned about losing my leverage over Daniel. But given what Nina Tiegs told me, there's no way I can justify withholding anything any longer."

Whitmore leaned back in his desk chair and regarded me with narrowed eyes. We were in his small office at the SLO County Sheriff's Department in San Luis Obispo, down the hall from where I'd spoken last week with with his colleague, Deputy Selma Barker.

"The wife will give us a statement?" he asked.

"If you lean on her. I'll ask my client if she's willing to pay more for the information about her mother, and that may loosen Nina up somewhat."

The detective continued to stare at me. "You remind me of my sister," he said. "She's a lawyer in Seattle. Specializes in divorce for women. Her clients call her 'Old Hard-as-Nails,' but they know that the reason she goes toe-to-toe for them is that she cares."

"Ah, you've found my weak spot. Kittens, puppies, children, grieving widows."

"Isn't a weak spot—it's a strength. So how're we gonna do this?"

"*We*? I assume you'll pick up Daniel. You'll have the information on this tape, Nina Tiegs's statement about the extortion attempt, and my statement about seeing him return home last night in a disheveled and distraught state. Yes, the tape isn't admissable in court, but even though Daniel's egotistical, he's not very tough. You people can break him easily enough."

"Maybe. But the kind of money and local prominence he has builds a thick wall around a person." The phone buzzed. Whitmore picked up. "Yeah? . . . Uh-huh . . . I see . . . Well, canvass the neighbors and run a surveillance on the place . . . Yeah, thanks." He replaced the receiver and looked up at me, scowling. "You screwed up, McCone. The Tiegs woman has taken off."

I thought of the hundred dollars I'd left on her coffee table. Not a lot to most people these days, but traveling money to someone like Nina. "Damn!"

"Kind of puts a whole new slant on how we proceed, doesn't it?"

"I guess."

He thought for a moment, then smiled—fiendishly, I thought. "Okay, McCone, how d'you feel about wearing a wire?"

Ten-thirty that night, and the huge windows of Kev Daniel's house in the vineyards blazed with light. People in casual attire were scattered over the floodlit deck, sipping wine and conversing animatedly. From where I had parked my car I could hear their laughter, see their sometimes expansive gestures. A woman shrieked, and the shrill noise was followed by applause and more laughter.

Friday night party time in the mid-coast wine country, and here I was, alone and cold sober, with tape pulling at my skin where the sheriff's deputy had attached the wire and my bag hanging heavily from my shoulder. Jim Whitmore had been adamantly opposed to my going into Daniel's house armed, but I'd made an unauthorized stop on the way here and retrieved my .357 from the closet safe at the inn. No way would I place absolute trust in the sheriff's department for getting me out of there speedily and safely should the situation turn dangerous.

As I got out of the car, I wondered what was wrong with me. Why had I volunteered for this duty when I had a new husband hoping we could spend at least part of the weekend together? But as I approached Daniel's house the thought vanished in a rush of excitement. I lived for moments like this, and so did Hy. So what if we weren't a conventional couple?

A few people glanced at me as I crossed the deck to the front door, probably wondering who I was; the circle Daniel ran in would be a small, close-knit one, and an outsider was always interesting. The door stood open and I went inside. More people filled a large room straight ahead, where a bar and buffet table were set up. I went to the bar, asked the man behind it for Mr. Daniel.

"Out there, ma'am," he replied, motioning at the other side of the wraparound deck, which was accessible through open French doors.

"Thanks." I crossed the room, went back outside. Daniel was by the far railing, his arm around a woman in a bare-backed yellow dress with blonde hair cascading to her waist. I stepped up behind him. "Kev, I need to talk with you."

He started, swinging around, and a few drops of wine

from his glass splashed over its rim and onto his fingers. He recovered his poise quickly and said, "Can't this wait till tomorrow? As you see, I'm entertaining."

"It's to your advantage that we talk now."

". . . All right, then. Will you excuse us, darling?"

The woman nodded. "I see Marnie and Bart have arrived. I'll go catch up on all their news."

Daniel watched her go, then turned to me, his face stony. "Let's take this into my study." He grasped my elbow and guided me inside, through the big room, and down a hallway. Shoved open a door and motioned me into a room that was furnished in massive leather pieces and lined with shelves of books in elegant bindings—the kind that pretentious people buy in quantity to impress others, but not to read.

After he shut the door behind us, he said, "All right, what's so important that you've come out here and crashed my party?"

I selected a chair, sat down, took my time about settling into it. "Laurel Greenwood. I know you arranged for false identification for her. I want to know if she confided her plans to you, or if you know her present whereabouts."

"The old case you're working on? How the hell would I know anything about that? It happened twenty-two years ago. I was—"

"A recent parolee, right here in SLO County."

He set his glass on a side table. Ran his hand over his chin. "Okay, you've got me there. It's a matter of public record."

"But it's not a matter of public record that you met with Laurel at the Sea Shack in Cayucos the day she disappeared and gave her the identification she needed to assume another woman's name."

"I don't know what you're talking about."

"Yes you do. About six months ago Emil Tiegs, the man who forged the ID, tried to extort money from you to keep silent about it. He recently sold the information to me."

Daniel sat down across from me, spread his hands on his thighs, and rubbed them up and down. "When?"

"Noon yesterday." When he didn't speak, I added, "I have a tape of my conversation with Tiegs. It won't stand up in court, but it will make the sheriff's department take a close look at you."

". . . All right, I helped Laurel. When I got out on parole, I called her, gave her my phone number in Cayucos, thinking she'd help me get some more of my work into this San Luis gallery that had sold a couple of my pictures. A few days later she called me back, asked if I had any contacts who could doctor an ID. I'd run into Tiegs the week before; I knew he was her man.

"I didn't want to get mixed up in something illegal, but Laurel was a wonderful woman and, from what she said, trapped in a miserable marriage. She'd been very good to me when I was taking her class in prison, and I felt I owed her. And I suppose in my young, impressionable way, I was a little in love with her."

Sly glance from under his thick eyelashes. Kev Daniel was probably used to charming his way out of sticky situations—particularly situations involving women.

I asked, "Did Laurel tell you where she was going?"

"She said it was better I didn't know."

"She must've said something. Jacob Ziff saw the two of you with your heads together at the Sea Shack."

"Ziff." He shook his head. "When my partners insisted on using him to design our new tasting room, I was afraid he'd recognize me, but I should've known better. Way back then, all he saw was a scruffy young biker, not the man I am today."

"About your conversation with Laurel . . . ?"

"It was so long ago, I don't remember much of it."

"But you do remember that I have the tape of my conversation with Tiegs."

"I'll deny everything."

"Still it'll be a hassle, could damage your reputation."

Silence.

"Look, Kev, you committed a minor crime, and the statute of limitations on it ran out long ago. I'm only concerned with finding Laurel, and I never reveal my sources."

"I've heard that before."

"From Mike Rosenfeld at the *Trib*."

Daniel raised his eyebrows. "He told you I gave him the story about you?"

"No," I lied. "He's as protective of his sources as I am of mine. I just guessed it was you. Why'd you do it?"

"I don't know; it was a dumb move. But at the time I thought the publicity might impede your investigation. I didn't want that shit dug up. All I did was help a friend."

"You also thought shooting at me would scare me off."

He tensed. "I had nothing to do with that."

"I'll accept that as the truth—even though we both know it isn't—and let it drop if you tell me about your conversation with Laurel."

"All right, let me think a minute." He relaxed some, leaned back in his chair, closed his eyes. "She said she shared the same profession with the woman whose name she'd appropriated—somebody Smith. The first name, I don't remember. She hadn't worked at whatever it was in a long time, but the other woman had, and her license was current. So it would be easy for her to earn a living. She had a fair amount of money, anyway. I asked about her kids—Laurel's, how she could leave them—and she told me her whole family would be better off without her because she was a terrible person. She wouldn't tell me why. Before she left, she gave me a postcard and asked me to mail it. That was the last I ever saw of her."

"Did you read the card?"

"Yeah. It was to her husband, telling him not to look for her. She sounded pretty much on the edge."

I pictured the postmark on the card; it hadn't been delivered to the Greenwood home until two days after Laurel's disappearance. "When did you mail it?"

"Not till the next day. I went down the street to the box by the liquor store, but they'd already made the last pickup, so I decided to hold on to the card in case Laurel changed her mind. I mean, it was such an extreme step, running out on those little kids. I lost my mother when I was very young, and I know how badly a kid can be affected by something like that. I hoped Laurel wouldn't go through with her plan. But when I called her house the next afternoon, a guy answered and said she wasn't there and demanded to know my name. He sounded like a cop. As it turned out, he was. I hung up, took the card to the post office, and dropped it in the slot."

"Anything else you remember about your conversation?"

"Nothing of any importance. Laurel talked a lot about me, how I should keep up with my art, that I had real talent."

"Have you worked at it?"

"Nah, I'm too busy making money and having fun." Daniel grinned, once more the rich, self-assured vintner.

"Well, I appreciate the information," I said. "But we've got something else to discuss."

"Sharon, my guests—"

"Emil Tiegs."

Daniel's expression grew wary. "Tiegs? What about him? The little weasel came out here with that fat wife of his last February, trying to make trouble for me. I blew him off. I know you paid him five thousand dollars yesterday, but that's your problem."

Bad slip, Kevin.

"Yeah," I said, "I was pretty stupid to fall for that, especially since he had so little information."

"Tiegs was the one who was stupid. Thought he could rip off both of us."

"You mean when he tried to hit you up for fifteen thousand."

"How do you know about that?"

"His wife told me."

"Yeah, well, like I would just stroll into my bank at three in the afternoon and ask for that much in cash. Talk about calling attention to a problem."

"That was yesterday afternoon?"

"Right."

"I tell you, Kev, if I'd've been in your position, I'd've done exactly what you did."

"What I did?"

"Tiegs is dead. Probably murdered. It was on the evening news."

"I didn't have anything to do with it."

"His wife said he was meeting you at ten-thirty last night at the pier in Cayucos."

"That fat, silly bitch? You believe her?"

"I do, and as soon as they question her, so will the cops."

"They haven't talked with her yet?"

"Haven't been able to; when she got the news, she collapsed."

Silence. His eyes moved quickly from side to side as he assessed his situation.

I said, "Kev, I don't blame you for killing Tiegs, but—"

"I didn't kill anybody!"

I went on as if he hadn't interrupted. "But what about his seeing-eye dog—Blake?"

". . . The dog? What about it?"

"What happened to him? I can understand Tiegs, but a *dog*?"

I'd pushed the right button; Daniel's face reddened. "Shit, I wouldn't hurt a dog! Or a person—intentionally. What kind of a man d'you think I am?"

"I don't know. Tell me what happened."

I watched him struggle with himself. His need to justify his actions won.

"It was an accident. I told Tiegs he wasn't getting any money, and if he kept bothering me I'd go to the authorities. He attacked me and I defended myself."

"Tiegs attacked you? A *blind* man?"

"Damn right, a blind man. A guy with a white cane or a seeing-eye dog, you think he's weak, but a lot of them're stronger than people who can see. Have a better sense of what's going on around them, too. That dog—it went crazy, started jumping and barking. Tiegs and I tussled, he went over the railing, fell, and hit his head on something. The sound it made, I knew he was bad off. Dog kept after me, so I kicked it good a couple of times, and it staggered away."

So much for not hurting a dog. "And then?"

Beads of sweat appeared on Daniel's upper lip and forehead. "I'm not saying anything else till I talk to my lawyer. If you repeat any of this to the cops, I'll deny it. I'll say you came into the house acting like a crazy woman, scared my girlfriend, and I had to bring you in here to calm you down. She'll back me up."

"I'm sure she will. But in case you aren't aware of it, I have a damned good reputation as an investigator. And plenty of your guests saw me come into the house, looking sane and sober. No matter who your attorney is, you'll have a tough time proving it—or your accident story."

"Are you threatening me?"

"Take it any way you want to."

"Look, you bitch, you may have a good reputation up north, but down here you're nothing. Nothing!"

I stood, slipping my hand into the pocket of my shoulderbag and onto the .357.

"No, Daniel, *you'll* be nothing, once the criminal justice system is through with you."

He gripped the arms of his chair until his knuckles went white. The cords in his neck bulged, and he made an inarticulate sound as he tensed. I slid the Magnum out just before he started to get up.

"Don't even think about it, Kev."

His eyes, focusing on the gun, turned dull and glassy. Then he sagged back onto the chair.

"Whitmore," I said into the wire, "you've got your confession. Come get your man. And be thankful I didn't follow your orders about coming in here unarmed."

Saturday

·

AUGUST 27

Hours later when I got back to the Oaks Lodge, I had two messages on my room's voice mail. The first was from Hy: "Why don't you ever turn your cellular on? I give up. Call me in the morning."

The second, from Patrick, said, "I think I'm closing in on Laurel Greenwood, but I need your help."

The number he'd left was again in the 707 area code. I punched it in, and after several rings a voice said, "Econo Lodge, Crescent City."

The northernmost coastal town in the state, on the Oregon border. Now, that was interesting. I asked for Patrick.

"Neilan," his sleepy voice said.

"What the hell're you doing in Crescent City?" I demanded. "You're supposed to be coordinating this investigation in the office."

"Shar . . . What time is it?"

"After three in the morning. What're you doing there? And what were you doing in Santa Rosa?"

"Uhhh." A short silence as he fully woke up. "The other day, after Rae told me that Laurel Greenwood was Josie

Smith's heir and executor, I got this idea about how Greenwood might've pulled her disappearing act, and I talked to a
friend of mine who's a nurse. She dug up some information
that led me to Santa Rosa Memorial Hospital, where she had
a contact, and that contact pointed me toward Sutter Coast
Hospital up here. But I'm running into difficulties."

"You figured out that Greenwood assumed her cousin
Josie Smith's identity and used her nursing credentials to
start a new life."

Long silence this time. When Patrick spoke, he sounded
crestfallen. "You figured it out, too?"

"Yes—but I had quite a bit more help than you did."

"Well, I could sure use your help now. Can you come up
here?"

"Of course. I've been awake forever, though, and I need a
few hours' sleep—"

*Oh, God, Hy! He's down there in El Centro, waiting to hear
from me. I can't just take off for Crescent City.*

"Shar?" Patrick said.

"I'll need to rearrange my schedule."

*Nice way to think of your new husband—as a scheduling
conflict.*

"Okay, but how soon can you be here?"

I considered the flying time, the possible delays if the fog
moved inland. "Tomorrow afternoon, earliest. I'll call you
with my ETA, and you can meet me at the airport."

"Thanks, Shar. I think we're really close to locating her.
This idea I had—"

"We'll talk about it when I get there."

I was almost asleep when there was a knock on the door.
Dammit, it had better not be Jim Whitmore or any of the

other people from the SLO County Sheriff's Department. I'd more than done my duty for local law enforcement.

I crawled out of bed, felt my way across the room, looked through the peephole. The amber-shaded bulb outside showed shining eyes, a hawk nose, and an extravagant mustache. Quickly I opened the door and stepped into Hy's arms. God, it felt good to hold him!

"How did you get here?" I asked into his well-worn leather flight jacket, breathing in its rich, familiar odor.

"Dan Kessel flew out to El Centro in one of the company's jets. I borrowed it."

"Oh, that's great!" I raised my face to his, tasted his lips, his tongue, felt his hands cupping my face.

"Missed me, did you?" he asked.

"Missed you—most definitely. But the jet, that's wonderful."

"Why?"

"Because later this morning you and I are going to fly up to Crescent City."

After our wake-up call came at eight, Hy looked up Jack McNamara Field at Crescent City on AirNav.com while I showered, dressed, and packed. "Runways're in good condition," he said, "and they can handle the Citation. I'll check on the weather while you pay the bill."

"I've got to make a call first." Since he had his laptop hooked into the room phone—even though it was a relatively new hotel, they offered only dial-up service—I took out my cellular, saw it had lost its charge.

Damn, I was definitely going to have to spring for a new model; they held their charge longer, were smaller and lighter. This unit that a short time ago I had thought so sleek and high-tech now seemed clunky and primitive. And if I let that thought lead me to contemplate the built-in obsolescence and disposability of the products we Americans snap up so eagerly, I'd fall into a daylong funk. So I simply asked Hy, "Use your phone?" and when he nodded, took it from the bedside table and dialed Sally Timmerman's number.

"A question for you," I said after we exchanged greetings. "Terry Wyatt told me about finding a gift tucked in bed with her on her first birthday after Laurel disappeared—a stuffed toy called the Littlest Lamb. She said she could smell Laurel's perfume, the Passionelle that both of you used, and thought the lamb had been left during the night by her mother. But it was you who put it there, wasn't it?"

"Yes. Those little girls were hurting so much, and I wanted to do something to brighten Terry's day, but Roy had made it plain he didn't want me near them. I still had the key to the house that Laurel had given me years before, so I sneaked in at around five in the morning."

"You gave her that particular toy because Laurel had been reading her the Littlest Lamb series just before she disappeared?"

"Right. The night after Laurel vanished, Terry begged me to read the next installment to her, and I did. I also read *The Wind in the Willows* to Jennifer."

"But you didn't give Jennifer a *Wind in the Willows* toy when her birthday came around."

"No, I couldn't. Roy figured out I was the one who had left the lamb. He called me and told me if I ever entered his house again without his permission he'd have me arrested—and to ensure I didn't, he had the locks changed. I suppose he wanted to distance himself from me because I knew about his infidelity with Josie."

"He might also have thought you were raising false hopes in Terry's and Jennifer's minds."

Silence. Then: "You know, I never thought of that. All I wanted was for a little girl to wake up with a nice surprise on her birthday. But the perfume—of course Terry would think her mother had been there. I should've realized that! How could I have done that to her? And then for Jennifer not to receive a gift . . . She probably assumed her mother didn't love her as much as Terry."

Sally sounded so sad and self-reproachful that I was sorry I'd raised the possibility.

I said, "I think the lamb was a lovely gesture, and it probably comforted Terry."

"But what about Jennifer?"

"She unloaded a lot of stuff on me about that time, but she didn't mention the lamb or the lack of a birthday gift of her own. Maybe she didn't believe it was from Laurel any more than Roy did, or maybe it didn't make much of an impression on her." I paused. "Here's what you might do—call Terry and tell her the lamb was from you. It would mean a lot to her to know her Aunt Sally still cared and didn't just drop out of her life like her mom did. And when you call, you can also talk with Jennifer; she went to stay with Terry yesterday."

Another silence. "You know, during all the years Roy wouldn't let me near those children, I hurt for them. But then they went away to college, and after a time I put my memories of them aside. Now I'd like to renew our friendship."

"I think they'd welcome it. I'll give you Terry's number."

Hy and I arrived in Crescent City around one that afternoon. The low-lying beach town, which once thrived on lumber and fishing, was years ago plunged into depression with the decline of those industries, but is now becoming a destination for outdoor recreationists visiting the Six Rivers National Forest. It also has the dubious distinction of being the site of a 1964 tsunami that claimed the lives of eleven people—the only killer wave that has ever struck the continental United States. Last June, the Crescent City tsunami siren—which the citizens are used to hearing tested at ten a.m. on the first Tuesday of every month—was activated one evening when the National Oceanic and Atmospheric Administration issued a warning after a 7.2 offshore earthquake. Four thousand people rushed to higher ground, while their more foolish brethren headed to the seaside to await the show. Fortunately, the alarm was false, and Crescent City and the idiot thrill-seekers remained unscathed.

An hour after our arrival, Patrick, Hy, and I sat in a booth in a coffee shop not far from the Crescent City Econo Lodge. Hy was consuming a huge cheeseburger with all the trimmings; piloting the Cessna Citation—a fast, easily maneuverable aircraft—had given him a natural rush that apparently needed to be fed. Patrick was excited, but in a different way: his bowl of chili sat barely touched. I was grimly plowing my way through a Cobb salad; after days of eating hit-or-miss and mostly fast food, something quasi-healthy had sounded good. Trouble was, I'd ordered it at the wrong restaurant: the lettuce was suspiciously brown around the edges, as was the avocado; the bacon was limp and greasy; the chicken was underdone; and for all I knew, there was something wrong with the blue cheese. A note on the menu had said, "Health Advisory: This dish contains bacon." In my opinion, the warning should have read: "This dish may offend your taste buds."

I reached out for one of Hy's French fries, and he grinned at me.

"Okay," Patrick said, "here's where I'm at so far. When Rae told me that Greenwood was Smith's heir and executor, I thought back to when I was executor of an elderly aunt's estate. One of the things I had to do was notify Social Security of her death, so her monthly payments could be discontinued, but with a younger person who wasn't receiving benefits, that wouldn't be necessary. So that would leave Greenwood in possession of a legitimate social security card, a birth certificate, a driver's license, any credit cards and bank accounts, maybe a passport, Smith's nursing credentials—and a substantial inheritance."

I nodded. "Prescription for a new life."

"Right. But there's one snag. As you told me before, Laurel got the driver's license picture replaced with her own, but when it came time to renew it, wouldn't the DMV have noticed something was wrong?"

"Renewing it might've been tricky." I thought back to the eighties, trying to remember the DMV requirements at that time. "In those days, I think the DMV made you come in to have a new picture taken every time your license was up for renewal, rather than extend it by mail, as they do now for good drivers. But they've always been understaffed and overworked; when Laurel had to renew Josie's license the clerk probably wouldn't have questioned its authenticity. The pictures never look like you, anyway, and there was no reason for anyone to cross-check DMV records."

"But what about the discrepancy in fingerprints? Or did fingerprinting drivers start after that?"

"Don't know."

I glanced at Hy; he seemed more interested in his burger

than our conversation. "When was the first time you had to
be fingerprinted for a driver's license?" I asked.

He frowned. "I'm not sure."

I looked back at Patrick. "Well, let's forget that issue for
now. Even if they had both sets of fingerprints on file, there's
a good chance they wouldn't cross-check unless Laurel was
picked up on a moving violation. Maybe not even then, unless it was a DUI, manslaughter, something like that."

"Right."

"So," I went on, "you thought about the fact that Greenwood and Smith had both been nurses, and talked to your
friend."

"Yeah. She's also a nurse, and a member of California
Nurses Association. She told me the union doesn't require
any sort of photo identification, and dues are paid either by
the individual or deducted from their payroll checks. I asked
if there was any way I could find out if Smith's dues were
current. She said yes, provided I was smart enough and a
good liar. I was smart enough to ask her what questions I
should ask the union, and I guess I'm a good liar, because I
got the person I talked with to tell me that Smith was a member until nineteen ninety-three—over ten years after her
death. They wouldn't tell me how she made the payments or
where she was working, though."

"Okay, how did that bring you to Santa Rosa and Crescent
City?"

"I picked my friend's brains again, and she told me about
the Board of Registered Nursing. State agency. License renewal is every two years. You have to renew whether you're
working in the profession or not—so long as you're alive and
ever plan to work again. You can track a person through the
relicensing, if you have the right contact at CNA—and my

friend does. Smith's license was last renewed in nineteen ninety-one, and her address at that time was in Santa Rosa."

Patrick's saga fascinated me, because it mirrored so many strange, twisting investigative journeys I'd taken over the years. "So you went to Santa Rosa—a town of over a hundred and fifty thousand people and God knows how many hospitals and clinics and private practices—in the hope of getting lucky?"

"Nope." He smiled. "You know that mantra you've been drumming into my head—'Work your contacts, and your contacts' contacts, and their contacts, too?' That's what I did. Happens my friend has another friend whose fiancée is a doctor on the staff of Santa Rosa Memorial. It seemed as good a starting point as any. I drove up there, exercised some of my Irish charm, and she agreed to check about Smith with Human Resources. Their records show that she was in Pediatrics and left in ninety-two. *That* was when I got lucky. The doctor is also in Pediatrics, so she asked around, and one of the older RNs remembered Smith. Said she'd left to take a job as an emergency-room nurse at Sutter Coast Hospital here in Crescent City. It was brand-new at the time."

"So what's your problem?" I asked. "Why do you need my help? You can just call them up and ask about Smith. For that matter, why did you have to go through your friend's friend's fiancée, rather than just calling around to Santa Rosa area hospitals?"

Patrick's broad grin spelled out his delight in knowing something the boss didn't. "Because large health-care facilities are very protective of their employees' information. My friend said that any inquiry that didn't come from someone with a legitimate need to know would be handed off to

Human Resources, which then would tell me the information was confidential and turn me away."

"Sounds like trying to find out something from Social Security."

"Right."

Beside me, Hy said to the waitress, "The blackberry pie with vanilla ice cream, please."

I turned to stare at him. "You never eat pie."

"Today it sounds good."

"It's lucky that Citation belongs to RKI, and not to you. If you flew it all the time, you'd get fat."

He smiled benignly at me.

"Okay," I said to Patrick, "you came up here . . . ?"

"Hoping to exercise more Irish charm. Didn't work. As predicted, I was quickly turned away at Sutter Coast. So I called my friend, and she told me that the most gossipy and informative place in a hospital is the cafeteria. If you're there at breaks or the lunch hour dressed like an employee, and can walk the walk and talk the talk, you can find out pretty much anything."

"So why aren't you at the cafeteria today?"

"I don't think I can walk the walk and talk the talk."

"What happened to that Irish charm?"

"It's challenged by this assignment. For one thing, the majority of nurses are female, so a male stands out. I tried to place myself in the role of a doctor, orderly, EMT, or lab technician. None of it felt right, and I'm really afraid I'll blow it. But you can do it, Shar."

"Me? A medical professional? I don't know anything about those jobs."

"People on their lunch breaks don't necessarily talk about their work. Some of them stuff their faces"—he looked over at Hy, who was digging into his pie and ice cream—"but mostly they gossip. Besides, you can act. I've seen you do it. My friend gave me a perfect scenario for you, and she's willing to go over it on the phone. But first we have to pay a visit to the uniform shop I found earlier."

From the bathroom of Patrick's room at the Econo Lodge I called, "Are you sure this is the kind of outfit nurses wear? Why don't I have a starched white uniform and a little hat?"

"When was the last time you saw a nurse dressed like that?"

I thought. "In an old film on late-night TV."

"Right; their dress code varies from place to place. Sutter Coast uses hospital scrubs and white shoes or sneakers for nursing personnel. Let's see how you look."

I stepped through the door, and he surveyed my light blue V-neck tunic top, loose elastic-waist slacks, and athletic shoes. The top and slacks were courtesy of the uniform shop, the shoes my own.

"Perfect." He gestured at the plastic nametag holder that hung around my neck. "I'll borrow the typewriter I saw in the manager's office and put your alias on that, just in case. But remember to keep the tag twisted, so they can't see the front. My friend says the ID tags can be a joke, because they're always hanging the wrong way."

"Dress rehearsal's over?"

"Yeah. You look great."

"Then I'll get back into my own clothes, and we'll grab Hy and hit that country-and-western bar he discovered."

Patrick frowned. "You're not gonna drink too much, are you?"

"*What?*"

"Well, you wouldn't want to be hungover for your performance tomorrow."

First I've got Ted worrying about my owning a gun and flying a plane. Now Patrick's concerned about my drinking habits.

I said, "I'm only going along to watch over you. We can't have you exercising that Irish charm on the wrong women."

Two hours later, Patrick was definitely exercising his charm on a woman. She was tall, extremely thin, clad in tight jeans and a tank top, and she was beating him at straight pool.

"Must be true love," I said to Hy. "He doesn't seem to mind she's making him look like a klutz in front of all these strangers."

He glanced over from where we sat at the bar. "If his tongue was hanging out any farther, it'd interfere with his bank shot."

The bar, Tex's, was crowded and noisy. A band that was never going to make it to Nashville or even Bakersfield played—largely ignored—at the rear of the cavernous room. As they segued into a cover of one of Ricky's songs, "The Midnight Train to Nowhere," I grimaced. He would have, too, could he hear them.

Hy said, "So tomorrow you assume the persona of Nurse Betty." The reference was to a movie we hadn't much cared for.

"Nurse Patsy Newhouse, in case anyone asks." I often assumed my sisters' names when undercover; they were familiar enough that if someone called me by one of them I'd be likely to notice, if not immediately react.

Hy asked, "Is Sunday a good day to go to the hospital? Won't they be short on staff on the weekend?"

"Yeah, that's a drawback. Patrick's friend says a Friday would be perfect because people are always more relaxed and gossipy before the weekend. But I certainly can't wait around till Friday, so I might as well try my luck tomorrow. I can always go back on Monday."

"How d'you explain that none of the staff have ever seen you before?"

"There's a thing called the nurses' registry; it's like a temp agency, and it gives me a license to ask questions. I say I've just come from registry, don't know where anything is, that kind of thing. Deflect any of their questions by asking a lot of my own."

"Sounds tricky."

"It isn't going to be easy. I talked on the phone with Patrick's friend for a long time this afternoon. She says the nurses know everything about everyone, but it's a close-mouthed community when it comes to outsiders. They're smart and, if they're old enough to have known Laurel . . . Josie, whatever, they've been around long enough to know better than to talk freely to a stranger. But the friend prepped me well, and I'm a good actor. I'll haunt that cafeteria until I get the information I'm looking for."

"How long d'you think it'll take?"

"I don't know, but if you need to get the plane back to El Centro, Patrick and I can drive down to the city in his car. Later on I'll hitch a ride with somebody from North Field who's flying south, and pick up Two-Seven-Tango in Paso Robles."

"Kessell wants the Citation back on Monday so we can both go back to headquarters, but I tell you what: I'll ask him to detour to PRB, and then I'll fly Tango back to San Diego and up to Oakland midweek when my business down south is done. You get a lead here, there's no telling where it may take you."

I grasped his hand, twined my fingers through his. "Thank you."

"No thanks necessary. We're partners, remember?"

"That's not something I'm ever likely to forget."

We were silent for a moment, listening to the band mangle another of Ricky's songs.

"You know, McCone," Hy said when they'd finished and—mercifully—left the bandstand, "I've been thinking about your house, and I just may have come up with a solution to our living-space problems."

A tickle of apprehension ran along my spine. "And that is?"

"I don't want to go into it until I check some things out."

Such as the price it would bring on the open market? Call a real estate firm, ask for comps? It's my house, dammit! I bought it, put my own hard-earned cash and physical labor into it. I don't interfere with what you do with your ranch, so why should you—

Stop it! You're reacting as if he said he wanted to burn it down for the insurance money.

"What things?" I asked, keeping my voice level, the tone casual.

"Well, I'll need to look it over carefully, but—"

Shouting erupted from the area where the pool tables were. Alarmed, I swiveled around. A crowd blocked my view.

Both of us stood. I still couldn't see what was going on. I grasped Hy's arm. "What's happened?"

More commotion, and then one of the bartenders shouldered his way through the crowd. Hy moved forward in his wake. After a moment he came back and said, "I suspect Patrick and I will be making a visit to the Sutter Coast Hospital emergency room. I don't know what he said or did to her, but his pool-shark friend just decked him with her cue."

Sunday

•

AUGUST 28

Sutter Coast Hospital was reasonably well staffed for six-thirty on Sunday morning. I stood near the cafeteria doorway, surveying the various tables, and after a moment spotted one at which two women wearing nametags and dressed in scrubs were seated. They looked fresh and rested, probably having breakfast before going on the day shift, and they were old enough to have been working here at the same time as Laurel Greenwood, a.k.a. Josie Smith.

I crossed to the food line and got an English muffin and a cup of coffee, paid the cashier, and went over to the table. Plopped down and said, "Hi."

One of them, a short brunette in pink, nodded to me.

I asked, "Are either of you in Pediatrics?"

"No," they both replied.

"Can you direct me? I just came from registry. I don't know where anything is."

The other woman, tall and blonde, sighed. "Why doesn't that surprise me?"

I'd been warned by Patrick's friend that some RNs were unfriendly to the registry nurses, considering them more trouble than they were worth because they were unfamiliar with the hospitals they were sent to, and always asking questions. It also didn't help that they earned top dollar.

Quickly I said, "I felt the same way you do when I was on staff at Santa Rosa Memorial, but, hey, I've got two kids at home and need to make a living."

"Sorry. Yesterday was a rotten day, and I'm not expecting today to be any better." She looked back at the brunette. "As I was telling you, I said to him, 'Dr. Strauss, this patient is very anxious.' And he says to me, 'You think the patient's anxious? *I'm* the one who's anxious. If I don't finish my rounds in ten minutes, I'll miss my tee time.' The worst thing was, he meant it."

The other woman rolled her eyes.

In the vernacular provided by Patrick's friend, I said, "Docs!"

"Yeah." The woman in pink nodded emphatically. "Dedicated, huh?"

I sipped coffee, then asked, "How long have you worked here?"

"Twelve years."

"Then you might've known my aunt, Josie Smith. She was an RN in the ER."

She thought, shook her head. "Name's not familiar. When was she on staff?"

"She started in ninety-two, when the hospital was brand-new."

"Then she must've left before I came. Hey, Linda," she said to the woman on the other side of the table, who was staring into her coffee cup, "were you here in ninety-two?"

"I didn't move here till ninety-four."

"And you never heard of a Josie Smith?"

"No."

"Sorry," the brunette said, glancing at her watch. "Got to run. You want, I'll walk you toward Pediatrics."

Well, at least I'd proved to myself that I could walk the walk and talk the talk—even if I hadn't found out anything.

After the nurse had pointed the way to Pediatrics, I left the hospital, went to Patrick's car, which I'd parked a couple of blocks away, and read the morning paper. It was still too early to go back to the hospital, so I did the crossword puzzle, then took a walk. The morning was clear, but strong offshore winds gusted through the town and, from long experience with the vagaries of coastal weather, I sensed the fog would be in by evening.

When I got back to the car, I still had time to kill. One of my occupational hazards: too much waiting. Fortunately, I'd brought my briefcase along, so I opened it and reviewed the Laurel Greenwood files until lunchtime. Then I returned to the cafeteria, where I struck up conversations with various personnel, and in the process learned some interesting and not-so-interesting things.

Dr. Martin was getting a divorce from his wife of twenty-three years; she had run off with her personal trainer. Diane, in the pharmacy, was marrying her ex-husband—for the third time. Judy, one of the receptionists in the ER, was having an affair with an EMT, but nobody knew which one. An unnamed advice nurse spent her lunch hours in her van in the parking lot, working on a novel on her laptop; it was rumored to be something involving knives and guns. Marie was developing bunions; Nell had sold her home at a fifty percent profit; Dan had bought a new motorcycle; Trisha's cat had puked again—but on the hardwood floor, not on the white rug, thank God; Mike was goddamn glad to be starting his

vacation tomorrow; Kim's mother-in-law was coming to dinner next Sunday, and she was considering seasoning the roast
with strychnine.

I learned nothing about Laurel/Josie. Most of the people I
spoke with hadn't been on staff in 1992.

When the cafeteria began to clear out, I escaped the hospital and drove to a city park, where I sat on the grass, leaning against a tree trunk; I'd go back at two-thirty before the
swing shift started. My mind was cluttered with idle chatter,
and I tried to clear it.

Usually I found nothing wrong with idle chatter: we indulged in plenty of it at the pier, over coffee and sandwiches
or just hanging out on the catwalk; it helped us get through
the days that were mundane, boring, or just plain tedious.
But today my ears were ringing with voice-noise, and it kept
me from focusing. After a while it faded, but something
worse took its place.

*I've been thinking about your house, and I just may have
come up with a solution to our living-space problems.*

And what's that?

I don't want to go into it until I check some things out.

What things?

Well, I'll need to look it over carefully, but—

My God, what had I gotten myself into?

I shook my head to clear it, tried a few deep-breathing exercises. They didn't work. I was glad when it was time to go
back to the hospital.

"Just leave me the hell alone," the thin, poorly kempt
woman said.

All I'd done was set down my tray—more coffee, another
snack—across the table from her. I looked closely at her face,

saw eyes with dilated pupils and facial muscles drawn taut with strain. A relative of a patient with a life-threatening condition? No, she wore scrubs and a nametag.

"Sorry." I picked up the tray, turned.

She muttered something unintelligible.

A hand on my arm. I looked around at a kind-eyed, dark-haired woman in blue scrubs. "Come sit with me," she said, and led me to a nearby table.

"What was that all about?" I asked.

She sighed, sat down, nodded at the place opposite her. "What d'you think?"

"I don't know. I only came today from the registry."

"Well, she's up to her old tricks, and pretty soon she'll be outta here for good."

"Drugs?"

The woman hesitated, then her eyes flashed with anger. "Yeah. She's been through the rehab program once, and one chance is all you get."

"Too bad." I glanced over at the thin woman. She was crumbling the bread from a sandwich into tiny pieces and casting narrow-eyed glances at us.

"Yeah, it's too bad. She used to be a good nurse, till she started forging prescriptions." The dark-haired woman's mouth closed firmly; she'd realized she'd said too much to an outsider.

I said, "My name's Patsy Newhouse, by the way."

"Barbara Fredrick." She extended her hand. "How's it going so far?"

"Okay. This is a nice place, people are friendly. My aunt always said so."

"Your aunt worked here?"

"Yes, maybe you remember her—Josie Smith. In ER."

"Josie?" The smile took on a frozen quality.

"She started here the year the hospital opened."

". . . Right. But she left a year later."

"D'you know where she went after that?"

"She's your aunt, and you don't know where she is?"

"She broke off all contact with the family about that time."

"Oh." Barbara Fredrick looked down into her coffee cup. "That's a shame. I liked Josie."

"Were you a friend of hers?"

"Not really. She was kind of a private person."

"Why'd she leave, d'you know?"

Fredrick shrugged. "I guess she just needed to move on."

"Is there anybody else on staff who might've known her well?"

She thought, compressing her lips. "As I said, she was kind of a loner, didn't socialize much, but she had one friend on the staff, Debra Jansen. I think she mentioned to me that Josie had moved after the—"

"After what?"

Fredrick ignored the question, finished her coffee.

I asked, "Does Debra Jansen still work here?"

"No. She retired and moved away about seven, eight years ago. I think she and her husband bought a place up in Grass Valley."

Grass Valley—an old Gold Rush town in the Sierra foothills, now a popular destination for both retirees and people attempting to escape the crowded Sacramento and Bay areas. The last time I'd driven through the area, the proliferation of malls and subdivisions had attested to the concept that when you move you take your baggage with you.

I said, "Do you have a phone number for Debra Jansen, or an address?"

Fredrick was about to rise from the table, but she paused, looking into my eyes. "No, I don't. But if you do locate her and talk about your aunt, you should remember this: people make mistakes. Josie's was a bad one, but mistakes happen."

"A bad mistake? Did somebody die?" I didn't know why I asked that particular question, but I saw confirmation of its answer on Fredrick's troubled face.

She looked at her watch, grasped her tray, and stood. "I've got to get back. Good luck."

Remember this: people make mistakes.

Josie's was a bad one.

"How's your head?" I asked Patrick.

"Still hurts. I can't believe I needed stitches." He was stretched out on his back on the bed in his motel room, looking pale and squinting in the light from the TV.

"What in God's name did you do to that woman?"

"My assailant? Damned if I know. One minute she was beating me at pool, next she was beating me with her cue."

"You must've said or done *something*."

He rolled his head against the pillow and winced. "Not that I remember."

A rap at the door. I went to answer it, let Hy inside. He hugged me, turned to Patrick, and said, "Still feel like shit, huh?"

"Yeah."

"Women, whiskey, and wildness'll do that to you."

"Woman, beer, and what I thought was a civilized pool game. You talk to the cops?"

"I did. Seems this sort of episode is business as usual with Crazy Mary."

"*Who?*"

"The lady who bashed you. She was winning, you wanted to quit, she took offense."

"Well, have they arrested her?"

"No."

Outraged, Patrick tried to struggle into a sitting position, but fell back against the pillows. "Why not?"

"Because she fled the scene, and they haven't been able to locate her. Plus I told them you didn't want to press charges."

"*What?*"

"You don't. I guarantee it."

"Why not?"

"Because Crazy Mary is not only a pool shark, but a habitual filer of nuisance suits. Gets into altercations, takes her victims and her sleazebag lawyer to court, and lies— convincingly. She'll manage to turn this one around, say you sexually harassed her, and keep it tied up in the courts for years."

I exclaimed, "I hate litigious people!"

Hy looked at me, lines around his eyes crinkling in sympathy with my anger. "Me too, McCone, but what's to be done? Your health plan'll cover the costs of this doofus's injuries"—he motioned at Patrick—"and he'll never mess with anybody like Crazy Mary again."

From the bed came a moan of agreement.

"So now that we've got that mess cleared up," Hy said, "how did it go at the hospital?" He was lounging on the bed in our motel room, a beer in hand.

"Fine. I have a lead to a friend of Greenwood's in Grass Valley. Derek's trying to locate her."

"You going down there?"

"Yes, but I'm not sure how. Patrick's in no shape to drive. I considered borrowing his car, but that would leave him without transportation. Besides, I'm not sure it would make it." Patrick's car was an ancient Ford Falcon that spent more time in the shop than on the road; frankly, I was surprised it had made it as far as Crescent City.

"Here's a solution: why don't I fly you there first thing in the morning. You could rent a decent car, drop it off when you get back to the city."

"It won't make you late getting the Citation back to Dan?"

"Nah, it's only a slight detour. Plus it'll give us more time together. And now what d'you say to getting some dinner?"

"Fine, as long as we don't follow it up with a stop at Tex's."

Monday

·

AUGUST 29

Grass Valley once was the richest gold-mining town in California, but, unlike many, it did not fade into obscurity after the veins of ore were played out. Today it thrives on a combination of high-tech manufacturing, agriculture, and—of course—tourism. While the town has spread far beyond its original boundaries, the central district is filled with well-maintained buildings dating from the 1850s and '60s.

I drove slowly along West Main Street, taking special note of a handsome old hotel, and turned onto the appropriately named Pleasant Street, following the directions given me over the phone by Laurel/Josie's old friend Debra Jansen. Her house was in the second block, a large white Victorian with blue trim. As I started up the wide front steps, a voice spoke to me from the porch.

"Ms. McCone?"

I looked up, saw a woman with a pert face and silver hair that fluffed out around her head, the sun's rays turning it into a halo. "I'm Debra Jansen," she added. "Come on up here where it's shady. I've made us some iced tea. I always keep a pitcher of it in the fridge on days like this."

"Thank you. It *is* hot."

"Ninety-nine today. Actually, that's nothing for August."

"I have an uncle who lives outside of Jackson; he'd agree with you." I stepped onto the sheltered porch. An assortment of white wicker furniture with floral-patterned cushions sat there, a moisture-beaded pitcher of tea and two glasses on a tray table.

"Sit down, please," Debra Jansen told me, turning to the table and pouring. "I was surprised when you called and said you wanted to talk about Josie. I'm not sure what I can tell you. It's been years since I've heard from her."

I accepted the glass of tea, drank some, then took out my recorder. "Is this okay with you?"

"I don't know why not. But, as I said, I don't think what I know will help much."

"You never can tell." I turned the recorder on. "When did you last hear from Josie?"

"She sent a card at Christmas of nineteen ninety-four. She was living in Klamath Falls, Oregon."

"Did she enclose a note?"

"No. She just signed it. It was a special card, though, not one of the kind you buy by the box. A Hallmark with a long message about absent friends. That made me a little sad."

"Why?"

"Because the two of us weren't all that close—at least, not what I call close—and I knew the reason Josie went out and bought an individual card like that was she probably didn't have many people to send to."

"She was a loner, then."

"Very much so. Ms. McCone, before we go any farther with this, I must ask you: why are you looking for her?"

"Her daughter hired me to locate her."

"She has a daughter?"

"Two. They also haven't heard from her in many years."

"She never mentioned any children. I knew she'd been married and, from a few of the things she said, I gathered he'd been unfaithful to her. But now that you've told me about the daughters, it explains her rapport with the children who were brought in to the ER." She frowned. "But her children would have been young then. Why didn't she have them with her?"

"They remained with the husband."

"He got custody, after what he did?"

"It happens."

"Well, it shouldn't!" Debra Jansen's face grew pink with indignation.

I moved away from that line of conversation. "Do you have Josie's address in Klamath Falls?"

"No. I sent a card the next year, but it came back as undeliverable, so I removed the address from my book. I assumed if she wanted to get in touch with me, she would. But she never did. Do you suppose she died?"

"It's possible. Mrs. Jansen, would you mind telling me about your friendship with Josie Smith, from the beginning?"

"Of course not. There isn't a great deal to tell." She stood, poured us more tea, and returned to her chair. "I joined the nursing staff at what was then Seaside Hospital in nineteen-eighty. In eighty-six, the county leased it to Sutter Health, with the provision that a new hospital be constructed, and when it opened in ninety-two, we moved to the new facility. It was larger, and quite a few new people were hired; one of them was Josie. I'd see her in the cafeteria, always alone, always reading. She looked so sad and vulnerable. So one day when I saw she had a favorite book of mine—Steinbeck's *East of Eden*—I plunked myself down and asked if she liked it. She did, and it turned out we liked quite a few of the same books, so we began talking about them during our lunch and coffee breaks."

"Did you see her socially?"

"Occasionally we went out for drinks after work. When my husband was working night shifts—he was in law enforcement, a deputy with the county sheriff's department—we'd sometimes go to dinner. I never went to her home, though; it was a studio apartment, and I gathered it was too small to entertain in. Once I had her over to the house for dinner, but it wasn't too successful an evening; my husband didn't like her, and she must've sensed that because she turned down my next—and last—invitation."

"Why didn't your husband like her?"

"He couldn't pin it down. All he could say was that there was something 'hinky' about her. Suspect, you know? I had to respect his feelings, though, so after Josie turned down my second invitation, I kept my family life and my relationship with her separate."

"Did you also feel there was something 'hinky' about her?"

"No. While my husband was used to dealing with criminals, I was used to dealing with sick and injured people; I knew that what he sensed in Josie was her underlying sadness."

Sadness, yes. But the hinky feeling was also valid. Your husband sensed a woman on the run.

I said, "You were at Sutter Coast when Josie made the mistake that caused her to resign?"

Debra Jansen nodded.

"What's your take on that?"

"It was an honest mistake any of us could have made—any day, anytime. Nurses, doctors, it doesn't matter—the potential for deadly mistakes exist, and sometimes they happen."

"And this one . . . ?"

"Josie was on the ER in October of ninety-three when a patient who had sustained bad lower-body burns in an auto accident was brought in. I don't know if you've ever been in an emergency room or watched any of the TV shows set there, but when trauma victims arrive, it can get pretty hectic. They were starting an IV, and Josie grabbed a bag of dextrose, rather than saline. The patient went into cardiac arrest and they couldn't bring him back."

"And she resigned."

"Yes. She was deeply shaken by what she'd done, told me she'd never get over it, and that she didn't deserve to be a nurse anymore."

"And soon after that, she moved away."

"Yes."

"Did you see her before she left?"

"Once. We met for a drink at a motel bar on the highway. Not one of the places that the folks from Sutter Coast frequented. She didn't want to see any of them."

"What happened at that meeting?"

"We talked about what was going on in my life. She said she was leaving town. I asked her what she'd do; she said she didn't know, but it wouldn't be nursing. She didn't even know where she was going, she was just planning to get in her van and drive. She had a garage sale the following weekend and got rid of everything that wouldn't fit in the van, and then she was gone."

I was listening to her, and yet I wasn't, trusting the tape to do my job while I entertained a frightening possibility. I reached for my glass, drained the iced tea left there.

I said, " I won't take up too much more of your time, Mrs. Jansen, but I wonder if you remember anything about the patient who died because of Josie's mistake?"

"I'm not likely to forget. The man's wife was litigious, and it took the hospital's lawyers a long time to reach a settlement. They were a couple traveling through on their way to a family reunion in Seattle. Collingsworth, was the name."

"And where were they from?"

"Somewhere down south. He was a retired chief of police, as I recall."

"Was his full name Bruce Collingsworth?"

"That sounds right."

Bruce Collingsworth—Roy Greenwood's tennis partner, who had been chief of the Paso Robles force when Laurel disappeared.

I was willing to bet his death was no accident.

I was speeding toward Sacramento on Highway 99 when my cell rang. I fumbled the unit out of my purse, which lay on the passenger seat.

"Yeah, Shar. What d'you need?" Derek, returning the call I'd made to him before leaving Grass Valley.

"A couple of things. Seems Laurel Greenwood was living in Klamath Falls, Oregon, under Josie Smith's name, in December of ninety-four. Will you see if there's a current address for her in that area?"

"Closing in, huh? Sure thing. What else?"

"This is a lower priority, but still important. See if you can come up with any information on a death at Sutter Coast

Hospital in Crescent City in October of ninety-three. The deceased's name was Bruce Collingsworth."

"You want I should call you, or e-mail the info?"

"Neither. I'm on my way back to the office, should be there in two, two and a half hours."

"See you then."

I broke the connection, dropped the phone on the passenger seat. Checked my rearview mirror for highway patrol cars and, when I didn't see any, pressed harder on the accelerator.

It was after six when I got to the pier. Traffic on Interstate 80 had been brutal in both Sacramento and the East Bay, and I'd hit a major snag in Vallejo as well. As I passed Ted's office, he called out to me, but I kept going to Derek's. Mick was the only one there.

"If you're looking for your top research man," he said, "he's waiting for you in your office."

Mick looked a little sullen, and the absence of his usual cheerful greeting told me I was at the root of his displeasure—probably because I'd cut him out of the investigation. Normally I would have asked him what was wrong and talked the problem through, but right now I was in too much of a hurry. Let him stew for a while; maybe he'd work it out on his own.

"Thanks," I told him, and headed for my office.

Derek was in my armchair, staring out at the fog. When he heard me come in, he started and got up, looking guilty.

I said, "Usurping my place, are you?"

"Shar, I'm sorry—"

"That chair's not sacrosanct, you know. And it's not even all that comfortable." I dumped my purse and briefcase on the desk, dragged another chair over, and motioned for him to reclaim his place. "You get an address for Josie Smith?"

"My property search for Klamath Falls shows she's owned a house at one-thirteen May Street since March of nineteen ninety-five. Taxes're current. The stuff on that death in Crescent City is in the top file in your in-box, and I also e-mailed it, just in case. It's pretty routine. The guy was badly burned in a freeway crash, and then he was accidentally administered the wrong IV by a nurse in the ER. No follow-up on the story, except a brief item saying the hospital had settled with the widow for an undisclosed amount."

"Thanks. I want you to keep on that one. The widow may still be alive; check the Paso Robles area first."

"You're close to solving this one, huh?"

"No—*we* are. Has Patrick come in or called?"

"He spoke with Ted this morning and said he'd be in tomorrow. Told him a wild story involving a woman and a pool cue."

"It *was* wild. I know, because I was there."

"Then it's true. Ted thought he'd made it up."

"It's true, all right." I went to the desk and buzzed Ted. "Will you check with the airlines and find out when the next flight to Klamath Falls, Oregon, leaves? And while you're at it, ask about the current regs about bringing a firearm on board."

Disapproving silence.

"Just do it. Lecture me later."

When I turned back to Derek, he was standing. "You taking off now?" I asked.

"If you don't need me. I've got a dinner date, but I'll keep my cell on in case you have to get in touch."

"You seeing Chris?"

He shook his head. "New lady."

So Chris and Derek's involvement wasn't serious. Well,

that meant I didn't have to worry about Jamie getting her tender young feelings hurt.

"Have fun," I said.

"Thanks."

The intercom buzzed as Derek left the office.

"The last flight for Klamath Falls on any airline left at five-thirty," Ted said. "Your next option is Horizon Air, at six-thirty tomorrow morning. Arrives at eleven-oh-four."

"Why so long?"

"Stopover in Portland."

Damn! I didn't want to wait till morning. But it was a long, difficult drive, and I couldn't fly myself, since Hy had phoned earlier to say he'd picked up Two-Seven-Tango in Paso Robles and gone back to San Diego for a few days. Not that I could have flown anyplace, given this thick fog. Oh well, at least this way I could drop off the car I'd rented in Grass Valley at SFO tomorrow.

"Okay," I said, "book the six-thirty, please. What did they tell you about the firearms regs?"

"Disassembled, in a hard case, in your checked baggage."

"No lecture now?"

"Well, I'm wondering why you need a handgun on this particular trip."

"You'll learn about it when I get back."

Silence.

"Still no lecture?"

"Would it do any good?"

"No."

"I thought not. Have a good trip."

Eleven forty-five that night. I hung up the phone after talking with Hy—a conversation during which I'd studiously avoided any discussion about my house—took a sip from my wineglass, and stared into the fire that was slowly dying on the hearth. The cats were curled up on the sofa cushion next to me; Alice was snoring. I knew I should get some rest, but I was too keyed up to sleep.

After a while I went to the kitchen, where my briefcase lay on the table. Removed the original file on Laurel Greenwood and brought it back to the sitting room. The newspaper photo of her was at the back. I took it out and studied it.

What were you thinking, Laurel, when you smiled so radiantly for the camera? Were you looking forward to one of your visits to Josie, or to one of your mental health days? Were you planning a special surprise for your daughters? Or a getaway with the husband whom you didn't yet know was cheating on you with your cousin?

One thing for sure, you didn't realize the sudden, dark turn your life would one day take. Didn't know that Josie would die in a heap at the bottom of the stairway where the two of you stood arguing. Couldn't know you'd walk out on that husband and those daughters and never be able to return.

Or, as I suspect, cold-bloodedly kill an old friend so he couldn't reveal your identity.

And since then? What have you been doing, Laurel? What has your life become?

Tomorrow I'd find out.

Tuesday

·

AUGUST 30

After the sun-browned terrain of California, south-central Oregon looked lush and green. Klamath Falls, a small city of around twenty thousand, was nestled at the tip of Upper Klamath Lake and spread out over the surrounding, softly sculpted hills. My flight arrived at Kingsley Field on time, to clear skies and balmy weather in the high sixties. Before going to baggage claim, I hurried through the terminal to do the paperwork and collect the keys to the rental car Ted had reserved for me. Normally on a trip like this I wouldn't have checked my bag, but the firearms regulations made that a necessity. The bag came off quickly, however, and after taking it to the car and removing and reassembling my Magnum, I was on my way, the MapQuest directions to Laurel/Josie's house on the seat beside me.

The route took me through downtown, along a main street with a pleasant old-fashioned feel and lined by interesting-looking shops. Then I found myself in an area of shabby motels, fast-food restaurants, and strip malls. A right turn, and a mile or so from there I entered an older subdivision where the homes were of the same style, differing only in size and color, and set closely together on small lots. It was clearly an area in decline, and probably had been for some time: many of the houses were in poor repair and in need of painting; lawns were untrimmed, flowerbeds unweeded; some of the yards were surrounded by chain-link fences and posted with Beware of Dog signs. The houses mostly had one-car garages, but their owners had multiple vehicles; cars, trucks, vans, SUVs, campers, and trailers laden with jet skis and boats hugged the curbs. When I got to the 100 block of May Street I wedged my rental car between two pickups and walked down to number 113.

It was one of the smaller houses, a single story, of blue aluminum siding; the main part was set back and formed an L with the garage, which protruded toward the street. While the yard was tidy and the lawn mowed, there were no plantings in the flowerbeds, no other attempts at adornment. The single picture window next to the front door was covered with closed blinds.

I studied it for a moment, thinking of the pretty house in Paso Robles that Laurel Greenwood had abandoned twenty-two years ago. Thinking of how it would feel to come face-to-face with her, after prying into the most intimate aspects of her life for over two weeks now. Wondering how she would react when she realized she'd been found out.

Then I went up the walk and rang the bell.

No one answered.

I rang again. Waited.

No response.

There was a mailbox attached to the wall next to the door. I glanced around to see if anyone was watching me, then tipped its lid up and looked inside. A couple of days' accumulation of what looked to be junk mail.

Not home, then. How could I find out how long she'd be gone, and to where?

I went back down the walk, turned, and looked at the house again. Much like the others in this tract, it had an untended feel. But with the others I sensed that the owners were either too poor to keep them up, or too busy with their boats and jet skis and RVs to bother—or maybe they were simply leading disordered lives. Here I felt something different: it was as if outward appearances didn't matter because the life being lived inside didn't matter either.

I looked up and down the block. No signs of life on the opposite side, but two doors down to my right, at one of the better-kept houses, a woman was digging in a flowerbed. She knelt on the grass, wearing shorts, a tank top, and a sunhat. I moved along the sidewalk toward her and stopped by the low white fence that surrounded the yard. "Excuse me."

She rocked back on her heels abruptly. "Oh! You startled me."

"I'm sorry. I thought you'd heard me coming."

"I was zoning out, I guess." Her face was a wrinkled and weathered brown, her eyes a clear, bright blue, as if exposure to the elements had worked the opposite effect on them. "It happens when I weed. Often I think that killing things shouldn't be such a pleasurable activity. But, then, it enables other things, such as this fuchsia, to thrive." She gestured at a healthy, purple-flowered plant.

"It's a pretty one."

"Yes. Thrives on moisture. Of which we have plenty."

"So I hear from my Aunt Josie. Josie Smith. She lives two doors down." I motioned toward number 113.

The woman took off her gardening gloves, noticed that in

spite of them her fingers were grimy, and wiped them on her shorts. "Josie never mentioned having any family."

"Well, we haven't seen each other in a long time, but I had to come here from San Francisco on business, and I thought I'd look her up. It seems she's not at home."

"Never is, this week in August. Her vacation from the convalescent hospital."

"Oh, she's working in nursing again?"

The woman frowned. "She's not a nurse, just works at Hillside, assisting with the patients. Grunt work, she calls it. Personally, I think it helps her pass the time. There isn't much in her life since her husband died, besides the nursing home and her volunteer work for the hospice."

Husband? "Yes, his death was a shame."

"That terrible accident, those bad burns, and then some nurse at the hospital where he was taken gave him the wrong IV and he went into cardiac arrest." She shook her head. "A tragedy like that is what tests a woman's mettle. Made Josie want to care for others. And she does."

"I'm having a memory lapse. Where was it her husband died?"

"Someplace in northern California. It's why she came up here, she said. To escape the past."

"It sounds as if you're good friends."

"Not really. She keeps to herself. Stays in that house of hers, unless she's at work or volunteering. The way I know her is that I volunteer for hospice myself. One night I gave her a ride home because her van was in the shop, and asked her in for a glass of wine. I'm nosy, so I pried into the details of her life. I think she regretted what she told me, because she's kind of avoided me ever since."

"When did she move to this neighborhood? I had to ask

another relative for her current address, because the one I had—from Christmas of ninety-four—wasn't good."

"Spring of ninety-five, I think. Yes, it was the year my first grandchild was born."

"And you say she's on vacation now?"

"That's right. Every year, the last week in August, without fail. She has a standing reservation at the Crater Lake Lodge. Calls it her 'mental health week.' Says it's the only thing that keeps her sane, after all the illness and death she sees at work."

Mental health week.

Mental health day.

In spite of all that had come to pass, one thing hadn't changed for Laurel Greenwood.

Crater Lake, less than fifty miles northeast of Klamath Falls, was formed by a massive volcanic eruption that has been carbon-dated at having occurred some four thousand years BC; the blast caused the shell of then twelve-thousand-foot Mount Mazama to collapse inward, lopping off four thousand feet and creating a vast crater. I once read that no streams flow into the lake; its water is derived entirely from rain and snow, and its intense blue color is due to the water's purity reacting with the sunlight.

A few years ago Hy and I had flown over the lake at dawn. We crested the pines on the eastern side, and suddenly it spread below us—huge, ringed by stark volcanic outcroppings. The first rays of the sun moved across its glassy, still surface like a golden stain. Hy pulled back on power and, as we glided closer and closer to the water, a silence so great that it rivaled the whine and throb of the engine rose to greet us. This was the world as it had been in ancient times; this was eternity.

It was an experience that made me aware in a profound yet comforting way of my own insignificance and mortality. Comforting, because I realized I was part of a magnificent creation. I'm not particularly religious, but you don't have to be to partake of the feeling; you simply have to relinquish control and exist in the moment.

Today as I drove north from Klamath Falls, I suspected that this upcoming experience of the lake would be very different from my previous one.

The lodge was an imposing building composed of several wings, stone on the lower story, dark brown wood above, with a steeply sloping green roof punctuated by two rows of dormer windows. Sturdy stone chimneys towered above it, and pine-covered hills loomed even higher. I left my rental some distance away because the parking lot was crowded and hurried toward the main wing. Although it was warm outside, the interior was cool and dark. I paused for a moment to get my bearings.

The space was wide and long, with highly polished hardwood floors dotted with area rugs and rustic wooden furnishings, the chairs with wide arms and bright woven cushions. People in tourist garb wandered through, exclaiming at the huge fireplace and beamed ceilings. I located reception, crossed to it, and asked if Josie Smith was registered.

The clerk, a slender man with large hair and a small ring in his left ear, said, "Yes, she is, but she's not in her room. I saw her go by an hour ago with her book; you'll find her on the veranda. She's always there this time of day."

"My friend is a creature of habit, isn't she?"

He smiled. "You could say that. One of the long-term employees says she's been coming here this same week every year since nineteen ninety-five, when the lodge reopened after it was reconstructed. She reads on the veranda every day from four o'clock till sunset, then has dinner in the dining room."

"Is she always alone?"

"She sometimes converses with the other guests but, yes, she pretty much keeps to herself."

"Well, I'd better go find her."

The veranda was wide, concrete-floored, with a low stone wall topped by a wrought-iron safety fence. Rocking chairs of natural bark logs with caned backs and seats were arranged along the railing. Several groups of people sat there, their feet propped on the wall, sipping wine and talking. Farther down I spotted a lone woman in jeans and a T-shirt, her legs tucked up under her; she had a hardcover book spread open on her lap, but her head was raised, her eyes on the lake.

Laurel Greenwood.

I remained where I was, taking in what she saw: the tops of the nearby tall pines and the brilliantly blue water beyond. An island, with more pines clinging to volcanic rock, sat midway between the shore and the stark outcroppings on the far side—remnants of the mountaintop that had been blown away by the ancient eruption. The lodge faced west, and already pink traces of the sunset were streaking the sky.

Laurel sat unmoving. A light breeze caught her hair and ruffled it around her shoulders; it was straighter than it had been at the time of her disappearance, but just as long, and silver-gray streaks caught the light. She had once been beautiful, but she was not anymore. And it wasn't just the result of aging.

I watched her for a moment, but she seemed unaware of anyone else, barely aware of her surroundings. As I approached her, she seemed not to hear my footfalls.

I stopped two feet away from her. Put my hand on the .357 in the outer pocket of my bag, in spite of the unlikelihood that I'd need to show it. Said, "Laurel?"

Slowly she disengaged her gaze from the lake and looked toward me. I was reminded of the expression in her daughter Jennifer's eyes when I'd approached her at the overlook north of Cayucos: remote, dazed. The same expression Jacob Ziff had described on Laurel's face when he'd encountered her there.

As if she were waking up from a dream, or maybe as if I were pulling her back from some other world she'd been inhabiting.

Well, by now Laurel had been inhabiting that other world for a long time. Too long.

She stared blankly at me, and when she didn't respond I said, "Laurel Greenwood?"

Suddenly her eyes came alive, displaying a rapid succession of emotions: bewilderment, disbelief, fear, and— finally—resignation. I waited out her silence.

"Who *are* you?" she finally said.

I took my hand off my gun and pulled up a nearby rocking chair; sat and handed her my card. At the same time I switched on the voice-activated tape recorder I'd earlier placed in the pocket of my light jacket.

I said, "Your daughter Jennifer Aldin hired me to find you."

"I don't have to talk with you," Laurel said after studying the card I'd handed her.

"That's true. I have no official capacity."

"Good." She started to rise from her chair.

I put my hand on her arm, looked her in the eyes. "Do you really want to turn your back on your daughter a second time? She still remembers you with love."

After minor resistance, she settled down. "How much do you know about me?"

"Nearly everything."

"Then what do you want?"

"To fill in the gaps so Jennifer will finally have peace of mind."

"If I agree, will you go away and not bother me again?"

It troubled me that she hadn't asked a single question about Jennifer or Terry. There was a coldness in the woman, an almost robotic quality, perhaps the product of living a reclusive life or—worse—of her basic nature.

I said, "No, *I* won't bother you again."

Emphasis on the first-person singular. Throughout most of my investigation I'd tried to understand why Laurel Greenwood had caused such ruin to the people she supposedly loved, and I'd hoped for Jennifer and Terry's sake that my search would have a happy ending. Even before I'd come face-to-face with Laurel, I knew there would be no such ending, and that I would be legally bound to turn over everything I knew about her wrongdoings to the proper authorities. Seeing her in the flesh cemented that resolve.

"All right," she said after a moment. "I'll tell you my story from the beginning. And then you'll go away and let me be."

Laurel and I talked for more than two hours, and I recorded it all. She was alternately defensive, petulant, angry, and defiant. But eventually she confirmed most of what I'd already surmised. Reinforced my initial negative reaction to her as well.

"Josie was in the terminal stages of her illness, and at times she barely knew who she was. But at others, she was lucid, and completely herself. I'd always known she could be cruel; I'd seen her nastiness directed at others plenty of times. But until that afternoon, she'd never directed it at me."

"She taunted you about her affair with your husband?"

"Yes."

"And you shoved her down the stairs?"

"No! I would never have done that. I made a move as if to slap her. She ducked, and fell. By the time I got to the bottom of the stairs, she was dead."

"But you didn't call for the police or an ambulance right away. Why not?"

"What a question! I was in shock. And, I admit, afraid for my own skin. Wouldn't you be?"

"After Josie died, I couldn't stand to be around Roy. Didn't want him to touch me. And I couldn't deal with Sally, because I knew she probably suspected what had happened. And my little girls . . . I never wanted to be a mother. Roy forced that on me."

"You didn't love them at all?"

"God, don't look at me like that! I loved them in my way. I was a good mother. A *good* mother. That's why, after the accident with Josie, I was afraid I'd somehow contaminate them. I decided everyone would be better off without me."

"So you planned your disappearance for a long time?"

"Yes. And it was a solid plan; it worked like a charm. With the money from Josie's estate I bought a van, stored it at a facility in Morro Bay. I wore a red wig so if they asked for my identification I could pass for Josie. Later I had my own picture put on her driver's license. And then, after a trip to Cayucos to paint one last canvas, I took off."

"Do you still paint?"

"No. I gave it up that day. I'd read about how to disappear. If I was to make a new life, I had to give up everything from the old. I left my VW bus with the canvas and all my painting supplies in a public parking lot in Morro Bay, put on the wig in the restroom, so the people at the self-storage place wouldn't think a stranger was taking the van. Then I walked up the hill, and drove away from there."

"And never looked back."

"Oh, I've looked back. Believe me, I have."

"Santa Rosa was just a temporary stopping point. It looked like a nice place, the hospital was hiring, and it was far enough away that I didn't think I'd run into anyone who might recognize me. But I didn't like the summer heat there—too much like Paso Robles—and then I heard that Sutter Coast Hospital in Crescent City was opening its new facility and hiring. I loved Crescent City. Cool and gray a lot of the time, like the coastal areas down south. And I wasn't so lonely. I made a friend there."

"Debra Jansen."

"You talked with her?"

"She told me you were in Klamath Falls."

"How . . . ? Oh, the Christmas card I sent her. A stupid, sentimental gesture. Probably the last I ever made. And since that's how you found me, the worst. Trouble was, it was the Christmas season, and I was depressed. I had good reason to be."

"Because of what happened a year before to Bruce Collingsworth?"

". . . You *have* done your homework, damn you."

"Debra Jansen says his death was an honest mistake. That

during the confusion in the ER you started an IV with the wrong bag of solution."

"That's the truth. I grabbed a bag out of the wrong cabinet."

"But it wasn't the usual ER confusion that rattled you."

"Have *you* ever worked on an ER? Even a good nurse like I was—"

"Come on, Laurel. You couldn't have helped but recognize Collingsworth. What really happened?"

"A mistake! That's all—a mistake! Bruce was in terrible pain, but conscious. We were stabilizing him, and he looked up and recognized me. He said, 'Laurel, you're alive.' That's what threw me."

"And you're sure giving him dextrose instead of saline was an accident?"

"Of course it was! I'm . . . I was a nurse. I would never deliberately kill anyone. Never! . . . No, don't you give me that look. Bruce Collingsworth's death was an *accident!*"

"I decided to settle in Klamath Falls because my van broke down here, and I'd run out of the energy to keep going. The first year I lived in a cheap apartment, hoping I'd get it together and move on. Then I realized I wasn't going anyplace, so I bought a house. For the past ten years I've worked in a nursing home. Just grunt work—changing beds, wheeling the patients outside to get some air, cleaning up after them. I don't mind it. I like helping people. And I volunteer for our hospice. Easing the last days of the terminally ill, it's rewarding. And, I suppose, something of an atonement for the things I've done—to Josie, to my family, to Bruce Collingsworth. I live very quietly. One of my neighbors has been kind to me, and tried to forge a friendship, but I find

I've lost the ability to function socially. I'm only good with the dying."

"All right—I'm sorry I haven't asked about Roy or the girls. How are they?"

"Roy died seven months ago. Of pancreatic cancer. Terry's married and teaches at a cooking school in Davis. Jennifer is a textile designer; she was living in Atherton, but now is separated from her husband and temporarily staying with Terry."

No reaction to that news. "You said it was Jennifer who hired you to find me?"

"Yes."

"That makes sense. She was always the inquisitive one."

"And she loved her mother."

"Did she? I wouldn't know. Children are such voracious creatures. What we think of as love is often pure need. Of course, there's nothing wrong with satisfying a child's need. Someone has to fill it."

Until it becomes inconvenient or difficult, and then you just walk away.

"So now are you satisfied? You'll go away and leave me alone?"

"Yes, but I'm required to report any evidence of wrongdoing that I find in the course of an investigation to the authorities."

"You promised—!"

"I said *I* wouldn't bother you again. I can't speak for the police in San Francisco or Crescent City. Or the state board of nursing."

"You lied! You're going to turn me in to them, even though I've told you everything."

"It's the law, and if I don't comply, I'll lose my license. Even if you can convince them that your version of what happened is true, there will be consequences. You've committed fraud, practiced nursing under another person's credentials."

"I'll lose my livelihood. The nursing home will fire me. The hospice will turn me away."

"As I said, consequences."

"But my work is my whole life. I have nothing except helping dying people."

"You have something else, Laurel, or have you forgotten why I'm here?"

"What? Oh, my daughters."

"Yes, your daughters."

". . . Do they want to see me?"

"I don't know."

"Can you talk with them? Ask? At least do that for me before you go to the authorities."

"All right, if that's what you want."

"It's what I want. When will you do it?"

"I'll make a verbal report to Jennifer tomorrow. If they agree to a meeting, probably my office in San Francisco would be the best place."

She considered. "No. Not down there. Please. Ask them to come to Klamath Falls, to my house."

"Why?"

"Because maybe a visit there will explain a few things to them. Maybe it will be a new beginning for the three of us."

"You'd better not be using this as a delaying tactic so you can run again. Because I guarantee I'll find you."

Her eyes grew bleak and she looked away at the lake. "Run? How could I? I have no place left to go."

*   *   *

After I'd promised again—against my better instincts—to ask Jennifer and Terry to meet with their mother, Laurel went inside to her room. I remained on the veranda, staring out across the lake at the fiery sunset.

Given her character as I understood it, Laurel's demeanor had seemed natural throughout our talk. None of it had been scripted; it couldn't have been, given the circumstances.

But I wondered.

Her involvement in the death of Josie Smith. Her alleged mistake that had cost Bruce Collingsworth his life. Her desertion of her daughters.

I was the one who had had to prompt her to ask about those now grown children, and suddenly she wanted to see them.

I feared for Jennifer and Terry, should they decide to reconnect, but they were adults, and it was their prerogative to say yes or no to a meeting with their mother.

Momentarily I banished the investigation from my mind. Accepted the glass of wine I'd ordered from a passing waiter. Above the towering outcroppings on the far side of the lake, the sky blossomed with the last violent protests of the dying sun; purple clouds outlined in pink and gold billowed above them.

The end of a day for me.

The end of a reconstructed life for Laurel Greenwood.

Wednesday

·

AUGUST 31

"I am *not* going to meet with her!" Terry Wyatt exclaimed. She stood in the living room of her Davis home, hands on hips, eyes flashing.

From the sofa where she and I sat, Jennifer watched, wary of her sister's anger. I kept my expression noncommital; I was the messenger, bearing bad tidings.

But Terry's rage wasn't directed at me. It was aimed at her mother, and she vented it with full force. "What she did is unforgivable! And now she wants a *new beginning*? What does she think? That we'll just pick up where we left off? Maybe she wants to tuck me into bed and read me a Littlest Lamb book? Where the *hell* does she get off?"

Jennifer cleared her throat and said in a tentative tone, "Terry, I think we should give her a chance, hear her out."

"No, we should not! For years I've believed she's dead, and as far as I'm concerned, she can stay dead."

"But she had her reasons—"

"Oh, yeah, she had her reasons. She killed Cousin Josie and was afraid she'd get caught."

"She told Sharon it was an accident."

"I don't believe that for one minute. And neither should you. This is all your fault, you know. You should've left well enough alone."

"But Terry, just think—we could be a family again!"

I studied Jennifer, frowning. She certainly was cutting her mother a lot of slack. Of course, her life had been torn apart in the wake of her father's death and my investigation; it was natural that she'd cling to what shreds were left—one of them being her image of Laurel as a flawed but good person. It was an image with which she deeply identified, as evidenced by last week's journey back and forth across the territory where her mother had vanished.

"Jesus Christ!" Terry exclaimed. "*Family!* I can't believe you said that."

I stood up. Time for the messenger to depart before she became a target. "This should be a private discussion," I told them. "When you come to a decision, let me know."

I'd flown down to Sacramento that morning from Klamath Falls, rented a car, and gone directly to Terry's house. Now I got onto Interstate 80 and drove south. I'd drop off the rental at Oakland, where my MG was parked at North Field. It seemed like years since I'd left it there and flown for the second time to Paso Robles.

I was tired, mildly depressed, and looking forward to getting home, taking a long, relaxing bath, and going to bed. One of the downsides of my work is the toll other people's emotions take on me.

Let Jennifer and Terry go on from here, I told myself. *You've done your job. You're not involved anymore.*

*   *   *

Ralph and Alice were waiting in the front hall when I got home. They gave me surprised looks; obviously they were expecting Michelle to show up and feed them. I took my travel bag to the bedroom, then spooned out some of the evil-smelling food they so loved, and told Ralph, "You'll get your shot when 'Chelle comes over." Giving insulin shots was not my forte.

Multiple messages on the answering machine. I pressed the play button.

Jim Whitmore of the SLO County Sheriff's Department. "The DA down here'll be in touch with you next week. Kev Daniel's hired top legal talent, and the state'll need your testimony to make its case. By the way, he wasn't lying when he said he didn't kill the dog; apparently it went looking for someone to help its master. Didn't stay around to fight because it had two broken ribs. Hung around a restaurant near the pier, whining and trying to lead people out there. One of the busboys took it to a vet, and the vet called the guide-dog association number that was engraved on the plate on its halter."

I'm glad the dog's okay, but I really don't need another court appearance.

Hy. "I'm flying back to the city tomorrow. Hope your case is going well. See you at home."

You bet you will! At home, and in bed.

Ma. "Why are you never there or at the office? You'd better not be out getting in trouble again."

You ought to be used to me getting in trouble by now, Ma.

Patrick. "I'm still in Crescent City. My piece-of-shit car died. I'll try to make it in on Friday."

Junk the thing and buy a new car. Please!

Saskia. "It was so good seeing you, dear, and meeting your lovely family. Please call me when you have time."

Lovely family. Now that's a new one.

Ted. "Your cell's not on, and I don't know how to get hold of you. Things're really piling up here, and I'm working overtime. Call me when you get this."

Go home, Ted. There's nothing on your desk that can't wait.

Robin. "My new phone's finally been installed. Write this number down someplace where you won't lose it."

Good God, do I seem incompetent to her?

Jennifer Aldin. "Terry and I have reached an agreement. We'll meet with our mother, but only if you come along to mediate."

So you're not involved anymore? Yeah, right.

Friday

·

SEPTEMBER 2

It was cool and a light drizzle had started falling when Jennifer, Terry, and I arrived at Laurel's house in Klamath Falls. The overcast rendered the old tract even shabbier than it had seemed on the sunny day when I'd first visited there. Both women were tense, and their edginess had infected me on the trip up. Jennifer had insisted on sitting with me on the plane, had barely spoken to her sister. Terry acted as if she were being transported to prison. I gathered the "agreement" was more a case of the older sister exerting her influence on the younger one, and I hoped the outcome of today's visit wouldn't seriously rupture their relationship.

I pulled the rental car to the curb, turned off the ignition. Then we sat there in silence. After a minute, Jennifer asked, "*This* is what she left our home for?"

I said, "I don't think her life turned out the way she expected."

"No, of course not," Terry commented from the backseat. "She probably envisioned a new, rich husband and no bratty kids to bother her."

"Listen, Terry." Jennifer's voice crackled with anger. "We promised not to prejudge her."

"You mean, you *told* me not to."

"Stop that! We've got to go in there with open minds."

Terry didn't respond.

Jennifer twisted in the passenger seat and glared at her sister. "What happens in there"—she jerked her thumb at the house—"will be something we'll have to live with for the rest of our lives. Don't blow it."

"As far as I'm concerned, our mother blew it the day she left us."

I closed my eyes, drummed my fingertips on the steering wheel. Why the hell had I agreed to come with them? Oh, yes, I was supposed to be a mediator.

I said, "Look, you can do one of three things: you can sit here arguing all afternoon; you can tell me to turn the car around and drive back to the airport; or you can go in there and deal with her. But if you do go in, you have to be civil—to her, and to each other."

They were silent. Then Terry said, "Okay, let's get it over with."

The two stayed well behind me as we went up the walk and I pressed the bell. Within seconds, Laurel opened the door.

She'd styled her gray-streaked hair carefully and applied makeup, including lipstick. She wore a black pantsuit that once had been elegant but now was shiny from too many dry cleanings. Her eyes were apprehensive, and worry lines stood out between her thick brows.

Another long silence. She stared at her grown-up daughters. I glanced at them: Jennifer's eyes had begun to tear, but Terry's were hard and cold.

After a moment Laurel swung the door widely and said, "Please, come in."

The door opened directly into a small living room, sparsely furnished in what looked to be thrift-shop items. A small TV and VCR sat on a stand, dozens of videotapes stacked on the shelf below them. One wall was lined with bookcases whose shelves sagged under the weight of the volumes. Most of the books were in poor condition, and many of their spines bore library identification stickers, indicating Laurel had picked them up at bargain prices when they were taken out of circulation. Most if not all of Josie Smith's money must have been gone after Laurel bought this house.

She stood very still, pressing her hands together and studying her daughters, who were similarly frozen. After a moment she motioned at a tattered plaid sofa and said, "Sit down, please. I've made coffee. Or perhaps you prefer tea?"

"Nothing—" Terry began.

"Coffee's fine," Jennifer said, gripping Terry's arm.

"Good. Ms. McCone, will you help me?"

I followed her through a dining area and a swinging door into a tiny kitchen. As the door shut behind us, Laurel turned to me.

"You said when you called that Terry was opposed to coming up here. Which one is she?"

"You can't tell your own daughters apart?"

"Obviously they've changed in twenty-two years."

Saskia had never seen me; I'd been whisked out of the delivery room as soon as she'd given birth. Yet when I first saw her, lying in a hospital bed in a semi-coma, she'd sensed my presence and whispered words that would allow me to unlock the secrets surrounding my adoption.

I said, "Terry's the one with the attitude and short hair."

Laurel nodded, busied herself with putting cups and a plate of cookies on a tray. I carried it into the living room while she followed with a carafe of coffee.

Jennifer was sitting on the sofa, her posture very straight, hands clasped primly around her knees. She'd composed herself, and her eyes were no longer tearing. Terry stood by the far wall, studying a group of photographs that were arranged there. I set the tray down, went to join her.

So Laurel *had* taken keepsakes of her children with her. There were seven photos in all, each framed in silver: Jennifer on a pony; Terry in a wading pool; both girls in front of a Christmas tree. Jennifer mugging for the camera in a Halloween pumpkin suit; Terry hanging upside down by her knees on a jungle gym. Both girls posing in the opening of a drive-through redwood tree. And in the central photo of the arrangement, Laurel kneeling, an arm around each girl, the sea in the background.

Terry said, "She kept them all these years." When she looked at me, I saw her expression had softened.

"Okay," she said, "I'll hear her out."

For more than an hour Laurel explained to her daughters the things she'd told me on the previous Tuesday, but her demeanor was radically different. She spoke softly and with regret; occasionally she cried, and Terry looked distressed, but Jennifer had become silent, aloof. Occasionally she glanced at the picture wall, a puzzled expression on her face.

I understood the change in Terry's attitude; the display of photographs had affected her deeply. But I couldn't understand the change in Jennifer.

Laurel refilled our coffee cups, and Jennifer studied the carafe as she poured.

"We had one like that when I was little," she said.

"Yes, it's exactly the same. I found it in a thrift shop. It made me think of you."

"Not of our father?" Jennifer's tone was sharp, her expression unreadable.

Laurel said, "It's hard for me to think of your father, after what he did to me. But you girls were always on my mind."

"Really."

"Yes—every day. Especially on your birthdays. Christmases. The Fourth of July. Halloween. Thanksgiving. I missed all those occasions, and I deeply regret it. I missed your high school and college graduations. Terry's wedding day. Your wedding to Mark Aldin."

Red flag. I'd told Laurel Jennifer's married name, but not that of her husband.

Terry got up and went back to the picture wall. "This is so nice," she said.

"What else did you miss, Mother?" Jennifer asked. Her tone was even sharper now. "The big house in Paso Robles? I mean, this"—she gestured around us—"is quite a comedown."

Laurel compressed her lips before she spoke. "I suppose, given your two lovely homes and rich husband, you would consider it so. I admit, since I left you my life hasn't been much."

"And do you think it might improve, now that you've reconnected with Terry and me?"

"Of course it would. I'd have my girls back."

"No, I mean in a material way."

"I'm not asking anything of you—"

"Of course you're not. Not directly."

Terry turned, frowning.

Jennifer stood, went to stand beside her sister. She took down the photograph of the three of them from the wall and examined it, turned it over. "How long has this been hanging here?" she asked.

Laurel ran her tongue over her lips. "Since I moved into the house, ten years ago."

"Really." Jennifer continued examining it. "Odd that it's not sun-faded like the spines of the books on the shelves. That east-facing window lets a lot of light in here, even with the blinds closed."

She stepped back, surveying the wall. "It's also odd that there's a big rectangle on the wallpaper where it's not faded—as if something much larger had hung there until recently. And there's no smaller, unfaded place where this one was—such as there would be if it had been there for ten years."

So that's what made her skeptical. Trust an artist's eye. She's a better detective in that department than I am.

"I had the walls repapered—"

"No way, Mother. You forget, I inherited your artistic talent. My eyes don't lie." She held up the the frame, its back toward us, where a sticker with a bar code was affixed. "In your haste to curry favor with Terry and me, you left the price tag on. It's from SaveMart, a store that didn't exist ten years ago. Besides, anything that old wouldn't peel off"—she pulled it loose, stuck it on the glass over Laurel's face—"this easily."

Laurel closed her eyes, sighed. "All right, I was trying to impress you. The frames I had the pictures in were from a thrift shop and very shabby—"

"You're good at covering up, aren't you? But I guess you would be; you've been living a lie all these years."

Laurel was silent. I watched Terry's face undergo a slow

transformation from bewilderment to anger, as the harsh recognition of how their mother had attempted to manipulate them sank in.

I couldn't keep out of the family discussion any longer. "Laurel, how did you know Jennifer was married to Mark Aldin? And that he's rich? And that they have two lovely homes?"

"Why, you told me."

"I only told you her last name, and that they lived in Atherton."

"No, I'm sure you mentioned—"

"A little Internet research was all it took to find out your older daughter—separated or not—is well-off. And I imagine you also found out Terry isn't doing badly, either."

"That's preposterous! Why would I care?"

"Money to buy you a good lawyer. To make the rest of your life easier."

"No!"

"The real question is, did you ever care? Did you ever think about your daughters' feelings at all?"

For a moment I thought Laurel would protest again, but then she lifted her head defiantly, and arrogance flashed in her eyes.

"You want the truth?" she said. "All right. The truth is, I never much cared about anyone but myself."

And that's what isolates you from the rest of humanity.

Jennifer reached out to Terry, who was backed up against the picture wall, eyes hard with anger. At first she pulled away, but then she took her sister's hand. Together they walked out of the shabby house and out of Laurel Greenwood's wrecked life, leaving her to face the consquences alone.

After again warning Laurel not to run, I did the same.

Friday

·

SEPTEMBER 16

Six in the evening, and Rae and I were drinking beer on the patio at Gordon Biersch Brewery across the Embarcadero from Pier 24½. Fall—or what we city residents prefer to call "summer in San Francisco"—had arrived, and with it mellow sunlight and warm, balmy days. I wore a short-sleeved shirt, and she had on a tank top, a sweater tied around her waist by its arms.

"So," I said, "you didn't answer my question. Are you on staff or not?"

"Sorry. I was just thinking how pretty Treasure Island looks tonight. No, I'm going back to writing my book on Monday. Getting out of the house and working on the Greenwood case broke my block. Gave me a couple of good ideas, in fact."

"Don't tell me the book's turning into a detective novel."

"No. More of a psychological character study."

"Let me guess—a mother who cold-bloodedly abandons her children."

"Among other things."

"And what's this one called?"

"*A Wasteland of Strangers.*"

"Good title. But I'll miss you; it's been nice, though I think Patrick'll be relieved by your departure."

"Why?"

"All along he's been afraid you'd take his job away—in spite of my reassurances to the contrary."

"Well, he shouldn't be, after how he helped you break the case. Besides, your guaranteeing his car loan should've convinced him he's there to stay."

Patrick's old clunker had proved not to be repairable, and he'd eventually been forced to take the bus back from Crescent City. Last weekend I'd dragged him down to the auto dealerships in South City, where he'd found a five-year-old Chevy Cavalier with very low mileage and an attractive price tag.

I said, "I made him buy a cell phone, too—the same kind I replaced my old one with."

Rae rolled her eyes. "My, you *have* moved into the twenty-first century! Next thing I know, you'll be lusting after a Blackberry."

"Don't laugh, but I've already started to."

"So when're you replacing your decrepit MG?"

"What? That car's the love of my life, next to Hy! Speaking of whom . . ." I checked my watch. "Nope, plenty of time. He won't be up from San Diego till at least eight."

"He's spending a lot of time down there."

I shaded my eyes against the sun, studied her to see if her statement contained some hidden implication. Thought of Gage Renshaw's words: *We've got a situation coming up that's gonna require all our resources.*

I said, "RKI's business is expanding, and they're undergoing a reorganization, that's why." It was all the explanation Hy had given me.

She nodded noncommittally.

I changed the subject. "How's Jennifer doing?"

"Coping pretty well. She's almost got her new condo in SoMa furnished to her liking. And she's getting her design business up to speed again. She filed for divorce last Tuesday. A lot of Mark's clients got wind of Ricky's pulling his accounts and started taking good hard looks at Mark's business practices themselves. Some of them filed complaints with the SEC, and they're reopening their investigation of what went on in St. Louis."

"How does it look for him?"

"Not good. The partner's still missing, and if the SEC brings in the FBI—well, the feds're damned good at finding out where the bodies're buried."

"How's Terry?"

"Not doing so well. She always thought of herself as the hardheaded sister, and then she let herself be taken in by her mother, only to be disillusioned with equal speed. But she'll get through it, with her husband's and Jen's help."

"I'm sure she will."

Last Monday, the district attorney in Crescent City had launched an investigation into the death of Bruce Collingsworth, and the California Board of Nursing had initiated proceedings against Laurel. If she didn't do prison time, she'd certainly be under scrutiny for years to come. In addition, she'd been fired from her job at the Klamath Falls nursing home where she'd worked and banned from the hospice where she'd volunteered.

"I wonder what she'll do?" I said, more to myself than to Rae.

"Who? Jen?"

"No, I was thinking of Laurel."

"Don't know. She's tried to call both Jen and Terry several times, but they won't have anything to do with her."

I envisioned Laurel, shut away in her shabby little house in the slipping-down tract, alone with her books and videos. Wondered if she'd dismantled the picture wall that had been her undoing with her daughters. Wondered also if she'd abandoned Josie Smith's name, or if she would keep up the pretense of being the woman she had killed until even that was stripped from her. Not that I really cared what she did or what happened to her. I'd seen firsthand the looks of betrayal on the faces of the daughters she'd claimed to love. And I'd seen too many other victims of cold, calculating people like her.

Rae said, "So Hy's finally coming up. He going to press you about your living-space problems?"

"Probably."

"Whatever his ideas are, I don't think you should worry. If you don't like what he suggests, you two will work something out to your mutual satisfaction. You always have."

I frowned at her. "I thought you were the one who said marriage changes things."

"That's right."

"But you didn't mean for the better."

"Of course I did. As far as I'm concerned, it only gets better."

"Oh."

"Why would you think I meant for the worse?"

"I . . . I don't know. I guess I was just looking for trouble. And in the course of this investigation I've come up against two truly dysfunctional marriages."

"Laurel's and Jennifer's. But yours could never be like that. It's not the institution, but the people who come into it that make or break a marriage."

She was right, of course. "Oh," I said, waving my hand helplessly, "I'm so damn *new* at this stuff!"

Rae's freckled nose crinkled, and she tried not to laugh, but as soon as she did, I joined her. People at nearby tables were casting curious glances at us when her cellular rang.

She answered, and I watched as her face sobered. She said, "Okay. It'll be okay. I'm on my way."

"What?" I asked, thinking of Ricky, the kids, even Charlene or Vic.

She snapped the unit shut, looking dazed. "That was Jen. Mark's sailboat capsized outside the Golden Gate this afternoon. Another boater spotted it, notified the Coast Guard, and an immediate search was launched, but they didn't find him. Looks like he was swept out to sea."

"Accident? Or suicide?"

"Could be either, but I'd say suicide. Mark's a good sailor; he knows the currents there."

I shut my eyes, pressed the heels of my hands against them. Pictured the strong, vital man who had assured me he would do anything to bring his wife peace of mind. A falsity, like everything else about the case. And Rae and I had been instrumental in bringing him down—

Rae said, "Not our fault, Shar. Goes with the territory."

"Maybe I'm getting sick of the territory."

"No you're not. The good you do far outbalances crap like this. I've got to go now, be with Jen. You go home. Listen to what Hy has to say about the house with an open mind."

He was already there when I arrived, his classic Mustang in the garage, so I could have the driveway for the MG. I parked, ran up the front steps, and called to him from the hallway.

No reply, but his flight jacket was on the coatrack. He wasn't in the sitting room or kitchen, but his travel bag lay on the bed.

I went to the door to the deck. He wasn't out there either. "Ripinsky?"

A thump from below.

"Ripinsky?"

"Down here. Hit my goddamn head."

I went across the deck and took the stairs to the backyard. Still didn't see him. "Where *are* you?"

His dirt-smudged face peered around from the far corner of the house. "Hey, I was right. I've found our living-space solution."

I angled under the deck toward him, cobwebs catching at my hair and face. He wore rumpled jeans and a filthy T-shirt, had a tape measure in one hand, a flashlight in the other. When he encircled my shoulders for a hug, the light banged into my spine.

I disentangled myself and tried to look disapproving, but his expression was so like that of a kid whose Halloween goodie sack is overflowing that I had to smile.

"Okay," I said, "show me."

He led me down the narrow walkway between my house and the Curleys' fence, to a door that led into a tiny storage space behind the garage, where I kept a lawn mower that I seldom used on the small back lawn that seldom grew. After squeezing inside he rapped on the wall that separated it from the space that extended to the rear wall under the deck.

"What's beyond this, McCone?"

"Dirt. When one—God knows which—of the former owners decided to raise up the house for the garage, they shoveled all the dirt back here and walled it off. It's pretty much solidly packed, nearly to the joists of the kitchen and bedroom floors."

"Yeah, dirt. I know, because I ripped out a piece of the wall in the garage." He beamed at me. "Dirt that, should we have it dug out, would create a hell of a lot of space."

"For?"

"One big room. Call it a playroom."

"Oh." Now it was beginning to compute. "A playroom containing a big bed."

"Right. And an adjoining bath with a big shower and tub like we have at Touchstone."

"Closet space. Your own sock drawer."

"Your stuff not getting shoved to the side and wrinkled by mine."

A drawback had occurred to me. "How do we get to this room? I mean, in the winter rains, do we have to run across the deck and down the stairs and enter through this door?"

"Hardly. Interior stairway."

I tried to picture where it would go. Couldn't.

Hy smiled and hugged me again. This time the tape measure rapped against my spine.

He said, "Leave it to me, McCone. I'll get it done."

"It's in your hands."

I won't have to give up this house that I love. He won't have to give up his ranch that he loves. And this house will become ours.

Rae said it only gets better—and she's right.

Damn, I'm so new at this!